C000001652

Where the Echo Calls

Calls

A Book for Dog Lovers

Steve N Lee

Blue Zoo
England

For my four-legged best friends.
And yours.

Chapter 01

The car's rear door swung open as the vehicle took a bend and cold night air rushed in, bristling Razor's whiskers. He shrank away from it, but the hook-nosed guy at the other end of the seat twisted around, jammed a foot into Razor's back, and shoved. Razor's eyes popped wide open as the gloom-drenched city raced by, nearer and nearer.

What the...?

He thrust his paws into the seat to stop himself from falling out, grimacing as the blue vinyl scraped one of the wounds on his hindquarters. But it was too late.

Razor slid out into the darkness and crunched onto the asphalt. He yelped and tumbled, tumbled, tumbled...

Finally, he smacked into the curb and sprawled in a crumpled heap. There he lay, still as the night devouring him.

As the black mist engulfing his thoughts cleared, strange sounds and alien scents swirled from out of the shadows, clawing at his senses as if daring him to challenge them.

His eyes flickered open. He winced, pain slicing into his right shoulder.

Blurry gloom surrounded him, while noises smeared, each merging into the next.

He shook his head, and a world bathed in the yellowy glow of streetlights came into focus. He sniffed, but dried blood clogged his nose, so all he found was a quagmire of unidentifiable scents.

And down the street, red taillights grew fainter and fainter.

He gasped. They were leaving? How could they not know he'd fallen out?

Razor pushed to stand, but pain stabbed again from his shoulder. A high-pitched yelp escaped, and he collapsed into the gutter.

Gritting his teeth, he heaved up and hobbled down the street after the car. He barked.

They had to stop. Had to come back for him. But the lights grew smaller.

He barked again, but it made no difference.

Tensing his muscles, he lunged to race after the vehicle, but his shoulder gave and he crashed to the ground. Every part of his body screamed to rest, but he'd never find his way back to his cage alone.

He clambered up. Panting as if he'd run for miles, he tottered on.

A horn blared behind him.

He jumped, glancing back. An SUV tore at him, headlights blazing.

Razor lurched sideways, slammed into a parked sedan, and hit the ground again as the vehicle roared by.

Muscles shaking with the effort, he pushed up and lumbered onto the sidewalk in front of a darkened store. A few parked vehicles hugged the curb while dim light bled through the drapes of the two- and three-story buildings.

Razor sniffed. His car had vanished. But worse, no scents he recognized hung in the air. He whimpered. He had no idea how to get home from here. Was this punishment for losing the fight? He'd tried his best, but against two dogs that were both absolute monsters... how could he have ever won?

Maybe his man would come for him tomorrow. Yes, that was it. Being left alone tonight was his punishment, but in the morning, everything would be forgiven and his man would come. This time tomorrow, he'd be back in his cage, curled up on his cozy concrete floor.

The icy wind raked his back, and he shivered. But where should he go now?

Nearby, a car stopped and a man entered a building. Heat radiated from the vehicle, so Razor limped over. Wincing, he hunkered down and shuffled underneath the engine. It was warmer than the sidewalk, but the wind still clawed at him.

He trembled, hunching up to make himself as small as possible.

If only he'd won that fight. Stupid dog!

The adrenaline from the shock of his accident draining away, he slumped, all his bite wounds burning like he was being bitten all over again. He licked the gashes on his front legs, then twisted and licked his side.

A building door opened and banged shut. Footsteps clomped nearer.

Razor sniffed. Uh-oh, the driver. If the car moved, it could crush him.

He lunged to dart to safety, but his leg buckled and he yelped.

The man crouched and peered under the car. "What the...?" He lashed out with his fist. "Get out of here! Darn dog."

Razor growled. *If that hand comes near me, cupcake, it's mine.*

Only one man was allowed to punish him for being bad, and it wasn't this clown.

The driver jerked his hand away and stood. He banged on the car, shouting.

Squealing as pain speared him, Razor scrambled from under the opposite side of the vehicle. He lurched down the sidewalk. Under cars wasn't safe, so he needed to find somewhere better. Sheltered. Deserted.

But where?

Coming from ahead, one scent overpowered all others. A dark scent. A scent of destruction. Razor hobbled closer.

Near the corner, a building stood with shattered windows, its interior blacker than the sky. Razor nuzzled through a gap in the metal fence cordoning it off and poked his head through the broken door.

Was it safe?

He sniffed. The stench of charred materials plugged his nostrils. He shrank back and turned to run, the overwhelming smell making his head spin... but a smell wouldn't kill him — the cold could.

He leaned back in. No shuffling noises came from inside. Was it safe? Maybe. But like he had a choice. He doddered in.

A broken staircase lay ahead, while to the left was a room with a partially collapsed ceiling. Everything was black and reeked of fire.

Razor stumbled to the wreck of a sofa caked in soot — the only square yard of surface not buried under jagged debris. He clambered on and nestled into the corner, shivering, hurting, alone. So alone.

Tomorrow his man would come and life would be good again. It had to be. That was all Razor's world had ever been, so it was impossible it could ever be any different.

Yes, tomorrow would be a good day. Razor could sense it.

Chapter 02

The rumble of traffic crawled into the burned-out husk of a house, and muddy gray light struggled through the glassless windows. Waking, Razor peered about without lifting his head off the charred cushion. He was still here? He closed his eyes again. It was real.

He winced, his wounds once more gnawing at him without the sanctuary of sleep to hold them at bay. Yes, it was so very, very real.

He longed to linger on his impromptu bed, but his man would never find him here.

Pushing up, Razor yelped as pain sliced through him, and he crumpled back onto the sofa. He cringed as he licked his right foreleg, then pulled back, smacking his lips. What the devil was that taste? Dry, powdery, burned...

His wounds needed cleaning, so he licked again, struggling to ignore the taste. He washed the wound on his upper leg but, unable to twist enough to reach his shoulder, settled on cleaning his side. By the time he'd finished, he was gasping for water.

Grimacing, he shuffled around on his three good legs, then carefully dropped from the sofa. The impact of hitting the floor jarred him, and he winced.

He hobbled to the doorway, dragging his right foreleg, but stopped — he wasn't allowed outside alone. Sticking his nose through the gap, he gazed about, sniffing.

Yes, he'd been outside last night, but that was because he'd fallen out of the car, so he hadn't had a choice. Now, if he went outside, it

9

was because he'd chosen to go out, which was him choosing to be bad. And he never chose to be bad but always strove to be good for his man. Unfortunately, no matter how hard he tried, bad things just kind of happened to him. Like slipping out of the car. He was unlucky that way.

What if he went outside and his man beat him for breaking the rules? He hung his head. But what if he didn't go outside and his man beat him for leaving the place in which he'd left him? What should he do?

He whimpered. It seemed whatever he did, he was going to be beaten, so...

Stepping out, he squeezed through the metal fence. A bolt holding the wire mesh in place scraped a wound on his side, and he squealed. The pain cut so deep, he fell, his chin hitting the sidewalk.

A chubby woman strutting along clutched her mouth.

He gazed up at her, eyes as big and brown as bowls of beef stew. Maybe she'd see he was hurt, or lost, or thirsty.

Fear lined the woman's face, and she scooted to the curb to give him as wide a berth as possible. She dashed past, flinging him a glance as if to check he wasn't following her.

He glared at her. *Don't mind me, princess. I'm having the time of my life here.*

So he was a big dog, a fighting dog — he wasn't aggressive with it, so why the attitude? People. Why did he ever imagine one would help him? Maybe the best solution wasn't to expect help but simply to take what he needed. Now that was a plan.

Way down the street, the woman looked back.

She seemed genuinely unnerved. Why? All he'd done was look at her.

Glancing down at himself, he did a double take. What the...?

He was black. Completely black.

Except, he was usually black on only his back, the rest being a golden brown with a flash of cream on his chest.

Twisting this way and that, he stared at his legs — black. His sides — black. His belly — black. What the devil was happening? Was he ill?

Wait...

He sniffed himself. Was it soot?

Thank goodness his man would be coming soon. He'd know what it was and what to do.

Razor lumbered up the street but stopped at a puddle and lapped the cloudy water. Cold, fresh, invigorating. And it took away that nasty, burned powdery taste. Heaven.

Onward he lurched.

He hoped his man wouldn't be too upset with him. Losing the fight was bad enough, but falling out of the car — how stupid was that? He cringed. Please let his man forgive him. He couldn't take another beating on top of all his wounds, no matter how much he deserved it.

Gazing back toward his soot house, he frowned. He'd come all that way — on his own? And nothing bad had happened? Maybe the rules had changed and he *was* allowed outside by himself after all. Good to know.

Razor sat on the roadside where he'd slipped out of the car. And waited.

Traffic grumbled and people scurried, and the sun climbed higher, but the day didn't get any warmer.

All day, pedestrians shambled by, many glaring at him as if he didn't belong there — and they were right, he didn't. Strangely, no matter how many appeared to come to that conclusion, none tried to help him.

People were so strange. They could kick him one minute simply for being there, then pat him the next for exactly the same reason. It was that paradox that made them so fascinating and each day so special — he never knew what wonders lay in store.

Of course, he'd rather have more days filled with pats. But a life without beatings? Talk about boring. Not to mention that pats always felt so much better after he'd been hit. And though he didn't always know in which way he'd been bad, he knew he deserved all those kicks. Why else would he get them?

In fact, he probably deserved more than he actually received, so he was lucky his man was so tolerant. Other dogs weren't as lucky, especially if they were bad and lost a fight — he'd witnessed it.

That afternoon, tiny balls of ice pelted him. Hail wouldn't usually be a problem, but when they hit his wounds, it was like being whipped with a spiky branch.

Razor hugged the wall of the nearest building, gaze still fixed on the street. Waiting.

His stomach grumbled. Not surprising as three days had passed since he'd eaten. That was how he'd known a fight was coming — his man always starved him for two days before a fight, giving him only the odd scrap. Razor wasn't sure why. Hunger always put him in such a bad mood that all he wanted was to bite something, so trying to solve such a puzzle at the same time was impossible.

As the day began to darken, he gazed along the street. Why hadn't his man come yet? Razor gulped. Please don't say he was waiting in the wrong place.

He sniffed the ground. It smelled like the right place, but after hitting his head on the road the way he had... he gulped again. If this wasn't the spot, boy, was he in big trouble.

He shrank into the shadows. Not a kicking. Please, not a kicking. He hurt too much to suffer a kicking.

Razor peered into the distance. With no leash, he could run and hide.

He slumped. No, he couldn't, because if he'd been bad, his man had every right to punish him.

Sitting upright, he waited. Shivering. But proud he was being good.

Darkness returned. Blinded by headlights, Razor squinted at each car, studying its shape, scrutinizing its occupants, sniffing as it went by... where was his man?

His teeth chattering, Razor gazed into the night. What would he do if his man didn't come? He whimpered. No, he couldn't think like that. His man *would* come. He always had in the past, so there was no reason to think he wouldn't now. His man loved him. That was why his man punished him so often — to make him the best dog he could be. Without his man, Razor was nothing.

He whimpered again. But what if his man really didn't come?

Razor stared into the shadows. Hoping. Pleading.

As the cold started to bite, the growling stream of traffic faded to a trickle.

Razor staggered back to his soot house and clambered onto his charred sofa. He curled up. Shaking from the cold. From the worry over everything he'd lost.

When the sun once more clawed its way into the house, Razor woke. Tentatively, he eased up and tested putting weight on his bad leg. It held. Good. He was healing. But when he climbed off the sofa, the leg gave, and he crunched into a fallen beam.

He clambered up. Okay, so he was stronger, but far from better. Not that injuries were his only concern. His stomach clenched like someone was crushing it in both hands.

He needed to wait for his man, but if he didn't get food soon, he wouldn't have the strength to sit and wait. His man had always watched out for Razor, so he would understand how food had to be a priority right now.

Once more, Razor limped out of the soot house and along the street, scanning the drifting scents for anything edible. If he could home in on something and fill his belly, he could be back waiting on his curb in no time.

He sniffed but struggled to isolate scents. During the fight, while Razor had warded off an attack from the white dog, the brown one had grabbed him by the snout. Hard. Razor winced at the memory. Had that brown monster damaged his nose? How would he live without his nose?

Razor pawed his snout, then licked his nostrils. It had to work. It just had to. A dog wasn't a dog without a good nose.

He closed his eyes and breathed in long and slow through his nostrils, then in short, fast in-out-in-out breaths.

There!

Thank heaven. His nose was struggling, yes, but he could pick up some things.

Using his nostrils independently, he homed in on the direction from which the smell was coming and stumbled toward it.

The savory, floury smell lured him around a corner. As he drew closer, sweet scents drifted toward him, too.

He was only now smelling those? His nose was obviously more damaged than he'd figured. But he'd worry about that later because breakfast beckoned.

Ahead, people moseyed in and out of a store, some clutching paper bags, others noshing on pastries. Razor tramped over.

People were strange, it went without saying, but generally, he liked them. Why wouldn't he when they were so nice to him? They patted him when he won fights, gave him food and his own concrete to sleep on, helped him get better at being good by hitting him.

That last one was tricky, though. Sometimes, no matter how hard he tried, Razor couldn't figure out why he'd been clobbered. It was as if his man changed the rules, hitting him for something that earlier had been fine.

But that was crazy. His man only wanted him to be the best dog he could be, so if Razor didn't grasp why he was being punished, it simply meant he was too stupid to understand. It was *his* fault. Everything always was. It was one of the few things he could always rely on to be true – like how his pee always squirted down and not up.

As Razor neared the food store, his heart hammered. He'd seen people frequent such places from his man's car, but he'd never actually been in one. So how did they work? Could he simply stroll in and take whatever he fancied?

Obviously. How else could they work?

With large glass windows crammed full of more food than Razor could eat in a day, maybe even two, the store burst with savory delights. A long white sign above the window was emblazoned with black and gold squiggles. Oh, how people loved squiggles – they plastered them everywhere.

Everywhere.

Maybe it was their idea of scent marking. He'd never seen anyone pee on anything, but he'd seen lots of squiggles made on paper with little sticks, squiggles on walls with sprays, even squiggles made on him with a humming machine. He glanced at his rump where the fur had been shaved into a squiggle.

They seemed to put squiggles on anything they found important. His tail lifted at the warm thought of how that meant he was important to his man.

Two young girls waltzed out of the store, each holding a doughy ring and licking white powder off their lips.

Razor wagged his tail. Instead of the girls smiling, they backed off, brows wrinkled, then scuttled away.

14

Oh well, some people just weren't sharers. It didn't matter; he'd fetch his own.

As a woman in dark blue opened the door to leave, he strode in. The woman gaped.

Inside, a man in a suit shrank back, and a small boy clutched his mother. Behind the counter, a man in white shouted, "Get out! Out!"

White Man shot around, brandishing a broom.

Razor had come here as a friend, but if this clown wanted an enemy...

Razor snarled, glaring at the man and his weapon. *You want to try your luck, slick, go ahead. But come near me with that thing and one of us is going to have a real bad day. Capiche?*

White Man swatted at Razor.

Razor dodged and tensed to pounce, but his injured leg gave. He splattered across the floor and the broom hit his hurt shoulder. He yelped.

"Get out!"

White Man swatted again and again. Razor scrambled through the door still being held open by the shocked woman and lurched down the street.

At a safe distance, he collapsed against a wall, gasping for breath.

He hung his head. Running from a fight? What was this place turning him into?

He rested for a moment, then lumbered on to explore. Choosing food in a store was obviously trickier than he'd figured, but he'd fathom it.

More people bustled on the next street. Most swerved to avoid him, as if he was dangerous or something, but some seemed to be in a world of their own, especially those gazing at phones. A man in gray stumbled into him. Then a woman carrying a bag.

Razor moved over to hug the building wall. He was a big dog. Easy to spot. What was wrong with these people?

Okay, he'd figured out they couldn't smell scents to save their lives, but they had eyes. Why the fixation on those devices? People were strange. So strange. If he lived to be four, he'd never understand them. Never.

As he passed another store, a pack of giant cats roared at him in unison. He gasped and jerked away. But when he whipped around to savage the nearest one attacking him, they'd disappeared and foaming water cascaded over cliffs. He slumped.

Televisions. Across a row of TVs, the biggest butterflies he'd ever seen landed on the biggest flowers. His man had a TV. A huge one, but just the one. Why on earth would anyone want a room crammed with the things?

He gasped and his eyes popped wider than they'd ever been as, in slow motion, a black-and-white dog leaped high into crystal-blue sky and snatched a gold disk from the air.

Razor barked with admiration. Talk about talented.

Landing in a lush green meadow, the dog clutched the disk in its mouth, and a man with dazzlingly white teeth leaned down and hugged him. Not a pat. A hug!

Wow. So it was true. Frisbees *did* exist. He'd once seen a dog catch one after winning a fight, as if it was a reward, but Razor had been pretty beat up after his own fight, so he'd thought he'd dreamed it, but... it was true. And hugging a dog? Where was this place? This Frisbee heaven?

The picture changing again, Razor trudged away. Frisbee heaven was a nice idea. However, he had a nice cage and a lovely bit of concrete that was all his. The smart thing was to appreciate all the things he actually had, not dream of how much better he could have it. Strategy. That was the secret to success in life.

Besides, he had more pressing matters than the existence or nonexistence of Frisbee heaven — food.

Farther along the street, a young woman gawked into another huge window. Fake people gawked back. Gray eyes stared from gray faces, while gray arms made gray gestures. Eight of them. Not a scent between them. Talk about eerie. But that was people-stuff — no sense to any of it.

Seeing a break in the traffic, Razor darted across to the other side of the road, hoping his luck might change there.

And that was when he smelled it.

Chapter 03

In the middle of the sidewalk, Razor closed his eyes and sniffed, long and hard. Tangy, fruity, acidy, meaty, salty... he sighed. Could there be a more heavenly aroma than dog pee? Now there was a rhetorical question if ever there was one.

He was surprised women didn't dab it on themselves instead of that horrendously flowery stuff they all adored. Being a unisex fragrance, dog pee worked for men who liked smelling flowery, too — it was an aroma that just kept on giving. But... people-stuff. Enough said.

Razor homed in on the smell coming from a red fire hydrant ahead. If other dogs were in the vicinity, maybe they'd found a better place to sleep and, more importantly, something to eat.

Hope reinvigorating his hurting body, Razor hobbled to the hydrant. Leaning down, he drank in the scents to identify the individuals responsible: a large male who hadn't visited for some time; a female and... three pups, all of whom appeared to have been regular visitors but also hadn't been for a while; and... one other pup, who'd been here only yesterday. Razor focused harder. Yes, a young male pup, possibly related to the others.

Razor sniffed closer, deeper. The pup's concentrated pee suggested it was dehydrated but overall healthy. Well, if a pup could make it alone in the town, Razor sure could. Things were looking up.

Cocking his leg, he peed on the hydrant, too. Peeing was as good as a calling card could get: this one would announce his presence, let potential friends recognize him at a distance, and inform them about his health.

Of course, for getting better acquainted, it didn't hold a candle to sniffing someone's butt, but then, what did? Sticking his nose right up there and sniffing and sniffing and sniffing... boy, the things he could discover. He was stunned people didn't do it. A smile, a hand shake, a hug? What good were they? He could sniff a butt and know more about someone in seconds than days of handshaking could ever reveal. Yes, a good butt-sniffing session spoke volumes.

Content he'd garnered as much information as possible from the hydrant, he clomped on. Now that he'd introduced himself, he'd come back tomorrow and wait in the hope a new friend could give him pointers on town life, especially on how food stores worked.

As if to prove his luck was changing, another scent drew him toward black wrought iron gates. That couldn't be...

He hobbled over.

Crushed into the sidewalk near a concrete lamppost were four or five potato chips. Finally!

Razor munched the bits.

Okay, that wasn't even a snack, but it was a start. And evidence that food could be found if he searched hard enough.

His shoulder throbbing, he sat back on his haunches and blew out a weary breath. Every day he ran miles on his man's treadmill, yet the short walk here had exhausted him. He was in worse shape than he'd reckoned.

The wind whipped around him, its cold fingers burrowing into his fur. He shivered. Maybe the best strategy was to return to his waiting spot and hope his man wasn't much longer. And if that didn't pan out, at least he had a solid plan for tomorrow — find his hydrant friend.

He trudged back to his corner and waited on the roadside until the bitterness of the night forced him to his charred sofa.

When he rolled off his bed the next day, lightheadedness overwhelmed him, and he stumbled sideways into the wall. Four days without food was too long. His shoulder throbbed, his bite wounds stung, his stomach clenched, and his legs had lost all strength. He couldn't go on like this. Until he'd eaten, there'd be no more waiting. He didn't want to be bad, but he couldn't be good if he was dead.

The decision made, he headed out with a renewed vigor only to waltz into torrential rain.

He tramped along the street, sweeping his head from side to side to scan for something edible, raindrops *drip-drip-dripping* off his nose. Still, it wasn't all bad news — rain seemed to make smells come alive, as if bits of them hung in the air just waiting for him to suck them up.

Fewer people crowded the main street today, so Razor didn't have to be so wary of being trampled. However, approaching the TV store, he stopped dead, mouth agape. His friend again! The black-and-white dog sprang across the sky and snatched the disk out of the air. It was just as spectacular as yesterday. No, even better. His friend landed, and the man with all the teeth hugged him. Again.

Razor barked. That was incredible. He waited to see what other adventures his friend might share. But instead of a black-and-white dog performing marvels, tiny men chased a tiny ball around a field. Was this a joke? Who in the right mind would want to watch this garbage and not the sky dog with his death-defying skills?

Razor ran his gaze along all the TVs. Every single one showed the same picture — tiny men, tiny ball. Disgruntled, he lumbered on.

A scent drew his attention to a green trash can strapped to a lamppost beside the curb. Fries. And more than that — warm fries.

Razor tottered to the post, his mouth watering. He'd known he'd find something if he tried hard enough.

A large puddle sat on the road, so Razor lapped it. The best fries were wonderfully salty, which, while making them delicious, always made him incredibly thirsty, so it was best to get ahead of things.

Strategy. He was a master.

Having drunk enough, he rose onto his hind legs, hooked his forepaws onto the trash can's lip, and peered into its gaping mouth.

Oh yes, a good handful hid in the gloomy interior. Fantastic.

Drool stringing from his mouth, he sprang up to dangle from the trash can by his front legs. He hauled himself farther inside and nuzzled through the waste, searching for the treasure buried within.

Finally, his nose nudged a fry, and a salty, starchy sensation exploded in his snout. He gobbled it down. And the one next to it. Proper food. Heaven!

He stretched for another, but the fries lay scattered beyond his reach among other debris. Kicking his back legs, he heaved with his forelegs and wormed his way farther inside.

He lashed at one fry with his tongue to try to scoop it up, but it shuffled under a candy wrapper. He chased it. Caught it. Devoured it.

Sniffing out the next, he prodded it with the tip of his tongue, but it was just too far to scoop. He strained to reach, wiggling to get farther inside. Almost. Almost. Almost...

A vehicle zoomed through the puddle he'd drunk from, forcing a sheet of water to arc up through the air. It splattered down, drenching him.

Razor yelped with shock and fell to the ground. He scuttled away, forsaking the precious food in favor of safety.

Slowing near the fake people store, he shook himself. Water sprayed across the sidewalk.

A scrawny woman huddling with two children under an umbrella squawked as the shower hit them, and a passing old man swiped at Razor with a walking stick.

Razor dodged and hobbled away. Three fries. Three. So that was breakfast, lunch, and dinner, was it? And he'd thought things were improving. Still, at least there might be good news at the local message board.

Shuddering from the cold drenching, he skulked across the road and trudged toward the hydrant.

A faint scent drifting over made Razor's eyes light up. A new message! His tail twitched, daring to peek out from between his back legs as the tiniest spark of hope ignited within him. He limped quicker, eager to meet his new friend.

At the hydrant, he leaned down and sniffed. Yes, the male pup had visited yesterday, but so far, not today. Finally, some good news.

Razor peed on the hydrant again to let the pup know he was still around. He needed help, and this pup could obviously provide it if it was surviving alone.

His legs shaking with weariness, Razor staggered over to a black bench in sight of the hydrant and crawled underneath it, its laths affording some protection from the unrelenting rain. He waited.

For hours, people scurried back and forth, expressions as dark as the sky. And the rain fell and fell and fell.

So this was the world? He'd often wondered what lay beyond his cage from the glimpses he'd caught during car journeys. But this? It was a far cry from Frisbee heaven. Maybe that place didn't exist after all.

Either way, he'd be happier back in his cage. He knew where he stood there — he was fed, was out of the weather, was appreciated. Yes, maybe he'd already found heaven and simply hadn't realized it.

He waited into the afternoon, praying the pup would show, then tramped back to his corner to wait there instead.

Sniffing the ground, he found no trace of his man's scent, so Razor knew he hadn't missed him. But that made no sense. Why hadn't his man come? His man had to be sick with worry about him.

As the skyline darkened, Razor shuffled back to his soot house. Alone. Again. Huddled in the dark, he shivered. And howled for all he'd lost.

***

On his expeditions over the next few days, he sniffed out a half-eaten apple, a whole donut, part of a cheeseburger, and a handful of jelly beans. Enough to keep him going, but nowhere near enough to stop the grinding pain in his gut.

Bathed in sunshine for a change one day, he limped along the sidewalk past the sweet and savory store. His wounds were healing slowly, thanks to his licking; however, his right foreleg was a worry. That shoulder gave out regularly, and the wound lower down frequently bled. But he was still fighting.

He glanced at the corner where he'd slipped out of the car.

Yes, he was still fighting, but fighting for what? His man hadn't come for him. Why?

His tail wedged between his hind legs, he trudged on. What if his man never came?

Razor shuddered. *Never?*

His man had always been there for him before, so why wouldn't he come now? But in the past, Razor had never slipped out of the car to be lost in the town. What if his man was searching in the wrong place?

Razor whined.

What if his man never came? If he was alone forever? No home. No man. No purpose.

As he turned another corner, however, a lightness swathed him in warmth – the TV store.

He took up his usual spot next to the lamppost and waited. He had three waiting places now, but this was by far the best. On the screens, men pranced with strange equipment on a stage while hordes of people jigged about in front of them. It was a toss-up which was most boring – the tiny men chasing the tiny ball or tiny men prancing. Although, he'd discovered that if he waited long enough–

There! He sprang up and scurried closer, his heart pounding with anticipation.

A black-and-white dog leaped through the heavens and grabbed a disk.

Razor barked with glee. The sky dog just got better and better. It was incredible how it never missed. Incredible. He glanced about. People moseyed by, but none stopped to marvel at the feat.

Razor had always wondered why people were so fascinated with the strangest of things – cars, gold jewelry, crates of beer, dogfights, cigarettes, boobs and butts, phones... so many things, and all of such little consequence. Yet a true artist like the sky dog went completely ignored. Were people blind to the beauty in the world or was it just that they weren't that smart?

A fat guy strolling past dropped an ice cream cone on the sidewalk. He cursed, then waddled away.

Razor looked at him, then the ice cream, then back to the man.

So, picking that up would interfere with your packed schedule of overachieving, would it, hotshot?

At least that answered his question. Leaving perfectly good food on the ground to go to waste proved people just weren't that smart. But thank heaven they weren't. He sauntered over and licked it up.

Having seen his friend perform and having enjoyed an unexpected snack, Razor crossed the street and tottered to the hydrant. He sniffed around it. As usual, the pup had been again yesterday. It seemed to come only when Razor wasn't around. Like it was being awkward and trying to avoid him. Why would it do that? Didn't it want to help him and make a new friend to boot? Or was it simply greedy and wanted to keep everything it found for itself?

While there was logic in going it alone, it was skewed logic. Yes, the pup could eat whatever it found without sharing it, but he and the pup were both in a hostile town. A pack, even if there were only the two of them, had a far better chance of surviving than each of them struggling on separately.

Still, if that was the way the thing wanted to play it, so be it.

Razor trudged to the bench and huddled under it. He'd give the pup one last chance to do the decent thing and then that was it.

He waited. And waited. And waited.

But the pup never showed.

The wind changing direction, a smell wafted over. Razor's eyes widened. Mmm...

Chapter 04

Under the bench, drool strung to the ground as Razor drilled his gaze into two guys dawdling by, one bald, the other wearing a blue cap. Each chomped into a hot dog, ketchup oozing from the corner of Blue Cap's mouth. The guy dragged the back of his hand across his lips, then sucked it.

Razor licked his lips, then swallowed hard. Where had they found those?

Shuffling out, he tottered along the street, tracing the scent to its origin. Across the road stood a truck with a giant glowing hot dog above it.

Why hadn't he come this far before when delights like hot dogs were on offer?

He shambled onto the road, but a horn blared. Razor jumped, then lurched back to the sidewalk as a silver car growled past.

He panted on the curb. This town was a hellish place. What weird creatures people were to enjoy filling the world with such dangers.

Nearby, a woman and three children walked across the road on black and white stripes, a column of cars magically stopping for them. Cool. But, how did they do that?

With the traffic stopped, he doddered across the road.

At the food truck, people stood in line, then spoke to the man inside before carrying away steaming food. Razor had already tried and failed with the forward approach in the sweet and savory store, so this time, he had to work smart. If so many people were getting hot dogs, it was only logical that one or two might have accidents like the ice cream man. After all, stupid was as stupid did, and from what he'd seen of most people...

He stepped back, filtering out the scents of hot, fresh food in favor of older, colder scents. With his nose still recovering from the goring he'd received, he struggled to isolate some aromas, so he swung his head from side to side, scanning and scanning.

There!

He spun to a gloomy alley. On the right, a black metal staircase crawled up the side of a wall, dark green algae hiding the true color of the building. At the base of the other side, a blue van sat near two battered dumpsters.

While he couldn't smell any people, he angled his ears to check.

No one.

He peered into the shadows.

Somewhere down there lurked fresh food. Big food. Unguarded food. *His* food. But where?

He sniffed again. Usually, he'd know exactly where the food was, but his busted nose couldn't home in properly. Still, that didn't matter. The meal was there somewhere. And it was *his*.

Razor prowled into the shadowy alleyway. He'd thought it safe to go into the savory and sweet store, but that had backfired. The fries in the trash can — another backfire. This would *not* backfire.

Sniffing and listening, he stalked down the alley, wary of surprises. The smell of people grew fainter, while the smell of food grew stronger. The food was close.

A group of five trash cans stood behind the van. The smell came from the third or fourth. He glanced about to check no one had entered the alley.

Content he was alone, he stole toward the two suspect trash cans.

A few steps away, his nose finally gave him the news he was praying for — the food was in the fourth trash can. His nose might have been broken, but like he was, it was fighting to survive.

Razor nudged the trash can's lid with his snout to push it open. The weight of it exploded pain in his snout, and he jerked back.

If he couldn't lift the lid, he'd have to get at the contents another way.

Rising onto his hind legs, he raked the trash can with his forepaws, then jumped aside as it toppled over. Its contents spewed onto the concrete.

Razor nuzzled through the debris. Where was it? He shoved aside dented plastic bottles, damp paper, crumpled cardboard packaging, and empty cans... he gasped and froze, staring down at his prize.

Beside a squashed plastic container lay the biggest hot dog he'd ever seen. But why had something so perfect been abandoned? Had someone hidden it to eat later?

Who cared? All that mattered was it was here, and it was all *his*.

Drool stringing from his mouth, he chomped into the sausage. Meaty, salty, juicy, tomatoey... heaven! He severed another chunk and closed his eyes. It was possibly the tastiest thing to have ever existed. And it had been just lying here, waiting for him. Amazing.

He leaned down for another bite, but a scent drifting through the shadows made him freeze and the hackles rise on his back. The pup.

So *now* the thing had turned up? Razor snorted. Seriously?

Razor had peed on that hydrant every day for the best part of a week to announce he was in the area and looking to be friends, but had the pup shown up then? Yet the instant he'd found some fantastic food...

Be friends? Yeah, right. The pup obviously believed in every dog for itself, so that was exactly how things would remain.

Plus, the pup's scent had already told Razor everything about its size, age, and condition — it was no threat to him. He ignored it and ripped away another chunk of *his* hot dog.

But the thing stalked closer. The chemical cocktail in its scent screamed that, though it was frightened, it meant business.

Surely the pup knew how small it was and, more importantly, how big Razor was. What was it playing at? Did it really think he was going to share after he'd been so viciously rejected?

The pup crept closer.

Without looking up, Razor snarled. The thing might be young, but every dog understood a verbal warning.

However, the pup tottered another step nearer. As if it believed it could take the food if it wanted to.

The audacity. Razor had offered to be friends and been snubbed. Now this thing intended to challenge him?

Razor raised his head. He glowered at the small brown dog that barely reached his chest. *This* thought it could challenge *him? This?*

While the pup was only a few months old, every dog had to learn its actions had consequences. Time for a lesson.

Rearing over the small dog, Razor glared. The pup had guts, Razor would give it that, but he could rip it apart. Literally. Surely it was smart enough to realize that.

Just in case it wasn't, Razor snarled again, gnashing his teeth. *This is when you pee yourself, then run away squealing, champ.*

But the pup didn't flee. It glared back. Trembling, but with a darkness in its eyes.

Razor's gaze burned into the young dog and he curled his lip to bare his fangs. *Run, you stupid animal. Run!*

Shaking, the pup shrank back as if it was about to turn tail and scram, but it didn't. It lunged forward and clamped its jaws around Razor's right foreleg. Sinking its teeth into his bite wound, it stabbed the raw flesh that was healing so painfully slowly.

Razor yowled. Then struck back.

Chapter 05

Razor lay on the sofa, moonlight casting an eerie glow in the soot-caked room. He dragged his tongue over his foreleg where the pup had bitten it and grimaced. The wound was bleeding once more. That pup had gotten him good.

He had to hand it to the little fella, the pup sure had guts. In another world, they could have been friends. Or worst enemies if they were pitted against each other in a fight once the pup had grown. He winced as he scraped a hunk of gravel out of his raw flesh with his tongue.

Yep, an adult dog with the pup's spirit would be one mean fighter. Courageous. Relentless. Deadly. The kind an opponent had to kill to escape.

Luckily, Razor had met it when it was too small to be a threat. And luckily for the pup, Razor hadn't ripped it to pieces. Instead, he'd hurt it only enough to teach it a valuable lesson: that some battles could be won, whereas others needed to be walked away from. Strategy – the key to so many endeavors.

Wounds cleaned, Razor slept.

The next day, he hobbled back and forth, scouring the alley for more hot dogs, but found none. Nor the day after. Worse still, the following day, the man from the fast-food truck shooed him away before he'd completed a thorough search.

Strangely, hot dogs weren't the only thing eluding him – the pup never again peed on the hydrant. Maybe it had realized that part of town was too dangerous for such an inexperienced pup and had moved on. Razor hoped so. Hot dog aside, he hadn't wanted to injure it, only to teach it a valuable life lesson it would have normally learned from its mother or siblings. Hurting it had been a kindness because if the pup didn't learn and challenged the wrong dog, it could be maimed or even killed.

The sun bathing the sidewalk in heat for a change, Razor straightened his back as he sat outside the TV store when his friend appeared, leaped through the sky, caught the disc, and was hugged by his man.

Wow, if only such a world truly existed.

His show over, he toddled away and crossed the street. At the hydrant, Razor sniffed all around, but no matter how he strained, he couldn't find fresh pee from the pup. He sighed. He kind of missed the little fella, it being the closest thing to a friend he'd found since he'd slipped out of the car.

With no need to lie under the bench waiting, Razor glanced around for new areas he might search for food, the alley having been a bust recently and consuming far too much of his time.

Nearby, tall black wrought iron gates caught his eye, and trees swayed in the light breeze beyond, tiny buds of the freshest green peppering their brown skeletal branches.

Had that entrance always been there? He must have been so fixated on the hydrant and meeting new friends that this area had completely passed him by.

Razor limped closer. What was this place?

Through the entrance, more trees and bushes greeted Razor, and a metal statue of a man stood on a stone plinth. A man and woman dawdled through the gates, smiling and laughing. They didn't even glance at him, let alone give him a wide berth as would normally happen. A young woman strolled in, two boys running before her, also laughing.

How intriguing. People were so much happier in there than out here. What the devil was this place?

Razor sniffed, but the wind was blowing in from the street, so other than the nearest trees and shrubs, he couldn't sense much. Especially as his nose still wasn't behaving itself.

He tottered toward the gates, but at the threshold, a bearded guy sauntered out, gazing at his phone and holding a leash. A black dog with pointed ears and a stubby tail reared at Razor.

Razor jumped.

Behind a muzzle, the beast gnashed its teeth.

Razor shrank back.

"Heel, Titan, heel." The guy pulled the leash.

The beast stopped lurching at Razor but snarled and fixed its beady gaze on him.

Razor had fought one of those. They were vicious, having a strong bite and great stamina. He'd beaten that one, but he was in no state to handle another. Just as he'd taught the pup, some battles a dog could win, but others they had to walk away from.

Razor slunk away, tail wedged between his legs. He hated running from a fight because it gnawed at everything that made him the dog he was. But a fight wasn't only about who had the biggest bite; it was about strategy.

Razor glanced over his shoulder.

Standing tall outside the gates, as if guarding the place, the beast glared at him.

Razor glowered. *Give me two weeks to heal, baby cheeks, then we'll see who's going in there and who ain't.*

Lumbering along the sidewalk, he gazed at the food truck across the street and stopped. He sniffed.

Yes, his luck was finally changing.

Turning, he sucked in air through each nostril, homing in on the scent. There! Close to the line running down the middle of the road sat a lump of cheeseburger.

Cheese and beef. Could there be a more delightful combination?

Razor checked the traffic. A blue bus thundered toward him, while the other lane was quiet. He stared at the bus. Buses were slow, so he had time to dash across, snatch up the food, and sprint to safety. Maybe...?

Or maybe he should play it safe and wait for the traffic to die down.

With his injuries, it was wisest to wait. His leg often gave out when he was walking, so running...

He glared at the bus. He'd be crushed.

Yes, he'd wait. Strategy.

He sat at the curb and waited. And waited. Drool hung to the ground as vehicle followed vehicle followed vehicle...

He glared at the never-ending traffic. Was it ever going to stop?

Pacing along the roadside, he stared at the vehicles, then the food, then the traffic again. He couldn't risk missing out on a great lump of food like that. With the luck he was having, if he waited, someone else would get to it before him.

No, he had to run. Now.

His claws overhanging the curb, he watched the traffic. His heart pounded so hard, it thumped in his ears. A green car passed, then a silver one, then a red truck followed. Like buses, trucks were slow. This was his chance.

He tensed his muscles to bound into action. He tried to swallow, but his mouth was too dry.

This was it.

But what if his leg gave?

The vehicles didn't go fast in the middle of the town, so he had time, even with his bad leg. He was sure. Kind of.

But what if...?

The silver car passed.

No time. It was now or never. Now or never. Now or—

Razor lunged in front of the red truck. That cheeseburger was his. *His.*

He grimaced as pain stabbed his shoulder. Ordinarily, he'd have plenty of time, but today?

His right foreleg dragging and the wound on his side shortening his stride, he lurched across the asphalt with as much grace as if he was loping through mud.

And that truck was close. So very close...

A horn blared so loudly it shook his brain. Razor cringed.

The massive black tires ate up the ground, and the huge fender glistened in the sun like a mouth of giant teeth aching to sink into him.

It was so close.

He lurched forward as the metal giant roared toward him.

The cheeseburger only a stride away, he lowered his head to grab it as he darted for the far sidewalk.

The metal giant thundered closer. Too close.

Razor lunged, jaws open, but the truck growled past and clipped his tail. He yelped, more with shock than pain, but in so doing, he missed the cheeseburger. His momentum carried him on, and he dug his claws into the road to swing back for his prize.

As he skidded to a stop in the other lane, a black SUV tearing toward him honked its horn.

He spun his head from side to side. Food or sidewalk? Food or sidewalk?

The horn blasted again.

He did the only thing he could – he scrambled to the safety of the sidewalk as the vehicle flew by.

Gasping for breath, he hauled himself over to a building and slumped against it.

A dog had to know when to fight because a battle could be won and when to run because the only option was to lose. But how many times could he run from a fight? And if he ran again today, what would he run from tomorrow?

No, he had to make a stand.

Dragging himself back to the curb, he stared at the cheeseburger – *his* cheeseburger. He was going to do this. He was a fighter, not a quitter. A *fighter*. This would *not* beat him. Not again.

His mouth watered as he stared at the food through a gap in the traffic, but a silver car revved by and blocked his view, then a van. A gap came after the van, so he stepped into the road. That cheeseburger was his now. *His!*

But he froze – the spot on the asphalt was empty. Where the devil had his cheeseburger gone?

He sniffed. Jerking his head to the right, he followed the scent. His gaze roamed... there!

Stuck to one of the van's tires, his squashed cheeseburger appeared, then disappeared, appeared, then disappeared. It vanished into the line of vehicles.

He slumped. So much for making a stand.

Still, there was always the chance there'd be another hot dog in the alley.

As he tramped toward the fast-food truck, a man in a white apron rushed out and stormed toward him, brandishing a broom. What was it with men and brooms? The man swiped at him.

Razor leaped sideways, swallowing the pain that exploded in his shoulder. He hobbled into the alley and cursed himself for running from yet another fight.

"Go on, get!" The man flailed his weapon.

Lumbering into the shadows, Razor glanced back. *Real smart, skippy. Maybe I'll mosey back later and drop a deuce in your precious truck's doorway.*

He wandered over to the two dumpsters, squeezed in between them, and collapsed. Safe.

What the devil was wrong with people that so many were so horrible? He was going to have nothing more to do with any of them. Nothing.

He stared into space. What was going wrong? He wasn't healing, he was struggling for food, and the entire world seemed out to get him. Why? He'd fought to be a good dog and to do everything his man had asked of him. Why had he now been abandoned to this hell?

As for his TV show...

He snorted. What a lie that was. There was no Frisbee heaven. No place where dogs were cherished. He'd never seen it, and he'd seen enough men and dogs in the real world to know the truth. Dogs existed to serve and to suffer. That was it. Not to have fun and enjoy hugs. And to think how much time he'd wasted waiting for that diabolical show when he could have been searching for food. What a loser.

And there was his answer as to why his man had forsaken him. Loser. Loser. LOSER!

Chapter 06

Midafternoon, after resting and ruminating, Razor slunk from between the dumpsters and stalked down the alley, hunting for food.

Loser? Heaven help the next person to challenge him, because he'd show them, show the entire world, what a loser looked like.

He heaved over one of the trash cans and pawed through the garbage that spewed out. His nose said there was nothing edible, but it wasn't as trustworthy as usual. However, he found nothing.

A passing bus changed the air pressure within the alley, and a scent teased him from the far end where traffic tootled in either direction. He strode down and rooted through the litter underneath a black metal fire escape.

Aha!

He snatched up part of a candy bar and devoured it.

Loser? Yeah, right.

Another scent wafted from the end of the alley he'd just come from, near the food truck. A scent that stopped him dead.

No, it couldn't be.

Could it?

From the gloom beneath the fire escape, he peered back.

A small girl with raven hair cascading over her shoulders crouched and ran her hand over a little brown dog's shoulders. "What's wrong, Kai? Huh? What's wrong, boy?"

The pup!

Razor glared. So this was what being charitable had gotten him — an ungrateful wretch coming back for revenge. *Big mistake, champ. Big mistake.*

The girl hugged the pup.

Razor's jaw dropped. People really did hug dogs? It wasn't just on TV? *Really?*

With a gentle voice, she said, "It's okay, silly. There's nothing to be afraid of. Come on."

Razor prowled through the shadows as the pair moved down the alley. His nose was acting up, but it couldn't mistake the stench floating toward him — fear.

The pup was right to be frightened. Razor had gone easy on it last time, but returning to challenge him a second time? With backup? Talk about stupid.

Another scent floated in the air too, one that ordinarily would have tantalized Razor but was completely irrelevant now — they had a hot dog.

Razor growled. Deep. Guttural. Oozing malice.

The girl gasped and tensed as she obviously realized her companion was right to be so afraid.

And there it was — the stench of fear from her, too.

Loser? Who was the loser now?

With her breath coming in sharp pants, the girl stared at Razor. Terror twisted her face, and the leash shook in her hand.

Blocking their way in the middle of the alley, Razor lowered his head and snarled.

The girl held a hot dog toward Razor, as if to buy her way out of trouble. Her hand trembled as ketchup dripped to the ground. She was small, young, and her face was as pale as her hair was dark.

Why on earth would the pup bring someone so useless as backup? Was the thing really so stupid?

Way to go, champ. Ready for your next lesson?

Glowering, Razor bared his teeth and stalked closer, hackles raised.

Despite stinking of fright, the pup growled. Razor gawked as it stepped forward to protect her, as if it had realized the mistake it had made in bringing a timid girl to a vicious dogfight.

Razor stared at the pup. If it had come looking to fight with her, why was it now shielding her? That was honorable. Not the act of a coward who ganged up on someone.

The girl tightened her grip on the leash, pulling the pup to her side and away from danger.

Now *she* was protecting the pup? What was going on? It was as if they were a pack that cared for each other. As if they were equals.

But people and dogs were never equals.

There was a distinct hierarchy that kept everything in its place. The lowest level was strangers and strange things, then came dogs, then fighting dogs, then friends of the fighting dog's man, and finally, on the top level, the fighting dog's man himself. Each separate, and each dominant over those below it. Never, never equal. Anything else would lead to chaos.

What the devil was going on here? Hugging? Protecting? Caring? It was crazy. Crazy!

He gnashed his teeth at them in frustration. If they'd come here to fight, they wouldn't have been so terrified when he'd appeared. That meant they hadn't expected to find him.

This wasn't a fight, it was an accident.

The girl twisted around, heaved her arm back, and launched the hot dog into the air. It sailed up the alley the way they'd come.

Razor glared at the odd couple. To hell with whatever weirdness was going on here. He shot past them after the hot dog as it skimmed off a dumpster and splattered on the ground.

Behind him, the girl shouted, "Run, Kai. Run!"

Their footsteps pounded away in the opposite direction.

Razor gazed at the hot dog, saliva stringing from his jaws. It was gigantic. The biggest he'd ever seen. He chomped into his prize.

Oh, heaven. Warm, juicy, fresh, meaty... absolute bliss. Today was turning into a grand day after all.

Loser? Yeah, right.

Savoring every mouthful, he devoured his meal, then stretched out on the concrete, bathed in sunshine. With his belly fuller than it had been for days, he yawned. What a grand day. No, a day to end all days.

His eyelids drooping, he sighed. Whatever happened later could only be an anticlimax. Nothing could top a belly full of hot dog and a snooze in the sun. Nothing.

Maybe it didn't matter if his man never came back. After all, Razor was surviving just fine: he'd gotten a new home, found a semireliable place to find food, had his sky dog friend... he had everything he could ever need. Compared to his cage and a life of fighting, this was pretty good. Who'd have thought slipping out of the car that night would be the best thing to ever happen to him?

Yep, today, he was living the dream. Tomorrow? Razor drifted to sleep, dreaming of how things could only get better.

Chapter 07

Footsteps clomped along the alley, waking Razor. Bleary-eyed, he raised his head.

A man in a gray uniform stood nearby, holding a pole. Before Razor knew what was happening, a noose slipped over his head and constricted around his neck.

What the...?

Razor jerked up to shake off the noose, but it tightened.

Twisting, he clamped his jaws on the pole and savaged it, but the contraption wouldn't release him.

He glared at the Gray Man. *Boy have you picked on the wrong dog, chief.*

Razor lunged, snapping at the man, but the pole yanked him back.

"Stop struggling, you silly dog. I'm trying to help you."

Razor writhed and bucked to escape, but the noose choked him. Spluttering, he leaped left, ran right, then spun around and around. But the more he battled, the faster he was caught.

"Finished yet?"

Panting, Razor glowered. If he wasn't so injured, he'd have ripped this clown to shreds already. He lurched forward, but his shoulder gave and he smacked into the concrete.

As he scrambled up, pain clawed his body. He scoured his various fighting strategies for one that would see him escape, but the Gray Man hauled him toward a white van with squiggles down the side parked at the alley's entrance.

A beady-eyed second gray man opened the rear doors, revealing two empty cages. He reached for the end of a pole jutting out beside them. "Need a hand?"

The Gray Man shook his head. "He's strong, but he's pretty banged up."

Razor lunged to make a break for it but got nowhere. Luckily, fighting wasn't only about brute strength, but strategy — if he jumped into the van, he could spin around and defend himself far easier than battling in the open.

He leaped inside and spun as Beady Eyes slammed the cage door shut.

Razor snarled.

As if by magic, the noose slackened. The Gray Man pulled the pole out of the cage, shoved it next to the other, then waltzed away.

With a bark, Razor glared. *And don't come back, chief, or you'll get more of that.*

Strategy. Never failed.

He glanced about. Now, what was the easiest way out of here?

But Beady Eyes shut the van door and gloom enveloped Razor. What the devil was going on?

The vehicle rumbled and the stench of burning fuel filled the air. They were taking him somewhere? He only ever went places with his man. No one else. Ever.

His nose hadn't been working up to par recently, yet he didn't believe he knew either of these men. He sniffed toward where the men were sitting and consulted his library of scents. No, he couldn't place them as friends of his man, but what else could they be? Obviously, his man couldn't come, so he'd sent them. Why else would they abduct him like this?

Razor lay down. Finally, he was going home.

During the journey, Razor scoured the scents drifting in. He hunted for the smell of the gas station his man regularly visited, the restaurant where his man bought sweet and sour takeout, the gym where he waited in the car while people ran on treadmills just like he did...

Nothing.

If they were going to his man, they were taking a very puzzling route.

The van stopped, and the doors opened. The Gray Man stared at him. "Settled down, have we?"

Razor squinted. If they'd arrived, where was his man?

The Gray Man slid the pole out of the van and stuck it back in the cage.

"Things will go much easier if you play nice, okay?" He slipped the noose over Razor's head again.

Razor remained docile. He didn't want to cause a scene in front of his man — he wanted a happy reunion, not to be punished the moment he got home.

The Gray Man opened the cage and gave a gentle tug on the pole. Razor leaped down.

"That's my boy."

They stood at the back of a white concrete building where Beady Eyes opened a door. Warm air gushed out. And scents. So many scents.

Razor gulped. Oh no. Please no. Not now.

He shuffled backward.

"It's okay, boy. Nothing to be afraid of." The Gray Man smiled.

Razor peered inside. There were dogs in there. Lots of dogs. And there was only one reason a place had lots of dogs — it was a dogfight club.

He stared at the Gray Man. Hadn't they seen he was injured? They couldn't expect him to fight in his condition.

"Come on, boy." The Gray Man yanked the pole.

Razor sat down. He was going nowhere. While he didn't want to incur his man's wrath, if he lost another fight, he would suffer his man's rage anyway. So, it was best to make it clear this was not happening.

Beady Eyes said, "I'm on it."

He disappeared inside the building. A moment later, he returned with a box of kibble and a metal bowl. He tipped a small portion into the bowl and placed it before Razor, then handed the box to the Gray Man.

Razor frowned. He was always starved before a fight, not given free food. How odd.

"Go on," said Beady Eyes.

Razor squinted at the man, then back at the bowl. Seriously? That meant he wouldn't be fighting today.

He scarfed down the lot.

The Gray Man rubbed his chin. "It might be the pole that's freaking him. I'll try him with a leash."

"Do you think it's safe?"

The Gray Man handed his pole over. "You be ready just in case."

Holding a black braided slip leash, the Gray Man said, "Easy now, boy. We're only trying to help."

He slipped the loop over Razor's head and tightened it, then Beady Eyes released the pole.

The Gray Man smiled and shook a small box of kibble as he strolled toward the building. "Come, boy. Come."

The hot dog had filled Razor, but only a fool turned down free food. He tottered in, Beady Eyes following with the pole.

The Gray Man led him to a room with a metal table in the middle, beside which stood a skinny woman in a long white coat and glasses. Strange equipment lay on the counter behind her, and shelves and cupboards burst with chemically smells from bottles and packets — like the smell from the medicine he'd had in the past.

"Hey, Vera. This ain't a pretty case. Looks like he's been used for fighting, but darn if I know what he's gotten stuck all over himself."

She sniffed. "Smells like burning. Is it soot?"

"Could be. His fur is matted to heck."

"Oh, poor thing. Can he jump up, or do we have to lift him?"

The Gray Man patted the table's silver top. "Up, boy. Up."

Without his vicious pole, the Gray Man didn't seem that scary, and if Razor leaped up there, he'd have a far better view of what was going on. Especially if things went south — higher ground was always an advantage. Strategy strikes again.

He jumped up, the movement making his shoulder burn, but the strategic advantage too good to miss.

Higher now, he stared Vera in the face. She didn't look threatening, but looks could be deceptive.

Her brow furrowed. "Awww, the world hasn't been good to you, has it?"

Her tone suggested she wasn't a threat either. Maybe he was safe here until his man arrived.

Vera looked in his ears, peered into his eyes, inspected his wounds, put black tubes in her ears connected to a disk that she held to his chest...

She winced at the Gray Man. "You're right. He's been fighting, but from the size of the bites and the distance between the canine puncture wounds, it looks like they pitted him against two dogs."

"Two?" The Gray Man shook his head. "Poor little fella. Thank God we found him."

Vera hovered a black stick with a ring at the end over his shoulders and down his back. "No chip."

The Gray Man rolled his eyes. "Big surprise."

"I'll have Hazel bathe him so I can inspect the wounds properly, and we'll take it from there. Thanks, Ted."

The Gray Man patted Razor lightly on the back. "Good luck to you, fella."

He left.

A lanky woman in a green uniform and with the curliest brown hair entered.

With his leash, Curly Hair took him to another room, where a gray metal trough stood on legs against one wall. She slid open a small door in the side and patted the interior. "Come on, boy. Let's get all that muck off you."

Higher ground. He rested his front paws on the lip and jumped in.

Curly Hair fastened his leash to the wall and closed the small door. Taking a muzzle, she said, "Are you going to be good and let me put this on?"

He stared at her. His man had made him wear those things sometimes. They weren't fun because they stopped him from being able to use his mouth properly, but if it made his man happy, it made him happy.

Curly Hair eased the muzzle over his snout.

"Good boy!" She stroked his head. "I don't think we need it, do we? But I don't want to accidentally hurt you while I'm washing you and have you bite me."

She caressed his side where the black powder had stuck to him after he'd returned home wet.

"Where the devil have you been to get in this mess?" Her voice was soothing, like she was talking to a puppy, not a fighting dog like him. But he kind of liked it. After all the hostile looks and angry voices on the street, her voice made a glowing warmth swell inside him, like a light coming on in a darkened room.

She took a silver hose and jetted water into the trough. After putting her hand in the stream, she sprayed it on his back.

"How's that feel? Good, huh?"

Razor straightened. The warm jetting action kneaded his aching muscles like little fingers massaging him. Very nice. This Curly Hair might become a new friend if she continued this kind of treatment.

She doused him from his tail to the back of his head, then ran her hand over plastic bottles filled with different-colored liquids on a nearby shelf.

"Now, which one will be best for stripping this gunk off you?" She picked a clear one. "Shall we try hypoallergenic to be safe?"

Pumping the top, she squirted a glob into her palm, then massaged it into his fur.

He sighed as her fingers unknotted his fur and rejuvenated his weary muscles. Oh yes, definitely friend material. Not that he'd want to be treated like this every day — what was he, a poodle! No, a fighting dog had certain standards to maintain. However, she seemed to be enjoying herself, and he didn't want to offend, so...

Below him, black water swirled away.

Curly Hair moved down his side. He flinched as her fingers neared his worst wound.

"Don't worry, I see it."

As if she knew it was there, her kneading transformed into delicate dabbing around the area without touching the bite itself.

She winced and sucked through her teeth. "Dear Lord, whoever put you through this should be sent to the chair."

Finishing that spot, she moved on.

"Have you been sitting in black glue?" She snickered, pawing at his rump, where his fur and the soot had formed a solid mass.

She delicately worked her fingers through his coat, prying apart the matted fur, but stopped. "What's this?"

He glanced around. Oh, she was admiring his squiggle. Yes, his man took great care to recreate that every few weeks.

Curly Hair ran her fingers over his squiggle.

"R?" She frowned. "An initial? Does your name start with R?" She continued washing. "R...? Ringo? No, you don't look like a Ringo. Rebel? Roger? Oh, yeah, Roger." She snickered again. "R-r... Rocky? Ummm..."

She kept making an R sound as if she were about to say Razor. No one had said his name for so long, he'd thought he might never hear it again. He wagged his tail, and it swished water across her face.

She giggled and threw her arms up as a shield.

"Is that a hint I'm getting close?" She resumed shampooing. "You know, you're going to need a name in here, so why don't we pick one beginning with R and hope it's not too far off? Is that okay? Now, what would be a good fit for a handsome boy like you?"

She stared at the wall, biting her bottom lip.

"Oh, I know." Craning around, she grinned into his face. "Rio." She arched her eyebrows. "What do you think? Good, huh?"

She continued washing him. "If we're going to find you a nice home, a good name is a great start, and nothing says fun and excitement like Rio. I went there once. Didn't see the carnival, but... wow, what an awesome place." She nodded. "Yep, Rio — that's the one."

After shampooing him twice, she gazed at him.

"So that's what color you are. Who'd have guessed under all that filth?" She removed his muzzle. "Okay, you've been good so far, so keep it up, Rio."

Curly Hair washed his head and snout, then turned off the water and toweled him. Finally, she took a fatter black hose and blew warm air on him.

Razor couldn't remember the last time he'd felt so clean and so warm. He'd visit here again, if his man would let him.

Curly Hair opened the trough door and unhooked his leash from the wall. "Down, Rio."

She obviously had other treats in store, so ignoring the pain, he leaped down, eager to indulge her. Not that he enjoyed this pampering — he was a hardened fighting dog — but it seemed to make her happy. And as she'd been so nice to him, indulging her was the least he could do.

44

They went back to Vera.

"How was he?" asked Vera.

"Fine."

"No signs of aggression?"

Curly Hair stroked his head. "No, he's a good boy. Aren't you, Rio?"

"Rio?"

Curly Hair pointed to his squiggle.

"That's his name?" asked Vera.

"It is now."

"Okay, Rio, let's see what we can do with these wounds."

Vera poked and prodded him, both with her fingers and with tools. When she inspected the wound on his right foreleg, the one the pup had reopened, he flinched.

Shaking her head, Vera exhaled loudly. "He's going to need anesthetizing for me to clean some of these."

"I figured as much. Poor little thing."

Vera typed something into her computer. "I don't know about poor. He's probably the luckiest dog we've found in months."

Curly Hair frowned. "Lucky? I've never seen a dog in such a state."

"All that soot could've saved his life. Its germicidal acids and phenols give it antibacterial properties. If he hadn't been caked in the stuff, these wounds could've easily become so badly infected they were life-threatening."

"Seriously?" Curly Hair's eyebrows rose.

"Oh, yeah." Vera nodded. "Of course, we'll still be giving him broad-spectrum antibiotics."

"Wow, soot. Who'd have thunk it?"

Vera winced. "Well, before we start celebrating, the downside is that inhaling soot can cause things like bronchitis and heart disease. His lungs and heart seem strong, but he'll get a thorough check once he's under."

She reached for a syringe and a small bottle of fluid.

"We're doing it today? Not tomorrow after he's fasted?"

"These wounds are too old, so I don't want to push his luck." She drew liquid into the syringe.

Curly Hair scooped one hand under his belly and placed the other in front of his forelegs to hold him against her torso, as if she didn't want him to move. She smelled of the Mexican food his man ate occasionally.

Something pricked his butt, and he flinched.

Curly Hair stroked his neck. "It's okay, Rio."

Vera said, "Can you stay with him, then bring him to the induction room in twenty minutes, please?"

"Will do."

Vera left.

Releasing him, Curly Hair stroked his back. "Well done, Rio. You're being so good after what you've been through."

Her hand smoothed his fur over and over. For absolutely no reason.

He frowned. Why was she being so nice? *Is this a symptom of a mental disorder, sparky? Because it's not normal behavior.*

Though he had to admit, it did kind of feel good. But she was obviously getting far more out of it than he was.

"Don't worry. Vera will make you better, then we'll find you a nice new home with someone who truly appreciates you."

She talked far more than his man. Unfortunately. Silence was good. Comfortable. Normal. Silence meant the world was as it should be — leaving him out of it until there was a fight to be fought. No, he didn't like this incessant noise.

Curly Hair stroked him again and again.

She touched him more than his man too — in strange ways that made him feel warm inside. Maybe he could forgive her noise when she made up for it in other areas.

He didn't know if it was this strange touching, but the pain from his wounds subsided. A dreaminess overwhelmed him, as if he'd only half woken from an afternoon snooze.

"Okay, Rio, let's get you sorted out."

Curly Hair helped him off the table and led him to another room with another silver table. These people certainly had a thing for silver tables.

It didn't look any higher than the other one, but this time, Curly Hair and Vera lifted him onto a springy blue pad on the top.

46

While Curly Hair scooped her arms under him to squeeze him to her again, Vera lifted his left foreleg and wiped a white plastic buzzy thing over it.

Razor gasped as fur fell off. *Hey, be careful where you put that, sunshine. I'll be wanting it back later!*

Vera wiped a smelly cloth over the pink skin she'd revealed, and his leg tingled with coldness, then she stuck in a needle with a white lump at the end.

He bucked, but Curly Hair squeezed him harder, and for some reason, he didn't have the strength or aptitude to fight her.

Vera bound the white lump in place with tape and attached another syringe to it. Moments later, Razor's eyelids drooped. He was in a strange place with strange people, and while they seemed nice, he couldn't risk dropping his guard. He fought to keep his eyes open. But the world darkened.

Chapter 08

Razor's eyes flickered open and he stared at a white plastic wall. He frowned. That wasn't there before. His head lolling, he peered about, mind as fuzzy as the world was blurry. More white plastic.

Where was he?

He pushed to stand but rose only a few inches before slumping back down. He drew a long breath and tried again. Grimacing, he heaved up and stood, swaying from side to side.

Bleary-eyed, he squinted through the glass door at the front of his cage. A woman sat working at a desk with her back to him, and cupboards lined the walls in a similar fashion to the other room. He sniffed, but all the scents smudged together.

Strangely, no matter where he looked, a white halo encircled everything, as if he were looking through a round window in a white wall. He glanced left – white halo. Right – white halo. Up and down – white halo. He turned around, but the white halo was everywhere.

What the devil had they done to him?

Maybe if he escaped this cage, he could escape the halo, too. He pushed the door with his nose. It rattled.

The woman spun around in her chair. Curly Hair.

"Hi, Rio, how are you doing, boy?" She unlocked the door and tickled him under the chin.

Touching? Again? Man, have you got issues, kiddo.

She removed her hand and smiled.

He frowned. *You're stopping already?* He nuzzled her. *Hey, pain means nothing to a fighting dog, so if touching makes you happy, I can bear it.*

She tickled him again. "Feeling better, I see. Good."

He opened and closed his jaws a few times, his mouth tasting funny and his throat sore.

"Mouth gunky, huh? This should help." She placed a bowl of water in his cage.

He lapped. The cool liquid drowned the funny taste in his mouth and soothed his throat.

His head clearing, he gazed about the room. There were medicines in here as well. And food in the bottom corner cupboard. He licked his lips, staring at it. He couldn't remember the last time he'd eaten properly.

"You've smelled it already?" Curly Hair laughed. "No matter how many times I see that, it never fails to astound me." She opened the door and slipped a leash on him. "So, how about we see if your new accommodation meets your approval and, if so, if you can keep a snack down?"

She led him along the same corridor as before toward a door at the far end. He sniffed — dogs. Lots of dogs. The smell grew stronger and stronger while barking and whimpering grew louder and louder.

So much for thinking he wouldn't have to fight. Razor tensed. Smelling the competition was usually when his muscles flooded with energy and he felt invincible, but today...

He trudged on, each step an effort. How the devil was he supposed to fight when he could barely stand? He cringed. His opponent would eat him alive. Possibly quite literally!

The door opened onto a cavernous room with a number of aisles, down each of which were pens with a metal grille front and back, and separated from its neighbors by a three-foot-high white brick wall topped by another grille.

Curly Hair guided him down one aisle.

Head low, eyes as wild as he had the energy to make them, he glared into the first pen.

A petite dog with luxurious brown-and-white fur sat prim and proper on a blue bed, like some little princess.

Razor's jaw dropped. This was his competition? He snorted with relief. What kind of twisted dogfighting club was this?

Still, a dog was a dog. Razor curled his lip at the little princess. The thing's eyes widened, and pee pooled across the bed and dribbled onto the floor. Very aristocratic.

In the opposite pen, a puppy batted a red ball with its paw. Next door, a small dog with puffy white fur lay trembling.

And he'd been worried?

Even in his state, this wouldn't be a fight but a massacre. He almost felt guilty at how easy this was going to be, but nature was brutal – it wasn't the taking part that mattered, only the winning. There were no participation trophies in dogfighting.

His head high, he strode along the aisle, glowering at anything that dared to meet his gaze.

Curly Hair led him into a pen where a piece of red carpet, a blue bed, and two silver bowls lay on a cream floor.

She eased up his right foreleg and studied a bandage he hadn't noticed. "It doesn't look like this is bothering you. Good."

Where had that thing come from?

She lowered his leg as if it were made of glass.

He stared at the bandage. *Seriously, sparky. Like I won't be ripping that off the moment you leave.*

"Here's water and food." She slid the bowls closer. "I'll check on you before I go home." She smiled. "See you later, Rio." After patting him, she left.

Razor leaned down to rip the offending item off his leg, but the white halo followed him and got in the way.

What the devil...?

He tried again. But however he turned, the halo was there, a cone of white encircling his world. He shook his head, but the cone remained. He shook again, so hard he stumbled against the wall, knocking one of the bowls. Kibble scattered across the floor.

Razor gulped. The horrible thing went everywhere he did. How was he going to cope with this monstrosity strapped to him?

He frowned. If they were torturing him with this cone, what else had they done to him? He twisted left and gasped.

Another white dressing! Hadn't they seen he'd been bitten there? What kind of lunatic would stick such a thing on a wound?

He lunged to rip the white thing off, but the cone obstructed him.

Razor slumped. Had he been bad to be punished like this? He'd thought Curly Hair was nice — her overfamiliarity aside — but strapping this to him was just plain criminal. And then she'd shoved food under his nose? Like he could eat with this contraption. Criminal? It was outright evil.

He lowered to the bowl to prove his point, but his snout reached the kibble with ease.

Oh... he had not expected that. He munched a mouthful. Mmm... meaty. He shoveled up more.

This did not alter the situation, however.

It was outrageous that they were abusing him like this. Unforgivable.

He scarfed down another mouthful. Absolutely delicious. Somewhat nutty with just a hint of sourness.

But what gave them the right? They didn't even know him, so why torture him?

Boy, was it crunchy. Like chomping through wood — fantastic!

Hell. He was in hell.

He lashed the empty bowl with his tongue and it skittered about, then he licked all the pellets off the floor.

He smacked his lips. That was probably the tastiest kibble he'd ever had. Giving him that was an odd way to punish him, but these people were crazy, so who knew what they were capable of? All that touching, all that sweet tone of voice, all that poking and prodding... Crazy, the lot of them.

Belly full, he lay down. The concrete floor was good and hard, just as a bed was supposed to be. At least they'd gotten one thing right. His man couldn't get here soon enough to put an end to this craziness. Razor closed his eyes and dozed off.

The smell of Mexican food woke him — Curly Hair. He opened one eye as his pen gate squealed.

"You ate all your food. Good boy, Rio." She crouched. "I'm going home, but I'll be in tomorrow to check on you."

He lifted his head. *So no touching? This affliction of yours is passing, is it? Good, because I—*

She scratched under his chin. "You're a big softy, aren't you?"

He turned his head left. *Oh yes, just there, sparky. I can bear it if you can.*

"Whoever gets you is going to be so lucky."

He stared at her. *That's right. Take your fill while you can because I'm a hardened fighting dog who could rip your thr—*

She stood. "Bye, Rio."

Oh, so that's it, is it? Yes, well, good. I was getting bored with it anyway, you weirdo.

She left.

Still exhausted, Razor curled into a ball and closed his eyes. It had been the oddest day ever, which was good because it meant only one thing — tomorrow would see a return to normality. No way could there be two odd days in a row.

Chapter 09

The next morning, Razor clambered up, pushed his forelegs in front of him and stuck his butt in the air, then shoved his chest out and held his head high while his hind legs trailed behind him. Surprisingly, despite all the abuse he'd suffered in this place, he felt good. Better than he'd felt for days.

Barking and whimpering surrounding him, he ambled to his gate. The pen directly opposite was empty, but to the right stood an old sandy-colored dog with floppy ears. Left, a mottled brown dog sat cringing, trembling as if it was freezing cold. Farther along, a tiny brown-and-white thing with immense ears and huge eyes yapped and yapped.

Razor snorted. Seriously? Even injured, he could take out those three all at the same time. These people had obviously never been to a quality dogfight. Still, like he was going to complain about his fights being too easy.

He scanned his competition again. The old dog smelled diseased, so he'd take it easy on that – there was no glory in punishing something not long for this world.

The cringer? He'd probably spend most of the fight chasing that around the pit, then after a few nips, it would probably roll over and play dead.

But that yappy thing? Boy, that deserved everything coming to it. So small yet so loud. What was wrong with it?

He ambled to the other end of his pen and peered out. A thing so emaciated it looked like its legs would snap if it moved too quickly, a chunky dog with a square head — they could be dangerous — and a female with long white fur. Square Head was the only threat, but as Razor looked at it, it wagged its tail. Oh, yeah, real deadly.

He snorted. The fight organizers obviously didn't have a clue, so he'd be top dog in no time.

Curly Hair's scent drifted over. Hey, his nose was working!

"Hi, Rio." She entered his pen. "How are you feeling?"

Here we go again. Sitting, he lifted his chin. *Come on, then, you weirdo, get it over with.*

Weirdo scratched him. "How about a little walk later? Think you can manage it?"

He closed his eyes as she tickled his throat. The stuff he had to put up with.

She stopped. "So, breakfast now, then a short walk. Okay?" She refilled his bowls with kibble and fresh water, then left.

If they were feeding him, he wasn't fighting today. It was good they were giving him time to heal.

He dug into his breakfast.

Sometime later, Weirdo returned and guided him out and down the aisle on a leash. In each pen, dog after dog barked or ate or slept or cowered. A black dog with only three legs, a mop-like mound of fur, a shaggy cream thing, a blob so overweight it could barely stand... it was hard to believe this pathetic bunch were fighting dogs, but why else would they be here?

Razor glowered at each of them. Strategy. His scent and his glare said more than any growl ever could. In the past, he'd met dogs that never stopped barking, yet their scent screamed how afraid they were. Like they were ever going to win a fight. His way? No dog could mistake he was there to do one thing and one thing only — win.

Weirdo opened a back door onto a grassy compound. A wire mesh fence enclosed the area, parked cars lined two sides, and another building stood on the other.

In the doorway, Razor froze. The place reeked of dog pee. Old dogs, sick dogs, young dogs, small dogs, big dogs... every dog in the world must have peed here at some time.

"It's okay, Rio, you're safe here." Weirdo gently tugged the leash.

He ambled out.

"Good boy."

He'd seen the number of dogs inside, and that didn't explain how so much dog pee had accumulated. How long had this fight club existed?

But he had more pressing needs right now.

Razor squatted and pooped. And as if Weirdo couldn't get any weirder, she picked up his poop in a white bag.

He frowned. *Starting a collection there, sparky?* Unbelievable.

The leash slack, he led them to the fence and a concrete post in the middle. He sniffed up and down it. Yep, this was the spot – the place where the most dogs had peed. He cocked his leg and overmarked as much of the post as possible.

Strategy. The top dog needed top billing.

Lowering his leg, he glanced at Weirdo. *Want that for your collection, too?*

She wasn't remotely interested. Strange. Pee was so much more interesting than poop.

He wandered around, sniffing to get a feel for who'd been there, when, and what kind of condition they were in.

Weirdo yanked the leash. "Time's up, Rio."

She led him back to his pen, then took the yapping thing out. It yapped even more, as if this was some great treat.

Razor glared at Yappy. Did the thing ever shut up?

Leaning against his gate, he watched as Weirdo took out other dogs – sometimes two at once. She usually came back with a white bag of dog poop, which she dropped into a blue container. It was an odd place to store something she treasured, but she was an odd woman.

A shaven-headed man in a similar green uniform also took out dogs and returned with white poop bags.

Was this place not just for dogfighting, but a special club for people who collected dog poop? Who'd ever have thought that could be a thing?

Midmorning, voices drifted in from the corridor. All around, claws scraped on concrete and barks changed to excited yips.

Had the audience arrived for today's fights?

He curled up at the far end of his pen. They'd given him a pass on competing today, but he didn't want to get dragged into anything by accident.

Weirdo's voice drifted toward him. "We've got a number of small dogs in, but from what you're describing, let me introduce you to one of my favorites."

Footsteps clomped over and stopped nearby.

Razor craned to see around the corner of his pen's wall. Weirdo had stopped outside Yappy's pen. A scrawny woman waltzed up holding hands with two small girls.

Razor gaped. *This* was the audience for the dogfight? *Hold the beer and smokes, Weirdo, try Barbies and cotton candy.*

Weirdo said, "This is Milly, our gorgeous little four-year-old papillon."

Both girls gasped and crouched, then pushed their fingers through the grille. Yappy licked them and the girls giggled.

"She's great with kids, as you can see. She has no special dietary requirements and is completely housebroken."

The woman said, "Does she shed?"

"Not really. Papillons are single-coated dogs, so that's not usually an issue. If you'd like, you can spend some time with her in our meet-and-greet room."

The girl with the red bow in her hair said, "Can we, Mommy? Please, can we?"

The troop meandered toward the corridor, the girls with the biggest smiles Razor had ever seen. And Yappy... if Razor thought she'd yapped before, how wrong he was. He'd never heard a dog so excited to fight before.

Curious, he sloped over to his gate. Who was she pitted against? Square Head was out of the question — it would rip her in half in a second and short fights usually upset the audience. Yappy had to have a chance. So who could she fight? The puppy? Maybe the three-legged dog?

Strangely, Weirdo didn't fetch another dog.

Razor frowned at the laughter drifting in, mingled with Yappy's jubilation. Yappy had to be winning to sound so happy. How? What was she fighting? A blind rabbit?

When the door opened again, Weirdo was beaming as widely as the girls. "Yes, we can chip her before you pick her up. It's thirty dollars."

Both girls holding the leash, they led Yappy down the aisle, gazing at her instead of watching where they were going.

"That's fine," said the woman. "And we'll be able to pick her up this time next week?"

"If the home check is okay, which from what you've said should go without a hitch."

"Great. Okay, girls, say goodbye to Milly. We've got to be at Grandma's in a half hour."

"Can Milly come?" said Red Ribbon.

"Next week, sweetheart."

Both girls crouched and petted Yappy. "Bye, Milly. Bye."

Weirdo put Yappy back in her pen, then they all left.

How odd. Yappy didn't have a mark on her and there was no scent of blood. What the devil kind of fights were they staging here?

Sometime later, a man with thick glasses hobbled around, peering at all the dogs. Then a young couple did the same before taking the puppy away for a while. In the afternoon, a woman with braided hair took Three Legs into the yard.

What were these people doing? And why were the dogs so happy they were doing it? It was as if all the dogs were privy to some secret and were reveling in it.

Late afternoon, Square Head began to yap almost as much as Yappy. And a few minutes later, Weirdo came in with a man sporting a stud through his nose.

She grinned. "Guess who knows you're coming."

He laughed. "I had a shower today. Honest."

"It's not just your scent. Dogs have amazing hearing. He probably heard us talking outside."

Nose Stud crouched outside Square Head's gate. "Hey, buddy. Are you ready to come to your new home?"

Square Head jumped in circles, yipping and yipping.

Smiling, Nose Stud looked up. "Are they always this excited?"

"Not always, but Toby's been let down before, so I guess on some level, he was worried you might not show."

He frowned. "People do that?"

"Oh, we get no-shows regularly. You'd be surprised."

He turned to the aisle. "I tell you, I'd take all of them if I could."

"Just remember to tell friends and family about us next time they're looking for a pet."

"Way ahead of you." He held his phone up to the pens and tapped the screen. "Already on Insta."

Weirdo opened the gate. Square Head bounded out and slathered his tongue all over Nose Stud's face. The man laughed and laughed, then draped his arms around Square Head and hugged him. Hugged him like in Frisbee heaven.

Razor's jaw dropped.

It really happened. A child hugging a puppy was one thing, but this...? People genuinely hugged dogs. Not just patted them. Not just stroked them. Hugged them. *Hugged!* Seeing it on TV was one thing, but seeing it in real life...

Weirdo walked out with the man and Square Head, all three absolutely reeking of happiness. Razor had never smelled such joy. Never.

Razor gawked at the closed door to the corridor. Would it ever open and someone come in to hug him like that?

Chapter 10

Over the next few days, a seemingly endless stream of people moseyed along the aisles. Happy yipping always erupted, and most dogs greeted the people with licking tongues and joyful jumps. It was as if each new scent offered new hope, and what dog could resist a new scent?

Razor watched all of it, sitting at his gate, waiting to lick fingers pushed through the grille or to bask in the warmth of a hug.

A young man and woman sauntered up the aisle and stopped in front of his pen. Twirling her brown hair around her fingers, the woman smiled. "Awww... look at this one. He looks so pathetic in his cone."

Razor didn't know why, but whenever someone smiled at him, he felt an overwhelming urge to wag his tail. Today was no different.

Beside her, a man in a baseball cap studied a sheet of paper on Razor's gate. "Rio."

"Rio? Awww, how could you not love that sweet face?"

Rio wagged his tail harder as the woman gazed into his eyes with such care. Was this going to be his Frisbee heaven?

"Around four years old, German shepherd cross, recovering from... uh-oh."

"What?"

"He was used for fighting?"

The woman flounced away. "Oh no. I'm not risking something like that in the house."

Weirdo scurried over. "Rio's a real softy. Don't let his past fool you — it's not like he had a choice about what was done to him."

The woman screwed up her face. "Once a fighting dog..." She shrugged.

Weirdo said, "You won't find a more loving dog than a rescue, no matter their background. And the more they've suffered, the more they'll love you for giving them a second chance."

"Yeah, but I'm just not feeling it with him, you know?" She strolled on. "Awww, look at that one with only three legs."

The man read from the sheet on that gate. "Max. Eight years old... he lost his leg after being hit by a car but still loves short walks and playing fetch."

"Short walks is no good, is it?" She pointed elsewhere. "Oh, how about that one?"

She strolled out of sight.

Weirdo whispered, "You don't want someone like that, Rio. Trust me. But don't worry, I'll find you your forever home."

Later, a man in a suit ambled over and glanced at the paper on Razor's gate. "Rio, huh? You're a handsome dog, aren't you, boy?"

Razor gazed up, wagging his tail.

The man studied the paper. "Four years old." He nodded. "A dogfight, huh?" He winced but then shrugged and smiled at him. "Can't blame you for that, can we?" He tapped his phone, then read aloud, "German shepherds shed their coats all year round, with intense shedding during the spring and fall." He snorted. "No, thank you." He wandered away.

The next morning, Weirdo changed the paper on his gate.

Midmorning, a family stopped outside. A chubby woman read the paper while a balding man and two young boys crouched to Razor. They pushed their fingers through the grille, so he licked and licked.

The boys giggled, and the one with glasses wiggled his fingers. "Lick mine again."

"Excuse me," said the woman as Weirdo strolled by, "what's this one's story?"

"Oh, Rio's one of my favorites. He's had it tough, but he's on the mend."

"But what happened to him? Why's he in the cone?"

"He, uh..." Weirdo gazed at him with sadness in her eyes, as if believing she held his fate in her hands and didn't know what to do with it. She winced. "Listen, I don't want to color your opinion before you get to know him, so just look at him — look at how gentle he is with kids."

Everyone watched him licking the family's fingers.

"So...?" The woman arched an eyebrow at Weirdo.

"He..." Weirdo rubbed her chin. "He was used for fighting."

The woman yanked her sons' hands away from the grille. "Jake, don't do that, sweetheart. You too, Nathan." She glared at Weirdo. "It's outrageous you don't warn people about things like that."

"We would if we thought there was a problem. But you can see for yourself, he's a big softy."

"Yeah, a big softy until you're on the local news because he mauled your kid." She marched away, pulling her children along. "I told you we should've gone to Pet Sanctuary, Lawrence."

Weirdo slumped against Razor's gate. "Sorry, Rio. Sometimes I despair of people. But we'll find you the right one. I promise."

The next day, Razor smelled two young guys waltzing in. Instead of strolling to his gate, he rolled over on his concrete and stared at the wall. There was no Frisbee heaven — at least not for him — so there was no point in hoping for it only to be rejected over and over.

The men dawdled down the aisle, stopping at each pen. They came to Yappy.

One said, "She's such a cutie. Couldn't you just eat her?"

His friend said, "It says she's called Milly and— oh, she's reserved."

"Too bad."

Footsteps clomped to his gate. "You know, I never thought about a big dog, but maybe we should consider it. Can't you just see us all snuggling up on the sofa with popcorn and Netflix?"

"Can dogs eat popcorn?"

"I don't know. I'll google it."

"Don't bother. This one doesn't look like snuggle material, does it?"

"Would you feel sociable with a cone around your head?"

"A cone? With these pants?"

They both laughed, then sauntered past.

Staring at the wall, Razor didn't acknowledge anyone who came by. What was the point? He'd always suffered. Every day for as long as he could remember. Why had he believed things could ever be any different?

The days passed and people came and went. More than he could count, and he could count up to five when it was important, like counting the number of treats he'd been given. But this people-stuff? Not worth the effort.

Weirdo came into his pen. He didn't even raise his head.

She stroked him. "Come on, Rio, you have to try or people will just walk by. I changed your info sheet, but if people ask, I can't lie, so it's up to you to seal the deal."

He didn't move.

She shuffled around to look into his face and tickled under his chin as if she believed he liked that. "There is some good news, though."

He yanked his head away.

"Prepare yourself. You're going to be in a good mood whether you want to be or not because — drumroll — Vera says I can take this off." She touched his white halo. "Are you ready to be cone-free?" She fiddled with something at the back of his head. "Get ready..."

Dear Lord, this woman talked a lot. Didn't she ever shut u—

"Ta-da."

What the...?

He jerked up. The cone that had tormented him since he'd arrived had vanished.

"See, didn't I say you were going to feel better?" She ruffled the fur on his head. "Now, let's try harder today, shall we?"

Razor gazed around. The world looked so much bigger. Had there always been so much of it?

She cupped his face and kissed him on the forehead. "Today's the day, Rio. I can feel it."

Weirdo left, and Razor bent his neck this way and that. Even though the cone had weighed hardly anything, he felt lighter. Maybe his luck was changing. Well, it couldn't get any worse, could it?

Midmorning, a man in blue overalls strolled in, smelling of oil and cars. He stopped at Razor's gate and stared.

Razor didn't lift his head off his paws, but he met the man's gaze.

Oily Man wandered on. His footsteps clomped down each aisle, then clomped out.

Razor yawned. No one else stopped at his pen that day. So much for his luck changing.

The next day, after cleaning his pen, Weirdo dumped the piece of red carpet in his favorite lying spot. He couldn't be bothered moving it, so he slumped down. It was softer and warmer than his concrete. Completely unsuitable for a hardened fighting dog. Except, if he no longer fought, was that what he still was? And if not, what was he? He wasn't a fighter, wasn't a pet, he was... nothing.

He closed his eyes, but Yappy became even yappier than normal. Lying on his carpet, Razor sniffed long and hard. Yep, Yappy's friends were in the next room. The shaven-headed man in a green uniform like Weirdo's took Yappy out of her pen.

Razor shuffled to his gate.

As Shaven Head opened the corridor door, the two little girls who'd met Yappy previously smothered her with hugs. And Yappy yapped and yapped, her stubby tail wagging like it was going to fly off.

The door closed, and she never came back. So, maybe there was a Frisbee heaven for some dogs, but not for others.

Nice one, Yappy. Good luck to you.

Razor returned to his carpet.

The following day, Weirdo walked him around the enclosure. Rio peed on his favorite post and sniffed about, but it was such an effort that he trudged back to the door to go back in. He couldn't wait to lie on his carpet again and just let another day wash over him. The days all turned out the same, so why try to do anything with them?

Weirdo took him back to his pen. "Don't give up, Rio. Trust me, there's someone out there for you. You just have to give it time."

In the afternoon, a strange shuffling gait woke him as someone entered the room. Like someone with too many legs. Talk about odd. Not that he left his carpet. It wasn't worth it. Probably never would be.

An old man ambled down the aisle beside a frizzy-haired old lady who hobbled along using a cane like a third leg.

She stopped at his pen. "Awww, Billy, look at this little angel."

Billy smiled, his teeth as white as his hair.

She said, "He looks just like my Duke from when I was a kid. Remember, I showed you that picture taken at the lake?"

He shrugged. "Did you?"

"Last week." She shook her head. "Sometimes, I wonder if you ever listen to a word I say."

"Pardon?"

She chuckled and elbowed him.

Razor watched, his chin resting on his forepaws.

Weirdo approached them from behind. "Hi. Can I help you with anything?"

Billy said, "We're looking for a dog."

"Really?" said the old lady. "That's why we're here? Because I thought we'd come for flying lessons." She rolled her eyes at Weirdo. "You'll have to excuse Einstein here. I'd say it's a senior moment, but he's been like this for forty-two years."

Weirdo laughed. "So, what kind of dog is it you're looking for?"

"Point us at the one most in need and we'll take it. Doesn't matter about age, health issues, behavioral problems... whatever. If it's the poorest in the place, we want it."

Billy rested his hand lightly on Weirdo's arm. "That's how she got stuck with me."

"Ain't that the truth!" said the old lady.

They all laughed, then Billy doddered up the aisle, peering in at the dogs.

The lady pointed at Razor. "This one reminds me of my best friend when I was a kid. What's his story?"

Weirdo said, "If you're serious about accepting any issue as long as the dog is the one most in need, Rio is—"

Billy pointed into a pen. "There's a black Lab with only three legs here, Ellen."

"Just a sec, Billy. Go on, dear. Rio is...?"

"Rio is..." As she caught Razor's eye, sadness washed over Weirdo. She swallowed, then looked away. "... maybe not the best choice." She pointed along the aisle. "Now, Max lost a leg following a car accident because his owner didn't take him to the vet but let him suffer a shattered femur for weeks. Luckily, a neighbor reported it, and we rescued him. Unfortunately, it was too late to save his leg."

"Oh, the poor thing." Ellen's eyes teared. "Some people deserve a public flogging, they do."

Weirdo clicked her tongue. "You won't get any argument from me."

Ellen gazed a Rio. "He does so remind me of Duke." She sighed and turned away. "Let's have a look at that Lab, then." She hobbled away.

Strolling alongside, Weirdo said, "German shepherds are great dogs, but they need a huge amount of exercise. Without it, they can start barking or chewing or showing all kinds of behavior you don't want." She pointed at Max. "With a lab, you're looking at half the amount of exercise, and for obvious reasons, Max needs even less than that. We're talking about thirty minutes a day."

Ellen said, "I think you're misreading your audience, dear."

"Excuse me?"

"You see an old lady with a cane, so point her to a dog that will be happy to limp around the block, then lie on the couch the rest of the day. Don't get me wrong, I understand you want the best for your dogs, so you try to make the perfect match, but—" She lifted her left forearm. "My son bought me a smartwatch, so I get in my ten thousand steps per day to stop this thing from seizing." She patted her hip. "Had it three years now."

"I'm so sorry. I didn't mean to—"

"Don't worry, dear. This wrinkly old skin is very thick. Now, why don't you tell me about Rio?"

Razor turned to face the wall and closed his eyes. Talk about noise. And he'd thought Yappy was a pain.

Chapter 11

Moments later, Weirdo entered Razor's pen, behaving even weirder than normal. She grinned so widely, he thought her face was going to split in two.

Crouching, she cupped his face. "I told you, Rio." She slipped on a leash. "Someone wants to meet you. Someone perfect."

She smelled extraordinarily happy. Why? It wasn't dinnertime.

Standing, she patted her thigh. "Come on. Let's go see if this is your forever home."

Rio trudged after her. People. They were overjoyed by the most inexplicable of things — tiny men chasing a tiny ball on TV, a car that had wheels and doors just like every other car, clothes. Clothes! As if covering themselves in an artificial skin wasn't ridiculous enough, they got super excited about changing that skin, even if the later one was just as ridiculous as the earlier one. It was no wonder he struggled to understand them when they didn't understand themselves.

"Please, Rio, be the old you, not the new one who stares at the wall all day. Be the old one, and you'll charm them easily."

He plodded along. This wasn't the way to the yard but the way to the silver table. Had he been bad? Were they going to strap that cone on again? He stopped and sat back on his haunches.

"Rio, please, don't blow this." Weirdo's joy twisted into anguish.

He sniffed again to be sure. Yes, the emotions were as different as lying in the sun on a beautiful day and cowering in his cage while a thunderstorm raged.

Why couldn't people change their smell like this all the time? If they'd communicate primarily through scent, instead of relying on the incessant noise they made, the world could be a wonderfully harmonious place. But like that would ever happen. If people liked one thing more than anything else, it was making noise. Endless, meaningless noise.

"Please, Rio. Please."

Weirdo sounded so pathetic. And that thunderstorm surrounding her grew darker.

Well, it looked like he was going to have to make yet another sacrifice. He lifted his chin and tilted his head.

"Now?" She snickered. "You need a scratch now?" She rolled her eyes but tickled his throat.

He sniffed. The storm clouds parted, and a ray of sunshine broke free.

He nuzzled her. *You're welcome, sparky.*

"So can we go now?"

Razor stood, and she guided him into the corridor. Ahead, the left-hand door led to the metal table on which they'd poked and prodded him so much. He didn't want the cone again, but if it was that or having Weirdo suffer storm clouds... he turned for that door, but the leash pulled taut.

Weirdo smiled and opened the door opposite. "This way, silly."

He frowned. In there? That was where dogs made the happiest sounds he'd ever heard – the yip-yip room. And *he* was going in? She had to have made a mistake.

Standing outside the door, he craned his neck and peeped in. Balls, knotted ropes, and lumps of colored plastic littered the floor, and large pictures of happy dogs lined the green walls. On a cream sofa at the far side of the room, Ellen and Billy sat smiling.

Weirdo said, "Sorry, he's not usually shy."

"Awww, bless him," said Ellen.

Weirdo eased on the leash. "Come on, Rio. It's okay."

So, this wasn't a mistake? It really was his turn in the yip-yip room?

He stepped his front paws inside, then looked at Weirdo, half expecting to be chastised.

"Good boy."

He stepped all the way in, gazing at her from the corner of his eye, ready to dodge a kick if need be.

She patted him. "That's it. Now, come meet Ellen and Billy."

His head low and tail down, he tottered to the sofa.

"Awww, look at his side, Billy. Poor thing." Ellen stared at where Vera had shaved her own squiggle. It was just a blob, so not as pretty as his R, but it was a fair attempt for a beginner.

Weirdo said, "He had multiple bite wounds, as you can see by the patches we had to shave to treat him, but he's responded well to medication, so there shouldn't be any ongoing health issues."

Ellen shook her head. "Hanging is too good for monsters who can do this. I'd tie them down and set their own dogs on them, I would."

Billy laughed. "Ellen, it isn't only Rio who has to make a good impression, you know."

Weirdo smiled. "It's okay. My mom's just the same. She wanted the pandemic to wipe out the human race so nature could recover and animals could have the lives they deserve."

Ellen nodded. "She sounds a wise woman." She reached toward Razor. "May I?"

"Of course."

Ellen scratched Razor under the chin. "Hello, Rio, I'm Ellen and this is Billy. If you'd like to, we'd love for you to come live with us." She leaned closer. "What do you think?"

Razor stared at the couple. Their scents were strange — old and yet remarkably young, as if they'd lived in the world a long, long time, yet done it their way, so it hadn't aged them, hadn't jaded them like it did most people.

He liked that.

It was odd that so many people seemed so unhappy all of the time — he'd met enough on the streets recently to witness that. But why? The world didn't care about people, it just wanted to be left alone to do its thing. The problems only started when people forced it to do what they thought it should.

Dogs didn't do that. Dogs passed through the world, sniffing this, peeing on that, but pretty much leaving it just as they'd found it. But people? People fought and fought to mold the world into what they thought it should be. Crazy. It was no wonder the streets were filled with the stench of unhappiness.

Billy stroked Razor's side, staying clear of his wounds. "Hey, boy, been in the wars, haven't you?" He looked at Weirdo. "Does he play with toys?"

"Not really. I don't think his owner tried much, so he doesn't get the concept. Of course, he can learn."

Ellen frowned at his rump. "Is that an R?"

"Yeah. We're not sure, but I guessed it was an initial, either of his name or his owner's."

"Hence Rio."

Weirdo nodded.

All this noise was happening, but strangely, it washed over Razor. Two hands stroking him was so soothing, the whole world could've been in the room shouting, and he wouldn't have noticed. Silence was wonderful, but two hands? That was a game-changer.

For some inexplicable reason, he felt an urge to roll onto his back and kick his legs in the air. So he did.

Ellen tickled his belly, filling him with a glow like sunlight through fresh spring leaves.

He gazed at her. *You do know I'm a hardened fighting dog, so this is solely for your benefit, don't you, toots? I'm getting no pleasure from it whatsoever.*

"You like that, don't you, boy?" She scratched him a little harder.

Okay, so maybe a little pleasure. But I could stop at any time.

Weirdo backed away. "I'll leave you to get to know each other. Any questions, just holler." She left.

Razor spent ages with Ellen and Billy. The couple stroked and smiled, and when Razor occasionally licked a hand, they smiled even more. He'd never realized it was so easy to please people.

His man had rarely been happy. Or at least, rarely happy with him. Razor had always figured it was his fault, but feeling the happiness in the room today... was that true? Compared to fighting another dog, he was doing barely anything, yet the room reeked of joy. That couldn't be a coincidence.

So, maybe his problem with his man wasn't that he'd never done enough but that he'd done too much. Yes, that was it. The less he did, the happier people appeared. And he'd figured people were complicated and difficult to understand. Yeah, right. They were simple creatures, easily pleased. People... maybe he liked them after all.

Weirdo returned. "How are we doing?"

"Great," said Billy.

Ellen nodded. "It's a yes. Just tell us what to pay and where to sign."

Weirdo beamed. "Fantastic. I'll take Rio back, then walk you through the process and organize a home visit."

Ellen said, "Is that anything we should be worried about? We only have a small house, nothing fancy."

"Is your yard enclosed?"

"Yes."

"Do either of you work?"

"Not anymore."

"Do you have other animals?"

"No."

"Where would Rio spend most of his time?"

"In the house with us. Where else?"

Weirdo grinned as she slipped on Razor's leash. "You'll be fine, trust me. I sometimes do visits, so I can tell you, you've got the major points nailed."

Billy said, "Can we visit him while we're waiting for your decision?"

"Of course. The more you get to know each other, the easier the transition will be, especially for Rio."

Weirdo guided Rio out. As soon as she shut the door, she sank to her knees and hugged him. A proper Frisbee-heaven hug. "I'm so proud of you, Rio. I don't know what you were like as a fighting dog, but you're going to make a wonderful companion."

His tail swished across the floor, and he licked her ear.

Wow. This was turning into quite a day. And if what he'd seen happen with Yappy and the other dogs who'd left was anything to go by, tomorrow was going to be even better.

Chapter 12

The next morning, everyday life resumed. People came, stared, moved on. And all the while, Razor lay on his carpet. Occasionally, someone wiggled a finger through his grille, but he ignored it. All the times he'd lavished attention on people, they'd rejected him, but when he'd ignored Ellen and Billy, they'd invited him into the yip-yip room. That meant the best approach was obviously no approach.

The day crawled by.

And another.

And another.

Razor barely left his carpet.

The following day, voices drifted in from the corridor.

He jerked his head up and sniffed. He gasped. Was that...?

Razor scampered to his gate and pressed his nose into the corner, as close to the corridor as he could get. He sniffed again.

They were here.

His tail wagged. He didn't actually tell it to, the thing just started by itself. He glared at it. What the...?

His tail wasn't the only thing wagging — his whole rear end was swinging from side to side. What the devil was wrong with him?

Weirdo scurried in. "Rio, you've got visitors."

He liked it when she smelled of happiness. In fact, she'd smelled of happiness most days he could remember. Was that a coincidence, or was it because of him? Maybe that was his superpower — making people happy.

In the yip-yip room, Ellen and Billy waited on the sofa and beamed when Weirdo opened the door.

Ellen held her arms wide. "There's my little treasure."

Razor's whole body wiggled and he yipped.

Oh, this was ridiculous for a hardened fighting dog. What would be next? Letting little girls dress him in people clothes?

Billy patted his thigh. "Come on, Rio. I'm sure there's a chin that needs tickling."

Razor wiggled his way over. Immediately, hands lovingly swarmed over him. Another yip escaped.

Was he trying to embarrass himself? He was a fighting dog. A *hardened fighting dog!*

Weirdo sat next to Ellen. "I see you've got a home visit booked for next Wednesday."

Billy nodded. "It was the earliest we could get."

Weirdo winced. "Sorry, we have a couple of staff vacancies, so we're pretty stretched."

Ellen patted Weirdo's knee. "With all the good you do here, there's no need to apologize, dear."

"Is there anything else I can help you with? Dietary advice, exercise regimens, flea and worming schedules?"

Billy shook his head. "We've had dogs before, so we've got it covered, thanks."

"Great, then I'll leave you to it." She left.

Somehow, Razor forgot he was a hardened fighting dog. Before he knew it, he was lying on the floor with hands caressing him. He couldn't work out how it had happened, nor why he was allowing it to continue, but every time he determined to stand and glare at Ellen and Billy for taking advantage of his good nature, a little voice inside him said, *Just one more stroke. What's one more going to hurt?*

It was afternoon before he finally sauntered back to his pen.

Another day crawled by — crawled so unbelievably slowly. It was as if the world had gotten stuck that morning and didn't want to go any further. Puzzling.

A warm glow welled up inside him as he thought of the yip-yip room with Ellen and Billy. Were they coming today? He marched to the corner of his pen and sniffed toward the corridor. Where were they? Where were—

He frowned. He'd waited for his man, waited for the pup, waited for hot dogs... he was usually good at waiting, so what was different this time? Hmmm... his man had looked after him for as long as he could remember, yet his man had never made him glow inside. The pup? No glow. Hot dogs? Maybe. But only a glimmer, not this blinding beacon inside him now.

He slunk back to his carpet. As he stared at his white brick wall, he pictured the sky dog flying through the air, catching the disk, then being hugged by the man. Would Billy do that one day?

He closed his eyes and pictured himself leaping through the bluest blue sky, snatching the goldest gold disk out of the air, landing in the greenest green grass, and Billy hugging him, so, so tight. Frisbee heaven. It wasn't just a TV show, it was real. *Real!*

Another day plodded by.

And another.

Then while Razor gazed at his wall, picturing the leap, the catch, the hug... he gasped, eyes popping wide. He sniffed to make sure.

Yes, they were here!

He shot to his gate, shoving his nose into the corner nearest the corridor. Yes, that scent. It was—

Wait...

That wasn't right.

He sniffed again.

No, that wasn't right at all.

Ellen was there, yes, but where was Billy? Razor whined.

A few minutes later, Weirdo shuffled into his pen, her eyes red and puffy. She knelt and collapsed over him, sobbing.

"I'm sorry, Rio. I'm so sorry." She clawed her fingers into his fur as if she were in pain. "It happens, Rio. But we'll find you someone. I promise, Rio. I promise."

What had happened? His superpower was to bring happiness, so why wasn't it working? He willed it to work. Willed it and willed it. But Billy never showed, and Ellen's scent disappeared. And Weirdo sobbed and sobbed.

Chapter 13

Every time Weirdo approached him, that thunderstorm smell came with her. Something had changed, and he didn't know what. Despite her weirdness, he'd grown fond of her, so he'd nuzzle her. He even licked her hand twice. But no matter how he tried, his superpower failed him and those storm clouds remained.

Occasionally, he shoved his snout into the corner nearest the corridor and scoured the scents for those special two, but they never reappeared.

Maybe he'd been bad. He hadn't intended to be, so maybe they'd forgive him.

But they never did, because they never came back.

Days came and days went — they simply did. His bowl didn't care what day it was or at what time water was poured into it. His bowl simply lay on the floor. Doing nothing, being nothing, feeling nothing. Razor became his bowl.

Weirdo crouched at his gate. "Rio, come... Rio."

She glanced toward the corridor and the door through which people would soon come — he could smell them. She was trying to coax him forward, coax him to lick and wag and yip...

On his carpet, he turned his face to the wall and closed his eyes. His days of waiting were over.

Later in the yard, though Weirdo stank of sadness, she smiled as if she were happy and threw a red ball. He sat and stared into space. Weirdo fetched the ball.

She crouched to him. "I know it's hard, Rio, but you can't give up. Please try."

She scratched under his chin, but that anguished sadness still lingered. A disease destroying her life. And he couldn't save her. He'd tried, but failed. So what was the point in anything else?

Another day and another scent.

Staring at his wall, Razor consulted his library of smells when a man dawdled by. Not that Razor wanted to, but like his tail wagging without his permission, his nose often sniffed things without telling him it was going to. The man smelled of oil and cars — he'd been here before. He walked around the pens, then stood before Razor's gate.

Weirdo scooted over. "Rio's a great dog, but he's been let down too many times, so he's not quite as affectionate as some of our others. But given the chance, he'd make a great companion."

Oily Man nodded. "I like German shepherds. Loyal, loving, intelligent. And protective, of course."

"Yeah, they're great pets. He's the only one here right now. If you're interested, you could get to know him in our meet-and-greet area."

The man rubbed his chin and stared at Razor as if deep in thought. "So, how's he been let down?"

"He was all set for his forever home with an elderly couple, but the man fell off a stepladder and broke his hip. His wife couldn't manage taking on a dog with everything else she had to deal with, so…"

"That's tough." He pointed at Razor. "But what's with all the shaved areas? Has he been in an accident?"

"He, uh… there's no easy way to say it, so I'm just going to come out with it. He was used in dogfights." Weirdo thrust her palms out. "But he's a real sweetheart. I've never once heard him even growl, let alone show any aggression."

Oily Man nodded. "And what's the meet-and-greet area?"

Weirdo grinned. And the storm-cloud smell vanished.

Chapter 14

Weirdo paced back and forth outside Razor's pen. Pausing, she pursed her lips at him, her eyes filled with sadness, then shook her head.

Shaven Head strolled over. "No sign yet?"

"If he's another no-show, I don't know what I'll do."

He brushed her arm. "Relax. There's still time."

"We close in ten minutes."

"So there's ten minutes. How long does it take to sign a paper and walk a dog out the door?"

"He hasn't been near since he reserved Rio." Weirdo dragged her fingers through her hair. "People never see an animal they want only once. They always come back again."

"Look, he's probably caught up in traffic. It'll be fine."

She flung her arm toward Razor. "You've seen, Rio. He's completely given up, and who can blame him after the life he's had?"

"Hazel, you've handled hundreds of animals. Why is this one dog such a problem?"

"Because I know what he's been through and what it took for him to trust people again, so I promised I'd find him a forever home." She smacked her chest. "*I did.* So *I* can't be the one who lets him down."

Stepping closer, Shaven Head opened his arms. "Come here."

They hugged.

"I can't let him down, Miguel, I can't."

"How long is it since you had a day off?"

"What's that got to do with anything?"

"Everyone knows you're coming in for him, but that's not doing you any good. How are you going to help Rio if you're fit to drop?"

"You haven't seen how many people are interested until they learn about his past. It's not fair — it's not his fault, is it?"

"I know. But you need to have some time away to recharge, then you can come back refreshed and start over. There are always other adopters out there. You know that."

Her voice faltered. "But it just feels like this is his last chance."

The corridor door opened. Weirdo and Shaven Head jerked around. Vera smiled. "He's here."

Weirdo's jaw dropped. Then she cried as if she was sad, which was puzzling because she smelled the happiest Razor had ever smelled her. Hey, maybe his superpower was back!

Weirdo wiped her eyes as she raced to the corridor. A few minutes later, she returned, face glowing.

Razor sat up. Something was happening, but what?

She dashed into Razor's pen and flung her arms around him. "We did it, Rio. *You* did it. Pete's single, so he'll have lots of time for you. Plus, he has a nice house with a fenced yard, so you can play and be safe. You're going to love it."

She pulled back and stared into his eyes. "But I'll miss you." She kissed him on the forehead, then smiled. "Ready to start your wonderful new life?"

Weirdo was so incredibly happy, he couldn't help but wag his tail. He was pleased he'd helped her through this difficult patch. Maybe tomorrow he'd even fetch that red ball for her — she looked so pathetic tramping after it herself.

Alongside her on a leash, he ambled toward the reception area, voices growing louder.

Pete said, "Remind me about your follow-up visits."

Shaven Head said, "We don't do follow-ups. We don't have the staff."

"Okay."

"And remember, if you decide you want him chipped, it's only thirty bucks."

"I'm good, thanks."

Weirdo guided Razor in.

Pete grinned at him. "Oh, there he is!"

Shaven Head and a plump woman stood behind a cream counter. Leaflets burst out of transparent plastic pockets on the wall and shelves of toys smelled like no dog had ever been near them.

Pete winced. "Again, sorry I'm so late, but the traffic…"

"You made it, which is all that matters." Weirdo handed him the leash, her voice breaking. "And here's Rio."

"Thank you. Come on, boy, let's go home."

"So long, Pete." Weirdo swallowed hard. "Bye, Rio."

Pete guided Razor through the exit and into the fading light.

Were they going on an adventure? How marvelous. He yipped. Was this what had happened to all the other dogs that had gone into the corridor and never come back? Was this when he'd finally find Frisbee heaven? He yipped again, remembering Ellen and Billy. Maybe Pete was taking him to them. Maybe they hadn't abandoned him but were waiting, longing to stroke and scratch and pet.

His tail wagged and his gait transformed into a bounce instead of his usual trudge. However, his nose told him something he didn't like — he and Pete were walking away from his pen, but no one else was. He glanced back. Wasn't Weirdo coming? He rarely left the building without her, so she had to.

But she wasn't. He whimpered.

Pete tugged the leash. "You can quit that for a start."

The man seemed kind of happy, but also kind of mad. Razor hung his head. Had he been bad already? He'd tried not to be, but with so many people wanting different things, it was impossible to make everyone happy. Even with his superpower.

Pete yanked open the door of a red pickup truck that was taller than he was. "In you go."

In the front? So it was an adventure!

Razor jumped in, and Pete looped his leash through the armrest. His man had one of these cars. Razor usually had to sit in a cage in the back, but occasionally, his man let him sit up front. Talk about a treat. So high up, he could look down on the world like a prince on a royal tour.

Were they going somewhere fun?

He watched Pete march around the truck and climb in the other side. His scent was a puzzle. He still smelled both happy and mad, as if part of his day was going well, but another wasn't. Although, if Razor was sitting up front, he couldn't possibly have been bad, so something else had to be troubling Pete. Poor Pete.

The engine roared, and the pickup moved off. Razor gazed out the window as the vehicle crawled through the town. In the center, he gasped — his TV store.

He turned as they passed, but unfortunately, his friend didn't leap across the sky. He snapped his head back around just in time to see the hydrant and the food truck, but then, places he didn't know sprang up.

At a red light, the pickup stopped next to a car with a brown-haired woman driving. In the back, a black-and-white dog rested its head in a boy's lap. Even through the two layers of glass separating them, Razor smelled the joy coming from inside the car, as if it was Frisbee heaven every day for them.

A green light appeared. The black-and-white dog went one way, and Razor went another.

The buildings became gloomier compared to those in the center, and fewer people walked the sidewalks. A few areas of wasteland sped by, followed by more gloomy buildings. Wherever they were going, there was going to be lots of interesting smells.

Finally, the pickup turned off and bounced along an uneven track into a compound with a high metal fence. The stench of oil and rust clogged Razor's nose. The pickup's headlights illuminated mountains of dilapidated vehicles piled on top of each other, forming canyons, rough tracks leading off between them in various directions.

Oh, this was wonderful. So many places to explore, so many things to sniff. What a nice man Pete was for bringing him.

The car stopped. Pete got out, then opened Razor's door and yanked the leash free. "Out, dog."

Razor leaped out and peered into the shadows drenching the metal canyons. He was glad Pete was there because close up, the place didn't look very inviting.

Pulling Razor behind him, Pete marched toward a wide structure where most of the front wall was missing. Various kinds of equipment and work benches lined one wall, while the other two had piles of metal items — some dirty and rusty, some shiny and clean.

A man with a bushy beard pounded a hunk of metal at one bench. "That the new guard dog?"

"No, it's your new butler." Pete rolled his eyes.

"They ain't going to be checking up?"

"Nope." Pete put a collar on Razor that already had a leash attached.

"Sweet. What's its name?"

"What's it matter?"

"Well, I can't just call it Dog."

Pete pointed at Razor. "Dog, sit. Sit."

Razor sat, gazing about.

Pete smirked. "Looks like you can." Without another glance, Pete strode for the outside. "Give it some kibble and lock up."

Moments later, the pickup growled away.

Bushy Beard pulled metal shutters down over the work area and flipped a switch. The overhead strip lights shut off, drenching the place in gloom.

Razor whimpered. What was happening? Was this part of the adventure? If so, he didn't like it. Could he go back to his pen now, please?

He stared at the entrance. Maybe Ellen would come. Or his man. Or Weirdo. Someone. Anyone. He sniffed but sensed nothing but dirty oil, grease, and decay.

At a sink at the back, Bushy Beard filled a dirty bowl with water, then set it and a scoop of kibble on the oil-stained concrete in the middle of the floor. Razor ignored him, staring at the entrance. Waiting.

"That's it, Dog, you guard the place." He walked out. Another engine roared, then drove away.

Silence descended.

Razor loved silence. But not this kind. He whimpered. What was happening? Why had he been brought here only to be abandoned?

Chapter 15

The overpowering stench of oil subsiding, Razor sensed another scent, a welcome scent – another dog. But it wasn't fresh. Maybe the dog was still around and knew what was happening.

Moving his head in an arc, Razor sniffed. Analyzing scents through each nostril separately, he pinpointed one worthy of investigation coming from around the corner outside. But outside was so black and scary now.

Scary? He was a hardened fighting dog – the dark should be scared of him.

He didn't know how far he could move on this leash, but the closer he got to outside, the more scent he could analyze to find this other dog. Tentatively, he padded farther and farther, claws *tap-tap-tapping* on the concrete. The leash never yanked him back, so he kept going. But the closer he got to the outside, the closer he got to whatever was lurking in the darkness. His heart hammered.

At the threshold, he froze. Traffic rumbled in the background, while something small scurried through the rusting canyons, its claws scraping on metal. Way, way in the distance, a siren wailed. He couldn't hear or smell any threat, so maybe it was safe.

He crept outside.

Eyes flashing through the night, ears angling independently to home in on the tiniest of sounds, he stalked around the corner. Behind a wheelless car that was more rust than metal, he found the source of the scent – pee and poop stretching back months, maybe years. The freshest was weeks old, which wasn't the worst of the bad news — the dog wasn't healthy. Razor couldn't tell exactly what was wrong, but he doubted he'd be seeing the dog anytime soon.

Okay, that was one mystery solved. He looked at his leash dangling into the dirt from his neck. How had an ordinary leash stretched so far?

He glanced about. His leash was the longest one he'd ever seen. It was fastened to a cable that ran along the ground from the back wall of the structure to deep into the darkness outside. A darkness that creaked and scraped and loomed. He shuddered.

Razor couldn't see, smell, or hear anything, but that didn't mean nothing was out there. If he were to stay here, he'd better ensure it really was safe.

He prowled forward, following the cable into the biggest canyon.

All around, aged metal hulks towered over him, twisted masses of smashed lights, missing doors, warped panels, lost wheels, broken windows...

He'd only ever seen shiny cars on the streets, so he'd figured that was all there was. And boy, how people loved them. Especially his man. Razor had once peed on the wheel of his man's car before he knew his man properly... whoa, talk about a mistake. He'd limped for a week after that. But it was his fault. He should've been more careful where he peed.

To his left, something clattered as it fell and scurrying disappeared into darkness. Razor jumped. Something was out there. Hiding. Watching. Maybe hunting. And if it was hunting, what was its prey? Dog?

The fur on his shoulders stood and his breath came in short pants. His heart beat fast. So fast. Faster than if he were running at full speed.

Moving each leg slowly, placing each paw on the ground so gently it made barely any sound, he stalked toward a towering heap of twisted steel.

He gulped as he crept closer, praying to hear a noise, especially a noise moving away. But silence devoured him.

Two paces from the heap, he froze and drilled his senses into it. What was in there? Lurking?

Metal creaked and he jumped. Some creature was in the heap. The tiny amount of noise and scent suggested it was small, so probably not a threat, but what the devil was it?

The night fell silent.

He waited. And waited. Nothing.

He prowled farther, listening, sniffing, watching.

More scurrying on his right. Scraping on his left.

His head dropped so low all he saw was dirt. Things lived out here. In this godforsaken mass of dead metal. And now he'd joined them.

That was another mystery solved.

He gazed up at the biggest mountain of metal. It stretched so high into the blackness, he couldn't see the top. This was where cars came when people didn't love them anymore. He'd wondered why he'd been brought here, and there was his answer — because no one loved him. His man had never searched for him. Ellen and Billy had never come back. Even Weirdo had sent him away. This was obviously where unwanted dogs were sent to end their days. Like the one he'd smelled earlier.

Head hanging, tail wedged between his legs, he slunk inside the structure. What did it matter if something dangerous was out there? Let it come. Let it eat him. Let it end his miserable life.

He collapsed onto the concrete. There wasn't even his white brick wall to stare at now. He whimpered. He must have been so bad to deserve this. So, so bad. If only he knew what he'd done so he wouldn't do it again.

Chapter 16

The gray dawn cast gray light into Razor's new home. Unmoving, he lay on the filthy floor, chin on his paws, watching the rectangle of light creep across the concrete toward him.

He pricked his ears. Was that...?

He jerked up and trotted outside, staring at the gated entrance. An engine was coming this way.

Without even asking him, his tail wagged.

It was Weirdo coming for him. Or Ellen and Billy. Or his man. It didn't matter who; it was someone coming. For *him*.

The gate opened, and a red pickup truck entered. Pete!

That wasn't Razor's first choice, or second or third for that matter, but who cared. Pete was coming. Coming to rescue him. Razor's tail wagged, and he didn't care.

He ran to meet the pickup, but instead of it slowing to greet him, the horn blasted. Razor leaped aside as the vehicle slewed around to park where it had the previous night.

Pete got out and marched for the structure. Razor raced over. He yipped.

"Not now, Dog."

Pete didn't smell happy, even though Razor was showering him with his superpower, so Razor hung back. He'd learned to sense when his man was unhappy and had quickly discovered that at such times, it was best to stay clear if he didn't want to get kicked.

Not that staying clear was any guarantee.

Strangely, his man often seemed happier after he'd beaten Razor, as if he felt he'd accomplished something, so occasionally, Razor took a beating for his man's benefit. It was the least he could do when his man took such care of him every day. But, until Razor learned if Pete liked to beat dogs, it was best to give him space.

Pete climbed a short run of steps to the left of the big opening in the structure and entered a door. No doubt he was doing important people-stuff. They all enjoyed that. Razor didn't understand it because, like clothes, most of it made no sense at all.

He'd once watched his man and one of his man's friends curse and strain to carry a huge sofa out of the house and dump it beside his cage. Then they'd carried another huge sofa in. Two huge sofas, lots of effort, zero change. What was the point? Didn't they sit on the new one in exactly the same way they had on the old one?

People-stuff — utterly baffling.

Soon after Pete disappeared into his room, Bushy Beard arrived. He threw kibble on the floor, and while Razor ate, the man took various bits of metal and banged and sawed and cranked and screwed... people-stuff.

Once Razor had finished eating, he loped around the corner and peed where he'd found traces of the other dog — if the old boy came back, Razor needed him to be aware of his presence.

Not wanting to be near people, Razor tramped into the middle of the yard and crumpled to the dirt. He stared at the entrance. If Pete and Bushy Beard had come, there was a chance someone else might come, too. Someone who enjoyed tickling him under the chin.

A truck arrived carrying a blue car with a mangled rear end. Bushy Beard played with the car for a while, wrenching off this, levering off that. When he'd finished, he sat inside a yellow machine with huge black wheels and a massive fork at the front. The machine roared like a million giant cats.

As the machine rumbled forward, the ground shook beneath Razor, so he scooted inside and peeked out from the shadows. The machine stuck its fork under the new wreck, lifted it up, carried it to a metal canyon, and dropped it onto a red car with a loud *crunch*.

Once the yellow machine juddered to a stop, Razor returned to his spot in the yard and stared at the entrance. They'd come. He could feel it.

At lunchtime, Pete sauntered out. "I've got a meeting in town. I'll be back around three."

Bushy Beard said, "No probs."

Walking to his pickup, Pete passed Razor.

"Guarding the entrance, huh? Fast learner." He patted Razor's side. "Good dog."

Not only was Pete's tone happy, but he smelled happy, too. And a pat, not a hit. Maybe this place wasn't that bad after all. For now. Until one of Razor's real friends came for him.

The sun high in a cloudless sky, Razor lay in the front opening of his new home, gazing at the biggest mountain that erupted from the middle of the writhing mass of canyons. What a beast. If he climbed that... boy, what a view. He'd be able to see the whole world from there.

And more pertinently, the whole world would see him. Maybe Ellen and Billy would see him and remember how happy they'd all been together. Or Weirdo would see and take him back to his lovely brick wall.

He frowned at the mountain. Was it climbable?

Most of the mountain's sides were way too sheer, but...

Bottom left, a silver car sat beside a green minivan, neither had a window that wasn't broken. Next to those, a crumpled blue vehicle lay atop another silver one. More vehicles climbed up and up in the adjacent pile, their battered metal not a wall but a precarious staircase to those courageous enough to risk it.

Razor stood. That mountain was big, yes. Dangerous, oh boy, yes. But he was a hardened fighting dog.

He raced at it. He leapt onto the silver car at the bottom, pounced onto the minivan's roof, then bounded for the pile next to—

The leash pulled taut. Yanked back, Razor yelped as his legs flew from under him. He crashed off the minivan and slammed into the silver car's hood. A jagged piece of metal slashed his snout, and he yelped again.

Limping, and with blood dripping from his face, he clambered off the car and slunk back to the structure. Unable to reach the wound on his snout properly with his tongue, he lay, rubbing it on his foreleg.

All the while, he stared at the mountain. He'd never be able to climb it. Never. That meant no one would ever see him, so no one would ever come. This was it. This was his life.

He dropped his chin onto his paws and he stared at the floor. At least it was concrete like at his man's. He liked that. Concrete was cold, hard, unforgiving. Like life. It was an easy way to stay grounded. Dreams caused only pain.

Night came and Razor was left alone again. Alone except for the sound of the nighttime critters. However, now he knew to expect their escapades, so their nocturnal scurrying didn't creep him out — it was only the metal mountain living.

The next day, once the gate opened, he resumed his watching and waiting.

And the following day.

And the day after that.

Before he knew it, weeks had rolled by, and the yard hadn't become only a home but a territory. And as every dog knew, a territory demanded guarding.

Whenever a stranger arrived, he barked, and if they came too close, he growled.

Pete seemed happier now, too. He didn't pat Razor like that first day, but occasionally he'd holler, "Dog!" with a tone that let Razor know whatever he was doing was going to get him a beating if he didn't stop. Razor appreciated the heads-up. But more importantly, it was reassuring to have things back the old way. Pete and his man would probably make good friends.

Long, lazy days stretched out in the sun transformed into long, lazy days stretched out in the wind and rain, then one morning, snow. Shivering, Razor lay watching the entrance. They'd come. He was sure. But they were obviously having a tough time finding this place.

Bushy Beard lumbered out of the structure, grabbed Razor's collar, and hauled him inside. "Are you trying to kill yourself, you stupid freaking dog? It's too cold to sit there anymore."

Bushy Beard dumped him near a portable heater that stank worse than the burnt filth that came out of the back of cars.

"Stay there."

It was nice that Bushy Beard cared so much about him, but he couldn't stay here — it was impossible to see the entrance.

He pushed up.

Bushy Beard held up a finger. "Stay."

Razor sank to the concrete. Until Bushy Beard turned back to his bench, then he lunged forward.

"Stay!"

He sank back.

Bushy Beard banged and wrenched again.

Keeping so low his belly scraped on the floor, Razor crept forward.

Bushy Beard turned. Razor froze, staring ahead to avoid eye contact. When the man twisted away again, Razor shuffled forward once more.

The man whipped around, so Razor froze midstride, trembling from holding himself in an awkward position.

"You little devil." Bushy Beard chuckled and shook his head. "Okay, you win."

He pushed the portable heater closer to the opening, then patted the floor. "Dog."

Razor shot over, checked he could see the entrance, then lay. Heat caressing him, he lounged, waiting.

He glanced at Bushy Beard. A typical person: confused, inarticulate, often miserable.

It was such a pity people weren't smart enough to communicate clearly because it would improve their lives immeasurably. But what did they expect when their preferred form of communication was oral? Like that could ever work. It was fine for dogs because dogs rarely said anything unless they had something to say, but people? Dear Lord, the noise they made. On and on and on. Most of it absolutely meaningless.

Still, being such simple creatures, they probably had no other option. A pity. If only they could appreciate the elegance of life the way a dog could, what a wonderful world they'd find around them.

Razor spent the rest of the day lying next to the heater to watch the entrance. Unfortunately, Bushy Beard turned it off before leaving, so Razor was forced to huddle in a ball at the back of the room, peering out at the world as snow fell through the darkness.

The snow stayed for more weeks than Razor could count, but every day, Bushy Beard set up the heater for him. Not that it achieved anything because no one he wanted to come ever came.

As the snow disappeared, the gray sun came back, then lazy days lounging in the baked yard returned. Each new day seemed to stretch on forever, making his waiting drag and drag and drag.

Time crawled by. More days passed than Razor had imagined there could ever be. Yet when he looked back on all those days that had lasted so unbelievably long, it was as if they'd been over in a heartbeat. All of them blurred together, and not one stood out. So many days, weeks, and months gone in an instant. Was that really what life was all about? Weren't there supposed to be things that happened? Things that changed? Things to remember that made him feel warm inside?

He kind of remembered someone stroking him once, imagined being tickled under his chin, pictured lying on his back as a hand scratched his belly... but it was so far away now, the memories were clouded.

He gazed at Bushy Beard from behind. The man grunted the odd word now and then, but that was it. No pats. No strokes. No tickles.

Razor whined. Had all those things really happened all that time ago, or had he ached for them so much he'd dreamed them all? If it was real, why had it never happened again?

Pete sauntered across the yard.

Razor slunk over, head down, tail down. Had he dreamed it, or could such things truly happen?

As Pete marched by, Razor whimpered.

Pete didn't even see him. He got in his pickup and drove away.

Razor slumped to his spot in the middle of the yard and sighed. As he'd thought — a dream. All that attention had been nothing but the fantasies of a stupid dog. He closed his eyes and hoped that dream might visit again.

As the weeks passed, even the dream became clouded. In time, Razor forgot about tickles and scratches. And Frisbee heaven.

The snow came again. Then the baking sun. Then the snow. And on it went. The blur of life. Until...

Chapter 17

Smothered by a clammy night, Razor dozed, stretched out on the floor. He'd learned that when there was a breeze, it was cooler outside, but when there wasn't, it was cooler to lie on the concrete.

A barely audible sound disturbed his slumber, crawling through his subconscious to alert him that something was wrong. Before he'd even opened his eyes, his ears angled to home in on the culprit — a tiny *chomp-chomp-chomp-chomp-chomp...*

What the devil was that?

His eyes flickered open. He gasped.

A yard away, a small brown rat sat on its hind legs, gnawing a pellet of kibble it clutched in its front paws.

Razor growled.

Eeek. The rat dropped the kibble and scampered toward Bushy Beard's collection of rusted debris piled against the wall.

Razor glared as it disappeared into the shadows. Coming into his home? Eating his food? The nerve! He'd heard them scurrying in the mountain since the day he'd arrived, and later, he'd seen them, too. On occasion, he'd even chased them, though more for exercise than from bloodlust. But to come into *his* home...

He lumbered over to the chomped pellet and ate it, then sniffed out a few other bits he'd missed earlier. Once he was sure no scraps remained, he slumped back down and closed his eyes. The coolness of the concrete caressed his hot body, coaxing him into sleep.

Chomp-chomp-chomp...

Razor's eyes snapped open. It was back? The freaking thing was back?

Five feet away, the rat munched another pellet, one beady black eye locked on him. Turning the food in its paws, it chiseled away another mouthful, then sat chewing.

Razor growled again.

The rat froze, whiskers flickering, that beady eye glaring at him.

They stared at each other.

When Razor didn't move, the rat took another nibble of its kibble. *His* kibble.

Razor sprang up and bolted at the thief.

Eeep. The rat darted toward the pile of debris. *Eeep, eeep, eeep.*

Razor snapped at it, but the thing dodged. He skidded on the smooth concrete as he turned, while the thing tore for cover again.

Razor dug his claws against the floor and hared after it.

He closed in. Almost, almost, almost...

He lunged, jaws craving flesh.

The rat dove into a black hole underneath a blue car panel. But Razor was too close, going too fast. He slammed into the panel, and it crashed down on top of him. Dislodged, three hub caps and various bits of metal clattered to the floor.

Clambering up, Razor shook himself, then glared at all the tiny black holes peppering the mound of junk. He was way too big to follow the rat into the heap, but he couldn't let the thing get away with invading his personal space.

He sniffed out another pellet of kibble and for the rest of the night stood guard over it, glaring at the rusting mound.

Despite the odd skittering sound, not a single whisker dared to show itself.

Come daybreak, and content he'd defended his territory, Razor resumed his daily duty – lying on the baked earth beneath an endless blue sky. And another day went on and on and on...

Before leaving that evening, Bushy Beard dumped kibble on the floor and refilled Razor's water bowl. Razor dined, then retired to his spot on the cool concrete.

The night quietened, but for the rumble of far-off traffic and the antics of nighttime critters.

Then the darkness blackened, the traffic dwindled, and the night became stiller and stiller. Until...

Chomp-chomp-chomp...

Razor's eyes snapped open. *Oh, you've got to be kidding me!*

His ears already having located the source, he jerked his head toward Bushy Beard's bench. The rat sat clutching a hunk of kibble in its front paws, gnawing away.

What was wrong with this joker? Couldn't it take a hint?

Razor glared at the demon tormentor. And growled.

Instead of running for its life, the rat finished its pellet, then scuttled over to another one and started devouring that.

What the...?

Razor growled again, but the rat continued eating. He glowered at it, but as he did, his expression turned into a frown. What a strange little creature. Last night, it had run on four legs like a dog, but now it was sitting up and eating using its paws like a person used their hands.

It turned the pellet and nibbled on another part.

Yes, just like a person. He couldn't use his paws like a person, so was a rat closer to people than to dogs? Obviously. That was probably why it didn't understand what his growl meant. How much easier life would be if everything was as smart as a dog.

Razor stalked over. The thing had evaded him last night, but if he got close enough...

He crept on while the rat ate.

Towering over the tiny creature, he tilted his head to one side and stared at it. So it had stolen a few pellets. Had it really committed such a crime?

Yes. That was his kibble in his home. *His.* This thing had no right to be here. Little thief.

Razor bared his teeth. *Gerrrowww.* He snapped at the burglar.

The rat didn't flinch.

Razor's eyes widened. *Never seen a mirror, half-pint? You get you're tiny and I'm huge, right?*

Wait, he was huge, wasn't he? He'd always figured he was, but maybe he was wrong.

No, he had to be – he'd been bigger than the pup, and the pup had looked bigger than this creature. Yes, he was big. And this thing was tiny. That meant, just as it was with people being bigger than dogs, he was the one with the power. Strategy.

He snarled.

Blanking him, the rat continued its contented munching.

How stupid could an animal be?

Razor leaned closer to be sure it was a rat and not some new super-dangerous creature he'd never encountered before. He sniffed it.

Eeek. The rat lunged and nipped his nose.

Razor yelped and sprang back. Cowering, he stared at the monster.

Okay, this was too weird. He was a hardened fighting dog who'd just lost the first round to a creature one-hundredth his size. What the devil was happening?

The rat meandered over to another pellet, picked it up, and sat back. *Chomp-chomp-chomp...*

Another pellet finished, the rat ambled toward Razor.

Whoa. It wasn't going to attack again, was it? Razor leaned away.

Ignoring Razor, the rat picked up more kibble and tucked in. Only inches away.

Razor stared from the corner of his eye, then, slowly, turned his head to watch.

Having dined, the rat licked its forepaws and washed its snout.

So that was how big and scary Razor was? So terrifying a tiny creature felt comfortable enough to clean itself in front of him – a hardened fighting dog – instead of fleeing in terror? Maybe he should reassess his life choices.

Sweeping its paws down from its forehead to its nose, the rat washed its whole face and ears.

Maybe it wouldn't be so bad to share his home. It was big enough. And those bits of kibble – he hadn't missed them when he'd been eating, so it wasn't like the rat was truly stealing. Maybe he could forgive the little fella. After all, it was something new to watch.

Grooming done, the rat scurried away into the junk.

Razor sighed. It had been nice to have a visitor. A pleasant distraction.

Excitement over, he curled up and went back to sleep.

The next day, Razor couldn't stop thinking about his nighttime guest and couldn't help but wonder if the little bandit might visit again. So much so, he eagerly awaited the day's end.

However, the sun crawled across the sky even slower than usual — torturously slowly. So slowly Razor regularly checked it hadn't got stuck.

As if that wasn't bad enough, when the sun had finally arced to the distant hills, Bushy Beard and Pete took forever pottering about before leaving.

Finally alone, Razor scampered inside and gobbled up his kibble, making sure he left a fair amount scattered across the concrete. Just in case.

He lay down. And waited.

Outside, a flock of small dark birds swooped and circled and climbed and spiraled, then left to roost in nearby trees. As the sky dimmed, so too did the rumble of traffic. The noise of daytime insects transformed into the noise of nighttime ones. And it all happened so, so, sooo slowly.

Eventually, faint dots of light scattered across the black sky.

Razor waited.

He sniffed and rotated his ears independently, seeking out the tiniest of smells and sounds.

And waited.

He yawned, then squinted into the shadows between the vast number of treasures Bushy Beard had piled inside.

And waited.

His eyelids drooped. Shaking his head, he pried his eyes open and gazed over the piles of debris.

He slumped. So, no guest tonight.

Well, it was probably for the best. Guests only made a mess and never knew when to leave.

Curling into a ball, he snuggled down and slept.

Chomp-chomp-chomp...

Chapter 18

Razor lay on the moonlit concrete, drilling his gaze into the black hole between a wheel and a heap of exhaust pipes. He stared and stared. Waiting.

Finally, a tiny pink nose surrounded by long curving whiskers poked out.

Warmth welled up inside Razor as Rat scampered to the kibble in the middle of the floor, packed pieces into his mouth till his cheeks puffed out, then scampered back into the darkness. A few moments later, Rat returned before once more disappearing with his bounty.

For five nights, Razor had left a pile of kibble in the open, then waited at a distance. And for five nights, the little bandit had swaggered over, stolen a mouthful, then scooted away to hide the food in his "secret" lair in a rusted gas tank — Razor hadn't seen it, but he could smell it.

Rat reappeared. His stash obviously filled to his satisfaction, he sat with another pellet and chowed down.

The night hotter than usual, Razor eased up so as not to scare Rat and padded to his water bowl. He lapped.

Something nudged his chin from below.

Frowning, Razor lifted his head. Rat nuzzled underneath, climbed up to lean over the side of the bowl, and lapped at the water, too.

So, they were doing that now, were they? Everything that had been Razor's was now communal property, was it?

Instead of Razor being upset, that warm glow inside him blossomed.

He ambled back to his spot and lay down while Rat returned to the pile of kibble and picked up another pellet. *Chomp-chomp-chomp...*

Rat only ever came to visit at night, which pleased Razor. He suspected Pete and Bushy Beard might not be overjoyed at sharing everything they owned with Rat, even if he was so tiny he hardly took anything.

After dining, Rat scurried into one of his dark holes. Razor angled his ears to follow Rat as he scurried through pipes and rusted gaps, until he disappeared.

Stretching out on the cool concrete, Razor closed his eyes. Already dreaming of the following night's dinner party.

***

Rat returned every night for another week. With every new night, he'd spend less time collecting his booty and more time eating in the open.

On the eighth night, Razor stood in the opening in the front of the building and watched Pete and Bushy Beard leave, then bolted inside to his spot. He yipped, then listened.

Silence.

He waited. Straining to pick up the tiniest sound.

Nothing.

He yipped again.

Scurrying came from behind the rusted treasures lining the wall, flitted under dented panels, darted through hidden pipes, trailed around grease-covered engine parts... finally, a tiny pink nose poked out between the wheel and exhausts. It sniffed, whiskers twitching, then Rat meandered out.

Razor yipped. He wandered over to his kibble, where Rat joined him, and they dined together.

After eating, Razor ambled back to his spot, Rat scurrying alongside. Razor sat back on his haunches, licking crumbs off his lips, while Rat sat grooming.

Razor gazed at his little friend. Rat's paws had to work like mad to wash him because they were so small. Crazy. Razor leaned down and nudged Rat with his snout. Rat dropped onto all fours, and Razor dragged his tongue across Rat from head to tail.

A flurry of squeaky whistling like a high-pitched birdsong erupted, and Rat shot away.

Oh, no. Razor hadn't ruined the entire night – and maybe even their friendship – had he? Please, no!

Rat spun around and doubled back, then stood under Razor's chin, as if waiting. What was the little fella doing? Surely, he didn't want...

Razor dragged his tongue down Rat's back.

Again, Rat bolted amid a cacophony of squeaky whistles, only to circle back and wait under Razor's chin.

Razor had once dreamed of being tickled on his belly, and when it finally happened, the sensation had made him want to leap with joy. Was this the equivalent of a belly rub for Rat?

He licked again. And again, Rat darted in a tight loop, squeaking.

They played the licking-tickle game until, panting for breath from all the excitement, Rat shuffled over to the water bowl, drank, then collapsed at Razor's front paws.

Razor lay down, taking care not to squash his little friend. He gazed at the metal mountain, the peak forever beyond his reach because of his leash. Moonlight glinted on the twisted metal like jewels glittering in darkness.

What must it be like to peer out from the summit? What wonders would he see?

He gazed at Rat. Wonders? He didn't need to climb a mountain to find wonders. He closed his eyes.

When Razor woke, sunlight poured in the front of the building, illuminating the empty space where Rat had lain.

Time no longer dragged the way it once had. Yes, waiting for their nightly dinner party took forever, but when Razor looked back, the days didn't all blur into a mass of meaninglessness. Instead, they created distinct pictures that warmed him inside. Was that the key to living – to fill it with pictures that made him glow?

Why had no one ever told him?

He rolled his eyes. No one had told him because no one knew.

That explained why so many people were so miserable so much of the time. How could they not be when they were so fixated on the nonsense of people-stuff that they missed opportunities to fill their

97

lives with pictures that warmed them? If only people would quit their noise long enough to see this simple truth. What a beautiful world brimming with joy it could be.

Razor determined to fill his life with as many glowing pictures as he could, so that night, as soon as he and Rat had eaten, they played the licking-tickle game.

Watching Rat shoot in a loop, squeaking, Razor wondered what kind of pictures Rat would have after this. He hoped they'd make his best friend glow, too.

Chapter 19

The next day, Razor lay in his spot of compacted earth. The sky seemed bluer, brighter, warmer; the birdsong more melodious, more charming, more friendly. He no longer watched the entrance but the shadows as they moved from pointing in one direction to arc around and point in a completely different one... marking the time Pete and Bushy Beard would leave.

Even this waiting time, which had always dragged, was now a time to cherish — it gave him the opportunity to conjure his glowing pictures or to imagine those yet to come.

This was the best time of his life. What he'd always been waiting for, even though he'd never known it.

The weeks rolled by, and Razor gathered more and more glowing pictures, then before he knew it, the gray days returned and a chilliness gripped the nights. But little indoors changed. A few yips always brought Rat scurrying; they'd dine, then play, then sleep.

One night, Razor called Rat and then followed his friend's approach with his ears. A nose and whiskers appeared in the hole near the wheel only to duck straight back in. Tiny eyes sparkled in the moonlight like black gemstones.

Razor frowned. What had happened? Had he been bad so Rat didn't want to be friends anymore? Was Rat sick? Why wasn't he coming out to eat?

Razor crept over, concern dragging in his gait.

The glistening gems spied him, but didn't move.

Fearing the worst, Razor lowered his snout to the darkened wheel hole. Please let everything be okay. Please let everything be okay.

Eeek. Rat shot out, bolted in a tight loop, and dove back in his hole. What the...?

Razor frowned as scurrying noises wove through the metal mass and stopped at another gloomy opening a few feet away.

He crept closer, so stealthily his claws didn't *tap-tap-tap* on the concrete. At the hole, he leaned down.

Eeek. Rat scurried around him, squeaky whistles filling the air, then dove back into the shadows. Tiny claws scraped on concrete, over metal and plastic, then stopped in another darkened gap.

How did Rat negotiate that rusted maze? Did he have pictures in his mind of all the routes to each tiny gap, like Razor had of the streets he'd lived on? That meant this was Rat's "town."

Wow. And Razor had believed this was his territory and that Rat was the intruder.

They played the hide-and-squeak game three more times. On the fourth go, instead of looping around to disappear into the shadows again, Rat ran too close to the kibble and obviously couldn't resist its scent, so he stopped. *Chomp-chomp-chomp...*

After eating and grooming, they lay together, Razor in his spot and Rat in his, a few inches from Razor's paws. They each curled into a ball to hold in their warmth against the creeping coldness that stalked in from outside. It smelled like it was going to be a cruel winter.

As if to prove the point, the following days grew colder and colder. One afternoon, while Razor lounged in the yard with glowing pictures swirling through his mind, something with such stinging coldness landed on his nose and jolted him out of his daydream. Cross-eyed, he stared at his snout as another white speck dropped out of the sky and rested upon it.

He looked up.

Snow fell. Flakes so large, he soon sported a mottled white coat.

He trotted inside for cover and shook himself. After showering the area, he lay before the heater, close to Bushy Beard.

"Too cold outside, Dog? Better get used to it. They're forecasting a bad one this year."

There was a time he liked to listen when Bushy Beard spoke to him because, for those few seconds, it made him feel he mattered, but these days... noise. Nothing but meaningless, unwanted noise.

Facing the wheel in the mound by the wall, he pictured Rat's glistening eyes peeking out. People? Who needed them?

That night, he called Rat and waited. And waited.

He called again.

Straining for the sound of tiny claws scraping on metal, Razor angled his ears this way and that.

Nothing.

He yipped a third time. Louder.

Nothing.

Creeping over to the mound of treasure lining the wall, Razor sniffed into the wheel hole.

No Rat.

He stalked along the heap, sniffing at the gaps where Rat had previously appeared. No sign.

Razor's heart thumped harder and twisted like someone was scooping it out. What had happened that his best friend — his only friend — hadn't come to visit?

He yipped again and again, his joyful tone tinged with urgency. Ears twitching, nose sniffing, he waited.

Something scratched in the depths of the mound. Razor gasped. Was it Rat?

Sniffing harder, he tried to home in on a scent to verify it was his friend, but the scent was too faint, too far away, and too overwhelmed by the oily stench of all the junk.

Slowly, so painfully slowly, the sound of claws scratching on hard surfaces wove through the heap, drawing closer and closer. Was it him?

Razor sniffed and sniffed, but he still couldn't isolate a scent. He whimpered. He couldn't lose his friend. Please, no. Not Rat.

While he ached to jump onto the heap and rip it apart to find Rat, if he dislodged something, he might crush Rat by accident. That was too much of a risk, so he had no choice but to wait.

Crouching next to the wheel hole, he shoved his snout in, praying for a scent to conjure more glowing pictures.

Eeep.

Rat!

A moment later, a pink nose appeared in the shadows.

With a yip, Razor leaped into the air and spun around. Rat. It was Rat!

They were together again. Everything was fine.

So, what would they play to celebrate? The hide-and-squeak game? The licking-tickling game? The chasing-around-the-feet game? No, to celebrate, they'd invent a new game. Something special.

But when Rat dragged himself from the wheel hole, Razor gawked. Something was wrong. Very wrong.

Rat didn't dash to Razor to say hello or dart in a loop, squeaking. Trembling, Rat doddered to the kibble, grabbed a pellet, and chomped.

Razor stared at his friend. What was wrong? Why was he shaking?

Rat finished one pellet and grabbed another, shivering and shivering.

Razor whined. His heart crumpled, the glow in his chest not one of warmth for the pictures they'd shared but one of dread for those that might now never come. It felt like he'd been bad and his man was kicking him, but not on the legs, or the side, or even the head – on the inside. He'd never known a pain like it. He whined again. What could he do to help?

He crouched beside Rat. Hoping he could solve the mysterious malady afflicting his little friend, Razor did what every dog knows can cure any sickness – he licked Rat.

Instead of running in a loop, squeaking like a crazy bird, Rat squealed and leaped out of the way. He scurried around to the other side of the kibble, grabbed a fresh piece, and bit into it, his tail swishing from side to side as if he was angry.

The rejection crushed Razor more than any kick or punch ever had. He shriveled inside. He'd been bad licking Rat – so bad – when all he'd wanted was to be so good. What if Rat couldn't forgive him? Was this the end of Razor collecting his beloved glowing pictures?

Head hanging, tail between his legs, Razor slunk away and slumped. But alone in *their* spot, he felt worse. He whimpered. Curling up, he tucked his head in toward his stomach to rest on his paws, then peeked over his tail through one eye. Was there any way he could repair the bad he'd done? Repair his cherished friendship?

Rat's tail stopped swishing, but he still shivered. He ate two more pellets, then scampered away from the kibble, his little legs pounding his claws into the concrete. But not toward his hole. And not to his spot. He ran to Razor. He nuzzled under Razor's tail and wiggled between Razor's paws. Cocooned, he snuggled next to Razor's stomach and closed his eyes.

Another glowing picture formed in Razor's mind. A picture that glowed so warmly it was like lounging on the baking earth in the summer sun.

Chapter 20

The next day, snow had buried the world. Bushy Beard bolted a scoop to his yellow machine with the big wheels, then spent ages shoving the stuff into piles. Razor yawned as he watched. Talk about boring.

That night, Rat seemed more his usual self. They ate and then played exploration by painstakingly circling the interior and sniffing everything. Not because it had never been sniffed — it had, many times — but to note any changes. Games were fun, but it was nice to occasionally have one that was also educational.

Later, they snuggled up together: Razor curled in his usual spot, Rat in his new one, burrowed into Razor's stomach fur to create a cozy nest.

The nights grew colder and colder, but Rat never seemed to suffer so badly as on that first one. Razor hoped it was because of his help. Rat even relocated to a new "secret" lair, probably hoping the closer he was to the heater, the warmer he'd be during the day.

For weeks, snow dominated the outside. As Bushy Beard plowed the drifts for the umpteenth time to create an umpteenth pile, Razor snorted. Lying beside the heater, he glanced at the piles of treasures inside that Bushy Beard frequently delved into. Boy, did Bushy Beard love piling up stuff. People were so easily pleased. But had no one told the man snow always melted?

Nice one, Einstein. Just don't blame me when you turn up one day and it's all been "stolen."

People. Real, real smart.

Bushy Beard continued playing his game for weeks and weeks. Inexplicably, he seemed happy when the days warmed and all his precious piles disappeared. People were so odd. Why spend so long collecting something only to be happy to see it go? Razor remembered his time on the city streets and seeing all the people collecting things in stores. Were those things cherished forever, or did they fall from favor as quickly as the snow?

Birds sang more happily, and trees no longer stabbed the sky with bony brown limbs — small green blobs dotted their branches.

One morning, Bushy Beard scurried in, leaving a trail of wet footprints across the concrete. Water dripped off his coat, his hair, even his beard. Before doing anything else, he flicked on the heater.

Razor ambled over and stretched before it.

Bushy Beard snorted. "Jeez, you live the life, Dog. You don't know how lucky you are." He began banging and clattering with his treasures.

Razor dozed for a while, then dawdled out to pee. On returning, he stood in the entrance and shook himself but froze. Oh, no...

Bushy Beard pawed through a pile of treasures against the wall. The pile into which Rat had moved his secret lair to be warmer.

Razor sniffed. His eyes widened as his nose gave him the answer he dreaded — Rat was in his lair, probably asleep.

Razor had to do something. Had to protect Rat. But how?

He barked.

Bushy Beard dumped two wheels to his right and pushed something black and heavy aside.

Ruff.

The man moved an exhaust.

Ruff. Ruff.

"Shut up, Dog!" He didn't turn but continued shifting things.

Razor didn't need to scare Bushy Beard away, only to alert Rat to the danger in case he hadn't sensed it.

Arrruff. Ruff. Ruff.

"I said shut the hell up!" Bushy Beard hurled a length of rubber hose.

Razor dodged, and it landed outside.

"Stupid darn dog." Bushy Beard shoved engine parts aside.

Razor lay on the concrete, watching Bushy Beard but angling his ears to track the tiny scratching claws that scampered through the pile. Their secret was safe.

"What the...?" Bushy Beard twisted a shiny cylinder and pulled out scraps of rag. Rag that smelled of Rat.

Razor arched an eyebrow. Maybe their secret wasn't entirely safe, but Rat was, and that was all that mattered.

Bushy Beard leaned across the floor and poked a screwdriver into the rusted pile. "Great. Just freaking great."

He stalked out, muttering.

Moments later, he and Pete wandered over.

"See for yourself." Bushy Beard pointed to the cleared area.

Pete crouched. He sighed. "Yep, rat droppings."

"So, why didn't he kill it? Isn't that part of his job?"

They stared at Razor.

Pete stood. "Maybe I forgot to put that in the job description."

"Very funny. So what do you want to do about it? Because I'm not working around rats with all the diseases they carry."

Pete sucked through his teeth. "What do you want to do?"

"Poison. Obviously."

Pete pointed at Razor. "And if he eats it?"

"Is he really so dumb?"

"He's a dog. What do you think?"

Bushy Beard shook his head. "Well, we've got to do something. I am *not* working around rats." He shuddered. "God, I can't stand them."

Pete patted his leg. "Dog... here, Dog."

Razor pricked his ears. There was a time he enjoyed their brief interactions because it made him feel wanted, but now he had Rat. He didn't move.

"Dog. Come here. Dog."

"Try his name," said Bushy Beard.

Pete squinted. "What is it?"

Bushy Beard shrugged. "Something with an R? Rocky, Rambo..."

Pete snapped his fingers. "Rio."

Razor frowned. That was the noise Weirdo always used to make. Was she coming? He hoped so. Though he hadn't thought so at the time, those weeks with her had been pretty good. And *she'd* be thrilled — he'd bet she didn't have a single sample of rat poop in her collection.

"Rio. Come here, Rio." Pete slapped his thigh.

Curious, Razor ambled over.

"Good boy." Pete patted Razor.

Razor wagged his tail. He didn't want it to because Pete meant so little to him, but it just moved by itself. When would the stupid thing learn?

Pete snagged Razor's collar and dragged him to the pile of treasures, then yanked the leash securing Razor to the cable that ran over the floor.

He said, "There's your problem — it's not long enough for him to clamber over all these parts. There could be a hundred rats and he couldn't do a darn thing about it."

Bushy Beard shuddered again. "Don't say that. One's already too many." He scanned the pile, brow furrowed.

"I suppose we could try him without the leash."

"Let him roam free?"

Pete shrugged. "Why not? He knows this is his home. Besides, would you want to run away in this weather?" He gestured to the driving rain.

"It's supposed to clear tonight."

Pete rolled his eyes. "So there's a sudden shortage of strays at the pound I haven't heard about, is there?"

Bushy Beard folded his arms. "As long as he kills the thing, I don't care. Something about rats... urghhh. They just creep me out."

Pete smirked. "Why do you think I chose him out of all the dogs there? Because he was a fighting dog."

"So?"

"So, like he's going to let anything invade his territory. Trust me, he'll nail the little sucker. So we good?"

Bushy Beard nodded.

"Okay, we'll let him off his leash for the rest of the day, and if he behaves, fine." Pete unclipped the leash from Razor's collar and dropped it. He jabbed a finger at the pile. "Kill! Kill!"

Razor looked at his leash on the floor, then at Pete. *That supposed to mean something, cowboy? Because I gotta tell you, it's pretty underwhelming.*

Pete snatched up one of the rags Rat had stolen for bedding. He shoved it against Razor's snout while holding the back of Razor's head.

"Kill, Rio. Kill," said Pete.

Razor shook his head but was caught fast. He didn't know what game this was, but he didn't like it. He growled.

Pete said, "That's it, boy. Kill. Kill."

Razor yanked back and broke loose.

"Good boy, Rio." He patted Razor.

Razor frowned. He'd thought they'd be upset if they discovered Rat was living here, but maybe they liked rats, too. Okay, some of the signals were mixed — their tone of voice wasn't happy, and the stink of fear mixed with revulsion oozed from Bushy Beard — but Pete had patted him for the first time in longer than he could remember. *And* they'd let him off his leash. On balance, it all seemed more positive than negative, so the next time the opportunity arose, maybe it would be a good idea to introduce everyone.

Razor sauntered back to the heater and collapsed.

Bushy Beard sneered. "Way to go, killer."

"Give him a chance. Once he gets the scent, there'll be blood and guts all over this place."

"There'd better be."

Despite having gained his freedom, Razor stayed inside most of the morning. Rain always made scents so much fatter, so much juicier, so much more delicious, but it needed time to work its magic.

Later, with the world sodden and a touch of sunlight peeking through the black clouds, Razor ventured out to test if the rain had done its job. The air popped with fresh, succulent smells. He drew in a huge breath, savoring the tantalizing scents energized by the rain.

It was strange not to feel something dragging behind him or to hear the chain scraping along the cable. In fact, it was unnerving. Like being in a noisy room for a long time and then going somewhere deathly quiet — it felt off, as if something was wrong when it actually couldn't be more right.

He glanced back to check he wasn't still tethered. No, nothing. Hmmm, that meant...

Unleashed, Razor broke into a trot.

Wow, that felt good. He'd forgotten how good running free felt. He quickened his pace. Then quickened it even more. Before he knew it, he was racing through the yard, zigging here, zagging there.

Wind blew past his face, ruffling his fur, and scents flew by almost too fast to smell. Almost.

He tore down the nearest canyon, around the curve at the bottom — a place he'd never been able to reach before — and back up the next canyon. Unencumbered by the leash, he ran, feet pounding into the ground, mud kicking up behind him. He was free. *Free!*

He circled the next canyon, tongue lolling, breath panting. Bolting between the glistening metal walls, on he flew.

But he stuck his claws into the ground and skidded to a standstill.

Razor gasped. Today was the day. He'd never thought it would come, but it actually had. Open-mouthed, he gazed at the sight before him.

The metal mountain beckoned.

His cable had never let him climb it, never let him see what lay beyond the enclosure's fence. But today...

He leaped onto the hood of the silver car at the bottom of the pile, then onto the roof of the minivan next to it. His claws slipping on the rain-slicked metal, he scrambled onward and upward, climbing, climbing, climbing.

Finally, he stopped, his claws scraping on the roof of a blue car — the summit. His breath billowed before him as, wide-eyed, he surveyed his kingdom.

Wow, the world was big. *So big.* Who'd ever have imagined there could be so much to it?

Traffic tootled along roads that disappeared into the distance. On two sides, dark factories reared out of the ground, while on a third, row upon row of parked cars gleamed in the sun. So, if this was where cars came to die, was that where they were born? People-stuff. He'd never get the hang of it.

However, it was the last side that snatched his attention. Immediately beyond the fence, trenches crisscrossed the ground in some spots, while in others, partly built walls struggled up, as if buildings were growing out of the dirt. More people-stuff. Boring. But what lay beyond that...

An ocean of green that seemed to stretch on forever, punctuated by only a few trees and bushes. Wow, he'd never seen such a vast expanse. What must it be like to run in a place so endless?

Strangely, tiny walls cluttered the area — so many tiny walls. Row after row.

He squinted. What were they? They were way too small to be of any use — he'd leap them with ease. And that would make running even more fun. Run and jump and jump and run. What a day that would be.

He looked back at his home. But Rat wouldn't be able to jump the walls, despite them being so small. Running and jumping would be fun while it lasted, but running and jumping alone? Those glowing pictures would quickly fade. However, if he found a way to take Rat with him... those pictures would glow for a lifetime.

That night, Rat came as soon as Razor called him. Obviously not happy his lair had been destroyed, he dragged bedding into the shadows to build a new home. After that, they ate, then played the over-the-mountain game — Razor curled up in his spot and Rat wiggled under Razor's tail, then up his belly, over his side, and down his back to the floor. Immediately, Rat scooted around to climb the mountain again.

Razor watched his little friend, glowing pictures already forming in his mind even though their evening together had barely begun. They'd each conquered a mountain today. Each achieved things they'd probably never believed they could. Razor's mountain had shown him the wonders of the world outside the fence. Rat's? Rat's mountain had revealed the wonders inside it.

Breathing hard, Rat wiggled under Razor's tail one last time. He pawed Razor's stomach fur, combing it into just the fluffiness he liked, then he snuggled down and closed his eyes.

Razor gazed at Rat, the only friend he had — the only friend he needed. He leaned over to lick him goodnight, but a tiny squeak stopped him dead, a squeak that came from the wrong end.

Razor frowned. That wasn't...? He leaned closer and sniffed. Yep, it was — rats farted. Who knew?

Chapter 21

The next morning, the rumble of Bushy Beard's car woke Razor. He remained curled in his spot and peered at his stomach. Cozy in his fur nest, Rat was snuggled in a ball. *Awww, so sweet.*

Normally, if Rat hadn't woken, Razor would nudge him to go hide. But Bushy Beard and Pete were obviously animal lovers, so what better time was there to introduce everyone?

"Still here, huh?" Bushy Beard waltzed in, scouring the floor. "So, where is it? Please tell me you got it."

Razor didn't move.

Bushy Beard shuffled around the room, tentatively peeping behind or underneath things.

He threw up his arms. "Oh, for crying out loud. You didn't get it, did you? Useless darn dog."

Pete moseyed in.

Bushy Beard jabbed a finger at Razor. "He didn't catch it, did he? I knew this was a mistake."

"Maybe the thing never showed."

"Poison. We need freaking poison."

"So we'll get poison. Quit your squawking." Pete nodded toward Razor. "What's with him?"

"Maybe he's exhausted after his hectic night of hunting." Bushy Beard snorted. "A fighting dog, my eye."

Pete strolled over. "Seriously, he's usually up and about, so why's he still lying there?" He squinted at Razor, then grinned at Bushy

Beard. "Maybe he killed a whole bunch of them, ate them, and he's too full to move."

"Oh, yeah, that's really what happened."

"Did you catch it, Dog, huh? Did you kill it?" Pete bent forward, frowning. "What is that?"

"What's what?" Bushy Beard slunk closer. "Did he get it? Please tell me he got it."

"He's got something." Pete crouched and eased Razor's tail aside.

Eeep! Rat lunged and bit Pete's finger.

Pete screamed and lurched backward, tumbling onto the floor.

Bushy Beard wailed and ran to the far side of the room.

Rat jumped out and darted for the safety of the rusty pile. But Bushy Beard hurled a wrench. It flew across the room.

Falling short, the hunk of metal skipped off the concrete, cartwheeled through the air, and clobbered Rat.

Rat squealed and crashed sideways.

"Yes!" shouted Bushy Beard. "Got you, you filthy vermin."

Razor leaped up. What was happening? Rat was their friend. This was Rat's home.

Pete clambered up as Bushy Beard prowled toward Rat, holding a metal pipe like a spear. He handed Pete a tire iron.

Rat hobbled for the sanctuary of the pile but collapsed, his hind legs giving way.

Brandishing his weapon, Pete gestured to his left. "Cut it off before he hides. If it dies in all that junk, it'll stink up the place for weeks."

Razor gawked at the unfolding nightmare. What were they doing? This was Rat. *Rat!*

The two men closed in, weapons ready, hungry for blood.

Rat lurched forward, but squealed and fell.

Razor shot over to Rat. Defiant, he stood between his friend and the men. *The only way you're getting to him is through me, you freaking monsters.*

Head down, he glared. A guttural growl shook the building.

"Easy, Dog." Bushy Beard shrank back. "It's not you we want to hurt."

Razor bared his fangs.

"Out the way, Dog!" Pete fired a kick at Razor.

Razor dodged, then lunged. He sank his teeth into Pete's shin. Pete screeched and fell backward, crunching into the concrete.

Razor leaped. He straddled the man. Lips curled, he snarled.

Pete threw his hands up to shield himself, face twisted in terror.

Bushy Beard rushed Razor. Holding the pipe like a bat, he hammered it down at Razor's head.

Razor ducked to avoid it, but just as the weapon came down, Pete shoved him up to try to escape. The pipe cracked Razor on the head and sent him crashing sideways.

Free, Pete scrambled across the room and sat holding his bitten leg.

Bushy Beard stabbed a finger at Razor. "Stay the hell away, Dog, or you'll get another one."

Razor was a hardened fighting dog. One tiny smack meant nothing. He sprang up and snarled at Bushy Beard.

The man backpedaled. "Oh, boy." He rubbed his face, so much fear dripping from him, Razor could suffocate on it.

Razor crept closer, fangs glistening.

"Easy, Dog." Bushy Beard threw his weapon away, and it clattered across the floor. His hands held up protectively, he backed away. He smiled, but fear creased his face more than joy ever could. "Easy — uh — Rio. Good Rio."

Stalking forward, Razor moved in for the kill.

Still smiling and backing off, Bushy Beard said, "Who gives you kibble every day, Rio? Who treats you so good?"

Razor lunged and snapped. Not to kill, but to scare — such cowardice was sickening. He wouldn't fight an opponent so unworthy.

Bushy Beard spun and ran, wailing like a little girl.

Razor shot Pete a glare. Even though Pete was beyond Razor's reach, the man pulled farther away, shielding himself with his hands.

The threat eliminated, Razor turned. Rat lay where he'd fallen. Unmoving. Razor darted over. Was he alive? Please let him be alive.

Staring down, Razor whimpered. He couldn't lose his only friend. Especially not like this. Pain tore through his chest worse than any wound he'd ever suffered.

As gently as he could, he nudged Rat with his nose.

Nothing.

Please don't let Rat be...

A tiny rasping breath broke the silence.

Yes!

But what could Razor do to help his friend? They obviously couldn't live here anymore, so where could they go? Well, there was one place...

Razor gazed through the opening to the world beyond his concrete hell.

The metal mountain glistened in the sun.

As tenderly as he could, Razor lifted Rat in his jaws, then bolted. He ran down the canyons that had imprisoned him for so long, the cable that had enchained him under his feet. At the far end, he jumped onto the hood of a yellow car, up onto a red vehicle, then finally onto a black one's roof.

Without glancing back, he leaped.

Razor and Rat soared through the air over the enclosure's fence. At the other side, they plummeted to land on a hill of muddy soil removed from the excavated holes. Razor slid down the mound and was already running before they hit the bottom.

Men in lurid yellow jackets gawked as he shot along a dirt track, Rat still clutched in his jaws. He raced between partially built brick walls to the far end of the site, then nosed through a gap where two sheets of the wire mesh fence met. Outside, he hunkered down and shuffled under a hedge that ran away into the distance in both directions.

His belly scraping through the muck, he wormed out the other side to stand in a new world — a grassy expanse dotted with trees and crammed with the tiniest walls he'd ever seen.

Free.

But what the devil did they do now?

Chapter 22

Razor gazed at their new world. They needed somewhere to hide. Somewhere Rat could heal. But where?

The odd person ambled the crisscrossing paths lined with tiny walls. Strangely, each wall had squiggles on it. Boy, did people love covering everything in squiggles. Why? Did they mean something? If so, the lack of people suggested no one was remotely interested in anything squiggled here. People-stuff: a constant source of mystery.

Razor crept along one of the deserted paths. People had caused enough problems, so the fewer they encountered, the better.

The walls were generally gray, black, or brown, with gray being the most common. Those wouldn't have been his choices to brighten up such a nice area, but what did he know about color coordination?

The majority of the walls were only a few feet wide and high, while being only a few inches deep. Some had flowers before them, either growing out of the ground or in decorative pots. However, despite there being so many walls — more than anyone could ever count — none provided any sort of shelter. Crazy. But that was people-stuff.

Prowling around the small walls to avoid people, Razor carried Rat deeper and deeper into this strange place, birdsong and the rumble of distant traffic accompanying them.

Finally, a building appeared, a hedge surrounding it on three sides as if trying to hide it. On the street, Razor wouldn't class it as a building because it was so small, but compared to the tiny walls, it was huge — big enough for at least three or four people to cram into.

Razor nuzzled the blue wooden door, its paint chipped and peeling. Locked.

Okay, so time for plan B. He squeezed between the hedge and the wall, then shuffled to the rear of the building. Secluded, sheltered, silent. Ideal.

Gently, he laid Rat on the flattened earth. He watched, praying Rat would squeak and scurry about to explore their new home.

Rat didn't move.

Razor whimpered. As tenderly as possible, he licked Rat. Whenever Razor was unwell or injured, licking always healed him. It had to work now. Had to.

Still, Rat didn't move.

Rat wasn't just his friend; he was Razor's world. That crushing pain returned inside Razor's chest, as if Bushy Beard were pinning him down while Pete stamped on him. Again, he whimpered.

He eased his tongue over Rat a second time, then stared. Waiting for a response. Praying for a response.

Rat's eyelids flickered. *Eeek.*

Rat!

Razor yipped. He leaped as happiness erupted inside him so strongly he simply couldn't stand still.

But Rat didn't scramble up. Didn't even lift his head. He lay panting, eyes once more shut.

Razor had to do something. But if the miracle of licking didn't work, what would?

He gasped. The next best thing: food.

Razor strode away to go search.

Eeek.

Rat still lay in the same position, but one beady eye stared at Razor.

The poor little thing didn't want to be left alone. Razor could appreciate that. He lay near Rat so his friend could sense him. Food could wait for now.

When the sun was high, Razor stirred. He licked Rat to assure him he wasn't abandoning him, then left.

Back on the paths, he sniffed. There weren't many people around, and he couldn't see a single food truck or store, but there had to be something edible somewhere. He angled his ears to pinpoint any people-

116

noise but frowned. Something was wrong with his right ear, because it didn't seem to want to do what he told it. He pawed it and winced. Blood was smeared across his foreleg from a gash across his ear where Bushy Beard had hit him.

He tried turning his ear again, but instead of standing pricked, it seemed to flop over. Great. How was he going to locate sounds now?

Still, that wasn't a priority. The only thing that mattered was lying behind the tiny building.

Razor trotted along, shoving his nose into the wind for the tiniest of clues. He zigzagged through the area, passing endless tiny walls with endless squiggles.

As he cornered a brown tiny wall, a tree appeared in the distance. The weirdest scent blew down from it.

He hadn't encountered a lot of trees in his life, most of his days having been spent training, but he'd encountered enough to know they didn't normally smell of ham. That could mean only one thing — someone was eating.

Razor trotted along, tail up. He hoped that the person would sense he was desperate so he wouldn't have to fight for food, but it was for Rat, so if need be...

Nearing the tree, he crouched behind a gray tiny wall. His nose had already told him there was a young man there, but he needed to judge if the person posed any threat, and if so, he needed to decide on the best escape route after he'd fought for the food. He peeked around the tiny wall.

A shaggy-haired man in blue coveralls sat on a black bench, a few tools beside him. He stuffed the last chunk of a sandwich into his mouth, then drank from a can before taking another sandwich from a white plastic box. The guy was so puny under his baggy coveralls, it looked like he could eat a hundred sandwiches and still not be a healthy weight.

Excellent. Food and easy prey. Everything a hungry dog could ask for.

Razor crept out of hiding, a strategy formulated — he'd try being a polite dog first in the hope the man was kind, but if that didn't work...

He bounced toward the bench, head up, tail wagging.

Puny Guy did a double-take, then grimaced at Razor. "Jeez."

Instead of tossing food to Razor, he scooped up everything and made to leave.

Razor darted to block his path, gazing up and making his big brown eyes as forlorn as possible.

Blood dripped from his ear and splattered on the white gravel.

Uh-oh. People generally didn't like blood. Unless they were the type who liked fighting. He stared at Puny Guy. Did he like fighting?

Puny Guy gripped his things tighter, his eyes widening.

Razor's hopes crumbled. So much for trying to be nice. He stalked forward, curling his lip.

Puny Guy retreated but backed into the bench and automatically slumped onto it. His face contorted and his gaze flashed around as if he were looking for help. Then, realization flickered across his features.

He fumbled his stuff. A canned drink, some tools, and a phone tumbled to the ground, then he feverishly tore open his sandwich box.

Hand trembling, Puny Guy held out a sandwich. "D-do you like ham?" His smile shook as much as his hand. He threw the food. "G-good d-doggy."

Talk about easy. Razor snatched the food and bolted.

Back behind the tiny building, he wolfed down half the sandwich — he had to keep his strength up now that he was the provider — then placed the rest before Rat and sat back on his haunches. He didn't want to lick Rat and wake him because sleep was almost as good for healing as licking, so he waited.

A glow welled up inside him as the sight he ached to see manifested — Rat's pink nose twitched and his whiskers quivered.

Razor yipped to encourage him, so Rat pushed to stand but squealed and crumpled. Razor winced at his little friend's pain. But Rat was a fighter, just like Razor. The little brown critter heaved onto his forepaws and nibbled the bread, then chomped into the ham and lettuce.

Cocooned in the warmth emanating from inside him, Razor lay down, chin on his paws, and watched Rat dine. This would become another glowing picture he'd treasure forever.

When Rat had eaten his fill, he again tried to stand but squealed and collapsed. Razor gingerly shuffled to lie beside him, pushing out his belly so Rat could lie in his special furry nest.

Rat feebly raked the fur with his forepaws to fluff it, then snuggled against Razor and closed his eyes. They slept.

Everything was wonderfully tranquil. Until the day drifted toward evening.

Banging and clattering came from the other side of their building.

Razor's pulse raced. Was it Pete and Bushy Beard out for revenge?

His blood pounding in his ears, he crept around to investigate. If they'd come looking for trouble, boy, had they found it. After what they'd done to Rat, he'd tear them to pieces and then some. He couldn't risk them returning and finding Rat alone while he was hunting for food, so he had no choice but to savage them so badly they'd be terrified of coming near them again.

But as Razor neared the front of the building, a scent both reassured and confused him — Puny Guy. What was he doing here? It was too late if he'd come to reclaim his sandwich.

Peeping around the corner, Razor spied on the man as he carried tools inside the building, then locked it and left.

The next day, Puny Guy banged and clattered again in the early morning. Razor didn't bother investigating — the wind blowing in the right direction carried the man's scent to him.

Rat still couldn't stand, but he managed to eat more of the sandwich, which was good. Razor could go days without food, so as long as there was enough for Rat, he saw no need to venture out of their secret lair and leave Rat unprotected. They slept together most of the day.

The third day, Rat squealed when he tried to stand. It wasn't good that his friend was taking so long to heal. Razor couldn't help but worry.

Midmorning, he licked Rat to tell him he'd be back, then snuck out of their lair. Better food might be the answer. Or maybe not. Either way, he had to try. And he knew just where to start.

Razor lounged behind the gray tiny wall near the bench. Puny Guy had banged and clattered again that morning, so hopefully, he'd be eating in the same place.

People came and went, many carrying flowers, but not one carrying food. That was odd for people. Most didn't seem capable of walking down the street without stuffing something into their mouths. Maybe that was why this place was so quiet — the lack of fast-food outlets.

Around midday, someone ambled up the main path, whistling a tune. The wind blowing the wrong way this time, Razor couldn't tell who it was, so he peeked out.

Puny Guy strolled toward a piece of paper on the ground, a black plastic bag in one hand, a metal stick in the other. Instead of bending to the paper, he reached with the stick. Its end opened up and grabbed the paper, just like a hand.

Razor gawked. Wow. Imagine being able to reach things that were unreachable. Maybe people-stuff wasn't all crazy after all.

Puny Guy dropped the paper into his bag and moseyed on. At the bench, he set down his tools and sat, stretching out his legs. He sighed as though he'd achieved something memorable.

Well, mastering that grabber was impressive. Maybe the guy had invented it and was some kind of genius. That would explain how he'd landed such a cushy job to be in this idyllic place. Some guys had all the luck.

Razor winced. It was a pity Puny Guy's had run out.

As Puny Guy unpacked his sandwich box from a small blue backpack, Razor stalked forward.

Being nice hadn't worked last time, so there was little point in wasting time now — Razor growled. But Puny Guy didn't quake and throw food.

"You again!" He leaped up, brandishing his grabber. "Come near me and you'll get another bloody ear." He swiped with the stick.

The man smelled of fear, but he didn't reek of it like last time. And his body language was far more aggressive.

Razor glanced at the sandwich box, the scent of beef making him salivate, then at Puny Guy. Razor could easily take the sandwiches, but what if the man got in a lucky shot that saw Razor laid up for days? What would happen to Rat if they couldn't get food?

It wasn't worth the risk. Not when they already had a scrap of sandwich left for Rat today. No, he'd hunt again tomorrow. Find an easier target.

Razor slunk away.

Strategy. That was how fights were won and lost. He'd just lost this one, but would he win tomorrow?

Chapter 23

Rat ate the rest of the sandwich that night, but though they slept curled up together, Rat didn't fidget or shift positions as much as normal. Talk about worrying. What if Rat never recovered?

The next morning, Razor prowled the paths, sniffing and sniffing for food. He scrutinized all the people he found, yet not one had anything edible. What was wrong with them? Up to now, people had constantly stuffed their faces everywhere he'd been. What was it about this place that made them starve themselves?

Not wanting to leave Rat alone and unprotected for long, Razor skulked home.

Eeek. Rat greeted him for the first time since they'd gotten there. Razor yipped with joy. But when Rat tried to stand, he squealed and toppled sideways. Razor's heart crumbled.

What could he do? Rat needed help, but nothing Razor did worked. Stupid dog. Stupid!

Razor nestled beside him, and Rat nuzzled his stomach. Not as if Rat needed to get warm or make himself cozy, but as if he wanted to feel the closeness of his best friend.

Razor shut his eyes, relishing the moment, the scent of his little friend, and the sound of his breathing. Maybe he was stupid, but not for the reason he'd imagined — sometimes, the best thing to do was nothing but be present.

They lay together into the afternoon, then Razor licked Rat to reassure him and left for another hunt.

He hated leaving Rat. Even though he crammed glowing pictures into his mind, he couldn't help but imagine Pete and Bushy Beard ambushing Rat while he was away. He cringed at the squeal Rat would make as they...

He shook his head, struggling to cast the image so far away it never came back. As long as he found food and found it quickly, everything would be fine.

Tramping the paths, he scoured the scents on the wind. Patience was the key because as he'd learned the hard way that most people coming here didn't carry—

He froze. Sniffed. Food!

Wow, that was easy. He sniffed again to verify it. Yes, someone was eating. Chocolate wasn't his first choice, but food was food. And maybe a change of diet would help Rat.

Razor trotted toward his prey, mouth watering, stomach clenching as the scent taunted him. He hadn't eaten for days, so he needed nourishment to give him the strength to continue caring for Rat.

As Razor prowled along the rows of tiny walls, the smell grew stronger and stronger. He drooled. Boy, he ached to chomp into that food.

One row over, his prey came into sight — an old woman with white frizzy hair. Her scent drifted over.

Razor's jaw dropped. Frozen, he gawked at the woman. It was her. Her!

But, it couldn't be. Why would she be here?

He gulped and stalked closer. His nose had to be wrong. Had to be. Closer.

But his nose was never wrong.

He sniffed again. It was her. *Her!*

She hobbled to one of the tiny walls, ran her hand over the squiggles, and placed a square of chocolate on the top before munching a piece herself.

"Oh, you'd love him, Billy. You really would. Of course, Ty tried to talk me out of it, didn't he?" She laughed. "Well, you can imagine how that ended. And thank heaven it did because Kai's a little godsend. A godsend, I tell you."

She broke off two more chocolate squares, ate one, and put the other on top of the wall.

"It's the first time our house has felt like a home since..." Her eyes teared and she gazed into space.

Razor glared. His pounding heart pumped anger-fueled blood around his body. All he wanted was to bite and savage and rip and tear.

She'd pretended to like him, then abandoned him to rot with Pete, to suffer years — years — of loneliness and neglect and hardship.

He snarled.

Ellen gasped and spun around.

Razor stalked toward her.

She clutched her mouth. "Oh, my." Staggering backward, she shouted, "Help!"

Razor glowered. The scent of other people drifted on the breeze, the aroma of chocolate hung in the air, even the smell of another dog floated over from not too far away... but it was all swamped by a cloud of fury.

"Help! Please, someone!"

She kept shouting, stinking of fear. And no one came.

Good. Now she knew how it felt to be desperate and forsaken.

He snarled again.

She threw what remained of the chocolate bar at him, probably believing it might placate him. Normally, it might have. But today? From *her?*

He gulped it down, then looked at the squares on the top of the tiny wall. He'd had his share, now he'd have his revenge, then take the chocolate off the wall for Rat.

Claws digging into the gravel, he crept toward the woman. Her face contorted, as if in pain.

His lip curled, teeth glistening in the afternoon sun. She needed to know what she'd done, to feel the same sense of powerlessness and abandonment.

Even though he was out of range, he snapped at her. She jumped.

With her arms up to shield herself, the woman tottered backward. She flung the empty candy wrapper at him. "That's all I had. You've eaten it all."

He snatched it out of the air and spat it back out. The stench of her fear clogging his nostrils, he prowled closer, but stopped.

No, no, no. What was he doing? He hadn't come looking for revenge but for food to save his friend. Revenge wouldn't help Rat, only himself. Revenge was selfish. Food was all that mattered. Food.

From out of nowhere, a big brown dog flew through the air and crashed into him. They tumbled across the ground, a mass of tails and flailing legs.

They broke apart and scrambled up. The brown dog was as big as Razor and powerfully built. But Razor was a hardened fighting dog — he could take anything on four legs if he had to. And he had to.

The thing snarled at Razor. He snarled back, hackles raised, but then frowned. He'd been so incensed by the woman's betrayal, he hadn't registered what his nose was screaming at him — he knew the other dog.

He sniffed again.

His jaw dropped. Champ! The courageous pup from the alley all those years ago.

Was that why the woman hadn't rescued him? Because she'd rescued the pup instead? Oh wow. That changed everything. She wasn't a monster but a savior.

Razor hesitated. What should he do? He had no quarrel with Champ and, it seemed, no quarrel with the woman, either. If they'd allow him to take the chocolate off the wall, he'd leave and—

Champ lunged.

Razor dodged and swiped with his paw, raking his claws down Champ's ribs, but Champ twisted and sank its teeth into Razor's shoulder.

Razor yelped. He headbutted Champ and they rolled across the grass again, all gnashing teeth and slashing claws.

The brown beast locked its jaws around Razor's right foreleg.

Razor squealed. Not just from pain, but desperation at what to do. He respected this dog, so he didn't want to win by hurting it. But he couldn't go easy on it and risk an injury that could prevent him from providing for Rat. That gave him only one choice. Strategy: sometimes it meant doing the last thing he wanted to do.

Razor writhed and broke the hold on his leg. He scrambled up and feigned an attack that drew Champ into charging, then Razor dodged and bolted past. He ran from the fight.

Instead of taking the victory, however, Champ shot after him.

What was wrong with this thing? Didn't it know when to give up?

Razor couldn't risk this monster getting anywhere near Rat, so he sprinted in the opposite direction, desperate to lose Champ. But that last bite to his foreleg had dug deep and slowed him down. Razor could smell Champ getting closer and closer.

What was he going to do? He had to lose this crazed monster. If the thing found Rat…

They hurtled down one of the wider tree-lined paths. And just when Razor thought he'd no choice but to turn and fight to the death…

A man leaped from behind a tree, holding a pole with a noose on the end. He caught Champ around the neck with his brutal contraption and yanked him off his feet.

The Gray Man!

The big brown dog crashed into the dirt.

Razor couldn't risk Champ getting loose and later seeking them out for revenge. He had to punish the monster. Prove to it beyond doubt that he was a hardened fighter who could rip it to shreds if it ever came near Rat.

Razor skidded to a stop, then leaped back. He clamped his jaws around the dog's neck. Bit hard, bit deep. The thing had to understand he could kill it, understand it could never come back.

Champ kicked and squirmed, but between the noose and Razor's hold, he couldn't break free.

"Let him go!" shouted the old woman. "That's my dog! Let him go!"

Hobbling as quickly as she could, she lurched up behind the Gray Man and battered her cane onto his head time and again until he dropped his pole.

No longer immobilized, Champ lashed out with its paws and bit at Razor. Razor fought the pain – he had to protect Rat – but the Gray Man stormed over and thundered a kick into Razor's side.

Razor cartwheeled through the dirt and crunched into one of the tiny walls. Dazed, he clambered up. He'd proved his point — Champ would never dare come near them again — so now it was time to retreat.

He lunged to run, but a noose snaked around his throat, pulled tight, and yanked him off his feet. A second Gray Man!

Razor bucked and spun, but the pole had him fast. And the more he struggled, the more it choked him. But he had to escape. Had to take care of Rat. He lurched this way, writhed that, but it was no use.

Meanwhile, the woman crouched on the ground beside Champ. "Oh, what have they done to you, boy? What have they done?"

"Fetch the van. Quick," said the first Gray Man to his bald colleague holding Razor. "We need to get this dog to a vet as soon as possible."

Hauling Razor away, Bald Man lumbered along the path toward big black gates in the hedge surrounding the area.

Razor jerked and jumped and tugged and lurched to break free.

Rat. He had to get back to Rat!

Chapter 24

Razor howled in the cage in the back of the van. For what felt like a lifetime.

Rat.

What would happen if Razor wasn't there for him?

The Gray Man finally opened the back of the van again. Daylight flooded in, so Razor launched himself at the cage door. He had to reach Rat. He clattered into the metal grille, but it wouldn't budge. He battered it again. Still nothing.

Sliding a pole out from beside the cage, the Gray Man said, "Looks like a two-pole case."

Bald Man took another pole. They inserted the noose end of each through a narrow gap above the cage door.

Razor backed away, snapping at the closest pole. These things were dangerous. He hadn't yet found a strategy to defeat them, but he would.

The pole neared, so he savaged it. He broke away, content it wouldn't dare come back, but the second pole's noose snared him.

He bucked to break free but thumped against the cage roof. And the pole pulled, drawing him toward the door, toward the men eager to stop him helping Rat.

Razor dug his claws into the floor and snarled. But the other pole swung over and snared him, too.

Together, the poles hauled him to the front of the cage. The Gray Man opened the door.

Sucker! Razor leaped to race to Rat, but the poles yanked him out of the air, and he crashed to the asphalt.

Razor snarled. He lunged at the Gray Man to rip him to pieces, but the poles kept him distanced.

He glared at the things. Which monster invented these hellish devices?

Bald Man said, "Quit fighting, you stupid dog. You're only making it worse for yourself."

The Gray Man clicked his tongue. "After what he's done, I don't think it can get any worse, can it?"

On either side of him, the men heaved him inside a white concrete building.

Razor glowered. Brute strength wasn't going to free him, so strategy said he had to try something else. Not least to conserve his strength for when an escape opportunity arose. As he negotiated a white corridor, Razor tugged and jerked, in case the men's grips failed and that chance came, but he stopped fighting so hard to save his energy. Waiting and watching for the right moment.

But he frowned.

He knew this smell, this place. Muffled yaps and barks came from in the distance. He sniffed. Yes, he'd been here — ahead on the right was a white door to a room with a silver table that he'd once jumped on.

Sure enough, the men carted him into that room in which stood a silver table.

"This the one?" said a woman in a long white coat and glasses.

Razor gawked. Vera! She'd helped him get better before. Surely, she'd see he needed help and oblige.

The Gray Man's voice strained as he struggled to hold Razor. "He's been battering the inside of the cage like crazy. I'm surprised he hasn't seriously hurt himself."

Vera shook her head. "If we put him in a crate or a pen, he'll probably injure himself." She sighed, her tone surprisingly sad. "Scott's already given the go-ahead, so we'll do it now unless he's chipped and we can reach the owner."

"Now?"

128

"The longer we wait, the more distressed he's going to get, and the more likely he is to hurt himself. It's not fair to him to wait and cause him more pain than we need to."

"Okay."

Vera hovered a black stick with a ring at the end over him. "He's not chipped." She peered under his chin. "No tag on his collar. We're sure this is the right dog? I don't want to put down someone's pet by mistake."

The Gray Man nodded. "I showed a photo to the guy at the cemetery who'd reported the problem. He IDed him straight off. That torn ear is a dead giveaway."

"Okay, let's get it over with."

"On the floor or up there?" The Gray Man pointed to the silver table.

"Here'll be fine." Vera laid a brown blanket on the floor beside Razor, then picked up a syringe from the counter. "Hold him as steady as you can."

Razor stopped bucking. The last time Vera had stuck a needle in him, he'd started to feel better. That had to be what was happening now. How nice of her.

Vera crouched, and he felt a pinch in his hind quarters. "Hold him tight till it starts taking effect."

The men renewed their grip while she clicked on a computer keyboard.

Strangely, the men's aggressiveness had vanished. Now, they looked at him with a sense of pity. So odd. Pity? That was something he wouldn't show them if they detained him much longer and they made the tiniest of mistakes.

Even more strangely, Razor no longer wanted to struggle as much. Though he ached to break away and find Rat, he didn't feel an overwhelming desperation to fight. In fact, fighting was the last thing he wanted.

Lying on this lovely hard floor, however...

He collapsed. He'd meant to lower himself slowly, but his legs didn't want to do what he asked of them.

What was happening? He was supposed to be breaking out to save Rat, yet here he was, lying on the floor like he had all the time in the world. Maybe if he had a short rest, he'd have more energy and so a better chance of escaping. He let his head drop to the blanket.

The Gray Man glanced at Bald Man. "I've got it from here. Why don't you go and finish the paperwork."

Bald Man left.

Vera crouched and lifted Razor's right paw. He didn't care.

She shaved a patch of fur away, her clippers buzzing. He didn't care about that either.

The door opened. Another scent he recognized flooded his snout. Weirdo!

His head on one side, he gazed up. It was kind of nice to see her, but also kind of... meh... Maybe after a nap he'd give her a lick and see if she'd help him get back to Rat.

Weirdo said, "Just wanted to let you know I've got your shift covered, so you're good to go Friday."

Vera smiled. "Great. Thanks, Hazel."

"That the dangerous dog?"

The Gray Man said, "Yeah, it was a hell of a job, this one."

"It sounds like it from what Scott said." Weirdo shook her head at Razor, sadness in her eyes. "Awww. No matter what they've done, they always look so sweet just before they go. You can't help but feel for them, can you?"

The Gray Man shrugged. "Yeah, but it's not like this one had any sort of life worth living."

Weirdo opened the door to leave but turned back. "Safe travels, little one."

Razor's eyelids drooped. He fought to keep them up. *Don't go, Weirdo. Help me, and Rat will give you some poop for your collection.*

She left.

Vera swabbed the shaved area. "He's a fighter, this one. They're usually well under by now."

The Gray Man clicked his tongue. "Makes it all the worse when they don't want to let go."

Vera stuck another needle in the cleaned spot. Razor hardly felt it. His eyes almost closed, he hardly felt anything, saw anything, heard anything.

But he smelled something. Something closing in fast...

The door burst open.

Weirdo shouted, "Stop, Vera!"

Vera gasped. "Jeez, you made me jump."

Weirdo jabbed at the needle in Razor's leg. "Please tell me that's not the pentobarbital."

"It is, yes."

Weirdo clutched her cheeks. "No!"

Vera held up her palms. "Don't panic, it hasn't gone in yet."

"Thank God." Weirdo slumped, holding her chest.

Gray Man said, "What's wrong? Has an owner shown up?"

Weirdo shook her head and crouched. "I need to check something." She cupped Razor's head and eased it up. She gasped. "It is. It's him."

"You know this dog?" asked Vera.

Weirdo stroked his head. "Rio? It's you, isn't it, boy? Rio?"

Rio? He hadn't heard that noise made with such affection for so, so long. His tail lifted and slapped down once.

The Gray Man frowned. "Was that a yes?"

"Rio? Rio?"

His tail wagged once again. If he had the strength, he'd lick her. Maybe tomorrow.

Weirdo hugged him. "I thought I knew you, but it just didn't click for a minute."

Vera touched Weirdo's shoulder. "Hazel, whether you know him or not, he's a dangerous dog. You know what has to be done."

"Not if I have anything to do with it. Have you completed a B3 yet?"

The Gray Man nodded. "From the van."

Weirdo marched to Vera's computer and clicked away. She scanned a document that appeared on the screen. "So, he didn't actually bite a person?"

"Not that we know of," said the Gray Man. "But he menaced enough for food."

"Then are we going to start euthanizing bums for hassling us for change?" She crouched next to Razor again. "Take this out, please, Vera."

"You're sure?"

"If we get any heat, I'll take it."

"You're the boss." Vera removed the needle. "I don't want to give him drugs unnecessarily, so we'll put him in a recovery cage till the sedative wears off. Okay?"

"Fine. But while he's under, treat those bites. That ear, too. In the meantime, I'll check where we stand legally, given the situation with the other dog and all." Weirdo leaned right down to Razor. "I don't know what went wrong, but I promise we'll get it right this time."

She kissed him on the head, then left.

The Gray Man and Vera lifted him onto a metal cart and wheeled him to another room, where they laid him inside a cage with white plastic walls and a transparent door.

He struggled to pry his eyes fully open to look about, but he couldn't. Though, after the day he'd had, it was hardly surprising he was exhausted. Even his nose didn't seem to want to sniff, which was a first.

Letting his eyes close, he drifted off to sleep. And glowing pictures of Rat filled his dreams.

Chapter 25

Groggy, Razor stood in the metal trough as Weirdo jetted water over his back.

"You'll have to excuse me if I'm a little rusty, Rio, but it's been a few years since I had shampoo duties." She turned his face to look at her. "But as if I was going to let anyone else do you?" She blew him a kiss.

He liked Weirdo. She had just the right weirdness to niceness ratio. He'd never imagined there was a correct proportion, which suggested people weren't quite as straightforward as he'd figured. Of course, compared to a dog, they were still all crazy. People-stuff — need he say more?

Scrubbing his body, Weirdo snorted. "I've never known a dog to get so filthy, Rio. What is it this time?" She sniffed him. "Is that oil?"

The water in the trough became dirtier and dirtier.

Washing his head, she winced as she cleaned around his injured ear. "What the devil went wrong for you to end up in this mess?"

She ran a finger over the scar he'd gotten on his snout during his first attempt to conquer the metal mountain.

"Never mind, we've got you now." She smiled. "And I promise, this time, I'm personally going to make sure you get the forever home you deserve. Okay?"

She bobbed a blob of bubbly lather on the end of his nose. He sniffed it. The bubbles went up his nostrils, and he sneezed.

Weirdo laughed and hugged him. "Sorry, Rio."

After drying him, she took him to the room with all the pens. "You'll be pleased to know we kept your old room just how you left it." She laughed again.

Razor studied her. Had she always been like this — happy? That was worrying because it wasn't normal. He'd met a lot of people now, both on his adventures and through his fights, and unless beer was involved, no one was ever so happy so much of the time. Did that mean she had mental issues? Poor Weirdo. He'd be more forgiving of her eccentricities in the future.

She filled one bowl with water and another with kibble.

"Before I leave today, I'll check your records and see who was supposed to take care of you..." She sucked through her teeth. "It's a good thing I'm not a guy, because I'd beat the living daylights out of a monster who did this to an animal. But don't worry, I'll see that he's blacklisted at every shelter within a hundred miles."

Cupping his face, she said, "This is the very first moment of your new life, Rio. Prepare for more food, more love, and more fun than you can handle." She tousled the fur on his head. "See you tomorrow." She left.

Razor looked at his beloved white brick wall. The times he'd dreamed of being able to stare at that. But now he could, he couldn't settle. Where was Rat? How would his little friend manage without him?

Amid a cacophony of whines, barks, whimpers, and snores, Razor lay down. Despite being surrounded by his own kind, he felt so unbelievably alone. He ached to feel tiny claws combing his stomach fur, to feel a tiny body nestled against his, to feel the closeness of a true friend...

He sniffed the air, not to search for a scent but to verify the time of day by studying how the air pressure, humidity, temperature, and the other environmental factors made the air smell.

Yes, it was that time — "Rat time."

He whimpered. A glowing picture formed of Rat peeping out of the rusty pile of debris only to duck back in to initiate a game of hide-and-squeak.

Pain clawed in Razor's chest. Like everything inside him was being crushed and twisted around and around.

He had no idea where Rat was, so how could he ever find him again?

The pain grew sharper, cutting and cutting so deeply, he believed he'd literally fall to pieces on the floor.

He stood, raised his face to the sky, and did the only thing a dog could do when his beloved pack was missing — he howled.

And howled.

And howled.

Other dogs joined in. Before Razor knew it, the whole place erupted, and a deafening sadness battered the room.

Shaven Head scurried up and down each of the aisles, peering in on the dogs, his voice drowned out by the wailing.

He scooted out of the room and returned with Weirdo.

"This can't be a coincidence," she said. "Give the others extra food to shut them up while I see the ringleader."

She entered Razor's pen, her palms up, voice soft. "Hey, Rio. What's wrong, boy?"

He howled. He wanted Rat. He *needed* Rat.

Kneeling, she stroked him. "It's okay, boy. Everything's okay. You're safe here."

Another howl.

She smiled at him, her voice as soothing as her stroking. "Shhh, Rio, shhh."

Soothing, soothing, soothing...

Cuddling him, she stroked his head. Her other arm draped over his back, the hand cupped under his belly, tousling the fur.

Fingers on his stomach... it was almost as if Rat had returned.

He gazed into her face.

She smiled. "It's okay. You're safe."

They sat together. And all around, the anguished voices calmed one by one.

A few minutes later, Shaven Head appeared outside the pen. He whispered, "Okay?"

She nodded.

Razor lay down. She continued stroking his shoulders but moved her hand off his stomach. He jerked his head up to her.

"What?" She frowned. "You want your belly stroked?" She smirked. And tousled his belly again.

Razor lowered his head and closed his eyes. Glowing pictures flooded his mind as he drifted off to sleep. And Rat came to him in his dreams.

The next day, Weirdo took him into the grassy compound and heaved her arm back, a ball in her hand. "Ready?"

He sat looking at her.

She hurled the ball. It soared through the air, then hit the ground and bounced away.

Razor yawned.

"Seriously?" She threw her hands up, then tramped over and retrieved the ball. Returning, she said, "Are you ever going to learn to play fetch?"

She held the ball against his nose. "This is a ball. I throw it, you fetch it. It's a game. It's fun. Believe me, you'll enjoy it."

Once more, she pulled her arm back. "Ready?"

She tossed the ball.

Razor lay down.

"Are you freaking kidding me?" She trudged across the grass for the ball.

So, this was what Weirdo did for kicks, huh? People-stuff — what an endless source of mystery. Still, at least it was good exercise for her.

Despite him letting her play her game, she didn't seem particularly happy today. Luckily, he knew how to cheer her up. He hunched over and squeezed out a poop. Sure enough, she gathered it up into a little bag. Good old Weirdo. Nice to know some things never changed.

He sniffed, and his eyes widened. Even better — he had something else for her collection.

He trotted over to the fence and sniffed through the grass. Yep, there it was. Lovely and fresh too, just how Weirdo liked it. He barked.

"Have you found something, Rio?"

He barked again.

She ambled over. "What is it, boy?"

He stuck his nose into the grass to show her the exact spot. She crouched.

"Bird poop? You're showing me bird poop?" She stood and dawdled away.

He frowned. Okay, he knew people couldn't smell as well as dogs, but couldn't they see as well either? Jeez, how did people negotiate the world?

He barked again.

"Rio, that's bird poop. I'm not cleaning up bird poop."

He barked louder.

She beckoned him. "Come on. We're either playing or we're going in. You won't believe the paperwork I'm neglecting to spend time with you."

He barked. Again and again and again.

"Okay, okay." She loped back. "Jeez Louise, and I thought I was missing all the good stuff spending my days in the office."

He pawed near the spot and whimpered.

"Yes, thank you, Rio. I can see it." She scooped it into a bag. "Happy now?"

Finally. He was starting to think she wasn't just weird but a little slow. He trotted toward the door, tail wagging, his job done.

Midmorning, people started drifting about the aisles and peering into pens. Owwwing and awwwing noises came from many, but none were directed at him.

Razor lay on the floor, staring at his brick wall. People. Who needed them?

In the afternoon, he smelled Weirdo nearby while two people hovered outside his pen for longer than usual.

A woman gazed at the paper fastened to his gate. "Awww, that's such a sad story, isn't it?"

"Heartbreaking, yeah," said a man.

"Rio?" The woman's voice was soft. "Rio?"

Staring at the wall, he frowned. That noise had to mean something for so many people to make it, but what could it be? He didn't glance around to investigate, didn't even raise his head. Whatever it meant, it was none of his business.

Weirdo said, "You'll have to forgive him. He's had a tough few years."

"It sounds like it," said the woman.

"Does he respond to people at all?"

"Yes, he's surprisingly affectionate considering what he's been through. I'll show you." She crouched. "Rio?"

He turned and locked Weirdo's gaze.

Weirdo patted her thigh. "Come, Rio. Show these nice people what a wonderful boy you are."

He dropped his head to his lovely hard concrete again. People. Why would she think he wanted to bother with people?

"Rio? ... Rio?" Weirdo sniggered, though she sounded more anxious than amused. "He's usually very attentive. Give him a second."

The man said, "Thanks, but I don't think he'd be a good fit."

"No, let's find another," said the woman.

Weirdo slumped against the gate and sighed.

That night, Weirdo gave him some supper.

"Once your ear heals, I'm sure there'll be more interest, so don't get disheartened, Rio. I know it's not your fault, but you have to try to get along with folks. They'll love you if they get to know you, but they can't do that if you ignore them." She tickled under his chin. "Can you try for me, please?"

Oh wow, he'd forgotten how much she enjoyed doing that. He twisted his head to give her a better angle.

"Still like that, huh?" She laughed. "Maybe we should add it to the list of requirements for a prospective owner. What do you think?"

He closed his eyes. Man, she loved doing that. It was a good thing he was as obliging as he was.

She stopped and stood up.

Oh, so that's it, is it? Well, if you're only going to half do a job, maybe I won't bother next time.

"See you tomorrow. Goodnight, Rio."

He wished he could tell her about Rat. He was sure she'd help, if she knew. But Rat was resourceful and smart. Razor would bet that when he finally got out of here and found that tiny wall place, Rat would have a cozy secret lair stocked with more food than he could ever eat.

A glowing picture formed of the time before they'd become friends when Razor had tried to scare Rat away, only for Rat to nip his nose. Oh yeah, Rat would be just fine. He was as hardened a fighter as Razor.

138

But as the day smelled like it was heading toward its end, that biting pain gnawed at his heart again.

Razor looked to the heavens and howled.

Quicker than the previous night, Weirdo showed up. This time, she didn't talk but immediately sat and hugged him, one hand stroking his head and with her arm draped over him, the other hand tousling his belly fur.

It was calming, soothing, relaxing. Almost like having Rat back.

He lay down and drifted off to sleep.

The next morning, a young boy with frizzy hair gazed wide-eyed at Razor. "Mom, Mom! This one. I want this one!"

A woman in a matching jacket and skirt ensemble ambled over. She glanced up from her phone. "No, Patrick. We want to snuggle at night, not get mauled."

Returning to her phone, she guided the boy away.

People came and people went. He ignored most, but when he did look over, all he saw were winces, frowns, or smirks before each person moved along.

As the light through the windows dimmed, Shaven Head looked into Razor's pen. "We could do what supermarkets do and offer a special."

"A two-for-one?" said Weirdo. "How would that help?"

"No, we give something free with him. Like free chipping or a month's supply of kibble."

Weirdo rubbed her chin. "I don't think so. We want someone to take him because they want *him*, not because they want free stuff."

Shaven Head nodded. "Hadn't thought of it that way. Could we exaggerate his pedigree?"

"Pedigree? You mean because the National Dog Show has introduced a dogfighting category?"

Shaven Head shrugged. "Sorry, I got nothing."

"If we start inventing stuff, it'll come back to bite us. And I'm not risking putting him in the wrong home again. Next time, it has to be just right. *Just right.*"

They wandered away.

As the day darkened and the need to howl once more consumed Razor, Weirdo dashed in before he even had a chance to get into the swing of it, as if she'd been waiting close by. She stroked and tousled, and before he knew it, his glowing pictures came and he settled down.

The next morning, a slim man with receding dark hair and a goatee stood at Razor's gate. He stared at Razor. Silent, unmoving, barely blinking.

Razor ignored him for as long as he could, but the guy just didn't leave, so Razor turned to investigate and stared back, silent, unmoving, barely blinking.

Although Razor liked silence, people usually didn't. They usually insisted on filling every environment with music or TV or radio or, worst of all, their own noise, believing if *they* were making the noise, then it had to be noise worth making.

But silence? Silence often said more than noise ever could. Silence was comfortable, normal, happy. Most of all, silence was the sound of forgiveness. No more shouting, no more hitting, just beautiful, beautiful peace.

No, people didn't usually appreciate the value of silence. Maybe this man was more refined than most.

Weirdo moseyed over. "Can I help you with anything?"

The man shook his head, focused on Razor, not her. "No, thanks."

"Have you been looking for a dog long?"

He shook his head again.

Razor studied the man. He hadn't stuck his fingers through the grille, hadn't whistled, hadn't puckered his lips and squeaked, hadn't made that stupid 'Rio' noise... He'd simply stood. Staring.

Yes, refined.

"Rio's a great dog, but he's been let down too many times, so he makes you work for his affection. Given the chance, though, he'd make a great companion."

The man nodded.

Weirdo winced, her right foot tapping as if she thought something was wrong. She was looking at the same thing Razor was, right?

She gestured along the aisle, her scent proclaiming her anxiousness. Why? Had the silent man done something bad?

"We've got plenty more dogs," she said. "I'm sure we have someone who'll be a great match. May I show you?"

The man peered along the aisle.

She smiled, but the lines around her eyes didn't crinkle the way they did when she smiled at Razor. "All fully vaccinated and eager for a loving home."

The man nodded, and they wandered away.

Razor lay back down. The guy was just like all the others. Big surprise.

Weirdo said, "What is it you're looking for? A family dog? A companion just for you? Something big or small? Active or lazy?"

"You know what…"

Razor's ears told him the strangest thing. He angled them to be sure. Yes, the footsteps were coming back.

At his gate, the man said, "I think I like this one."

"You don't sound too sure. German Shepherds need a lot of exercise. And boy do they shed, which, believe me, can drive you nuts."

"Him." He pointed at Razor. "I want him."

"I should warn you, there's a home check and some forms to complete. Then there's a flea and worming schedule to discuss, a—"

"You chip here, right?"

She nodded. "We do."

"What about health insurance?"

"I can tell you who I use. The premiums are a little higher than average, but the coverage is incredible."

He took out his phone. "What's the website?"

She smiled, and this time, her eyes crinkled. "How about we start with a meet-and-greet?"

Razor sat up. The scents coming from each of them reeked of happiness. How odd. What had suddenly changed to make that happen? Had he missed something important?

Weirdo guided the silent man toward the main door. Leaning behind him, she beamed at Razor and gave a thumbs-up.

Razor lay back down. The man had seemed nice. So wonderfully silent. It was a pity Weirdo had spoiled everything with all that people-noise.

Chapter 26

A few minutes later, Weirdo led Razor into the meet-and-greet room, where the silent man was sitting on the sofa. The man stood.

Razor trundled over, his blessed tail doing its own thing as usual by wagging like a loon. Strangely, it kind of felt right, so he didn't stop it.

"Ben, this is Rio." Weirdo patted Razor's side. "Rio, this is Ben."

Ben crouched. He didn't smile the way Weirdo did by showing lots of gleaming teeth but instead smiled the way he talked — almost not. Razor liked that.

"May I?" Ben looked at Weirdo, his hand outstretched toward Razor.

"Please, that's why we're here."

Ben patted Rio's side, then stroked over the back of his head to his shoulders, seemingly being careful to avoid his bad ear.

Weirdo said, "As you can see, he's had it tough, so he's not as handsome as he once was."

Ben nodded.

"And I should warn you, he's been exhibiting a little separation anxiety recently, resulting in howling when he's left alone."

Another nod.

"But it's not surprising he's got a few quirks, considering his history."

The man didn't say a word. Razor basked in the silence.

"Okay, I'll leave you two boys to get to know each other." She whispered, as if she believed doing so would mean Razor wouldn't hear, "He likes being scratched under his chin, but he pretends he's doing you a favor letting you do it."

"Got you." Ben tickled Razor under the chin.

Razor closed his eyes and tilted his head. Yes, this guy knew his way around a dog. Silence: it couldn't be beaten as a judge of character.

Weirdo left, and for the next hour or so, Ben and Razor sat together. Ben didn't say a word. It was wonderful.

When Weirdo took him back to his pen, she crouched and stroked him.

"Oh, Rio, fingers crossed he's the one." She rolled her eyes. "Sorry, I nearly messed it all up for you, but I had to be sure."

She topped up his bowls. "We'll see what happens over the next few days, and if it goes like I hope it's going to go, I'll do a home visit myself." She hugged him. "I'm so happy for you."

Weirdo left and Razor lay staring at his wall. What a strange day. Kind of nice, yet also kind of not. The experience had made him feel warm inside – the way spending time with Rat had – yet also made him anxious about being taken away from here and ending up somewhere lonely, cold, dark… somewhere that wouldn't feel like home no matter how long he stayed there.

As the smell of the day changed, bringing gloom with it, Razor sat up to howl. He missed those simple times next to the pile with Rat. But Weirdo appeared, as if she could smell the time of the day, too. Could people do that, or was it a fluke?

She spoke gently while stroking his head and tousling his belly fur. He settled beside her and closed his eyes.

Leaving, she whispered, "Goodnight, Rio."

Over the next three days, Ben came back every day. Razor had never seen Weirdo smile so much. Until the fourth day, then she could barely stop grinning.

Sitting on his pen floor, she combed his fur with a black brush. "You're going to love it, Rio. It's out in the countryside, so there're grasslands and woods to explore. It's near enough to hike to the lake. And you'll be going to work with Ben every day, so you'll never be alone."

She pulled the fur out of the comb and piled it beside her.

"But best of all, it'll be just you and him in a lovely big house. It's perfect, Rio. Perfect." She ran her gaze over him. "And now you are, too. Are you ready?"

Her eyebrows rose as if she'd asked a question and was expecting an answer, so he licked her.

She laughed. "Jeez, I'm going to miss you." Her eyes glistened, more moist than usual.

She slipped a leash on him. "Time to go."

Ben did his silent smile when they ambled into the reception area. Weirdo handed him the leash but then turned away and dabbed her eyes with a white tissue.

"Sorry, he's one of the special ones," she said.

Ben nodded and patted Razor. "I think you're right."

Weirdo handed Ben a couple of folded leaflets. "Here's that info I promised you."

"Thanks." He stuffed them in his jacket pocket. "Ready to go home, Rio?"

Razor yipped. Ben didn't usually say much, so when he did say something, it was obviously important enough to warrant a reply. More importantly, Ben had an odd smell today — one he hadn't had any other day, and one Razor didn't know. Such a tantalizing smell. What was it?

They strolled outside, Razor gazing up at him. What was that smell? It seemed to be coming from the right pocket of Ben's blue jacket.

Weirdo stood in the doorway behind them. "Look after each other. Bye, Rio!"

Ben guided Razor to a silver car and fastened him into a harness in the back, diagonally opposite the driver's seat. As Razor watched Ben stroll around to the other side of the vehicle, he spotted Weirdo still watching from the doorway.

After his misadventure with Pete, Razor eyed Ben warily. His heart pounded as they left the parking lot and Weirdo became smaller and smaller. Then, she was gone. Razor whined.

Ben leaned back and patted him. "It's okay, Rio. Everything's okay."

Pete had scolded him when they'd left here. Maybe Ben wasn't a Pete. But Pete had seemed nice at first, too. What if the same thing happened?

They drove through the town, but instead of heading to where dark buildings reared out of wasteland, Ben took another road.

The car circled a small island that had only a single tree and a bush on it, then went off on a road where the buildings became sparser and sparser. Soon, everything was vibrant color, with the green of trees that stroked hillsides and the blue of a sky that soared away forever.

Razor frowned. How was it possible that so much greenery and so much sky were so close to the town, yet he hadn't known about it? Maybe it was a secret place that most people didn't know of. That would explain why people stayed in the town, even though it made them miserable. Because who in their right mind would stay there when there was all this to explore?

He looked at Ben. Maybe he'd found someone special. Someone worthy of his trust. Especially if Weirdo trusted him. Maybe...

His heart rate slowed as his anxiety melted away.

He sniffed. That smell was still present.

They parked in front of a house that was literally a building sitting on its own plot. Not joined to lots of others, not higher than he could see, not surrounded by nothing but brick and concrete. A building — on its own — surrounded by green. Amazing.

Yes, this was a secret place. Had to be.

Ben released him from the harness, led him to the house, then opened the front door.

Razor ambled in. He gawked.

"Welcome to your new home." Ben unclipped his leash.

Inside, the house was just as special as it was outside. The huge room had furniture and a kitchen area, but it wasn't like any house he'd ever visited. Everywhere was color — blue sofa, yellow door, green rug, red drapes, white ceiling, pink wall, purple lamp... like a rainbow had exploded to fill the place with happiness.

Except, it wasn't happy.

It was empty. So unbelievably empty.

Razor's claws *tap-tap-tapped* on the wooden floor, the sound eerily loud. What had happened that a place with such potential to nurture life felt so much like a tomb?

Still, what did it matter? It was warm and dry. And while not concrete, the floor was good and hard to sleep on. All he needed was a place to eat and a place to pee, then everything would be complete.

A staircase curved up from the living room to a balcony, along which colored doors hid secrets to be uncovered. But first things first. Razor sniffed the right-hand newel post at the bottom of the stairs. Wonderful, that was one problem solved — the post was just the right size, right place, right material. He cocked his leg.

"Rio, no!" Ben darted over and eased him away by his collar. "Good boy."

He fished a ziplock plastic bag out of his pocket. Crinkly squares of reddy-brown meat nestled inside, looking like they'd once been strips that had been cut up.

"Do you like bacon?" Ben took one piece out and offered it on the flat of his hand. "Good boys get a piece for not peeing inside."

Razor sniffed it. *That* was what he'd smelled earlier. But what was it?

He angled his head and took it. Taste exploded in his mouth — meaty, salty, smoky, fatty... it was possibly the most wonderful thing he'd ever eaten. The problem was, it was gone in an instant.

Eyes big, brown, and begging, he peered up at Ben, mouth watering. There was more. A lot more.

Ben wagged his finger, pocketing the bag. "Nah-huh. You only get one when you've been good." He gestured to the door. "Come on."

Ben reattached the leash and guided Razor through the yellow back door. Outside, Razor's jaw dropped. This place just kept getting better and better.

He ambled across an elevated veranda and poked his head between two of the upright wooden bars supporting the handrail. Before him, an ocean of grass stretched away to what had to be the end of the world where mountains reared in the distance. To his right, trees crawled over a hillside, while left, more vegetation carpeted the world in green.

Ben gave a little yank on the leash. "Rio."

Razor dawdled down a wide wooden staircase to the grass, but at the bottom, he stopped. He sniffed the post on the left. Another dog had peed here. Many, many times. But long ago now. Being exposed to the elements, the smell had almost vanished, but the tiny trace remaining was unmistakable.

Wonderful. This would be his peeing-post, too. He cocked his leg.

Ben slapped his forehead. "Oh, for crying out loud, not you as well."

Razor relieved himself. Marking his territory and announcing his arrival to all those smart enough to know what a nose was really for.

Ben sniggered. "A million trees, but you choose the same post."

Having finished, Razor stooped to sniff around the base of a bush, but Ben fished another square out of the ziplock bag and offered it to him. "Good boy for peeing outside, not inside."

Razor wolfed the square down.

Ben tugged the leash. "Okay, come on."

Razor eyed Ben's pocket, imagining himself ripping it off the jacket to get at its contents, but other scents drew his attention from the bag.

He stuck his head in the grass and sniffed. It was good grass. Natural, fresh, juicy. His man had once presented him with a rectangle of grass growing in a shallow box and seemed to expect him to poop on it, then gotten mad when he hadn't. But it just hadn't smelled right — all chemically, as if someone were forcing it to grow where it didn't really want to. This grass? Oh, this grass was overjoyed to be here; the smell was a dead giveaway.

"Come on, you might as well have a sniff around while we're out."

Ben led them away from the grassy area to the tree line where a brown path snaked into the wood. He pushed a small branch aside and held it for Razor to pass.

Razor sniffed the earth in the middle of the path where a clump of grass had sprouted. He couldn't smell people, so while it was a path, it wasn't well used. Strange. If he lived here, he'd want to be off exploring this place every day.

Wait... he did live here. Wonderful!

They meandered by trees and bushes and rocks and flowers... so many new and exciting smells bombarded Razor, he struggled to categorize each one properly for his library of scents before another popped up. What a wonderful problem to have.

At a gnarled old tree that had drooping branches peppered with tiny green leaves, Ben stopped. "That's far enough for today, Rio. Okay?"

Razor was far too busy to take notice. He jammed his nose against the tree's trunk and sniffed.

Some kind of dog had peed here, but what kind? He consulted his library, scanning all the dog smells he'd ever encountered. He frowned. No, it wasn't anything he knew. In fact, while it was doglike, it wasn't actually a dog.

What kind of a crazy place was this?

"Rio?" Ben waggled the leash. "Rio?"

Razor looked over. It was a popular noise, that. Weirdo liked it, too. It didn't seem to mean anything because they said it at all manner of times when dealing with all manner of things. People! They just couldn't resist making noise.

Ben set off back. "Come on."

Razor would have liked to stay longer, but he'd already discovered more scents in those few minutes than he had in the last few weeks.

Back at home, Ben slipped the leash off, then strolled into the kitchen.

"Rio?"

That noise again.

"Rio?"

What was he making a noise about this time? Razor wandered past the table and brightly colored stools to where Ben had crouched in the corner of the kitchen area.

Ben emptied kibble into one of two silver bowls, the other full of water. He patted his thigh. "Rio?"

Razor meandered closer. The kibble smelled nice, but he wasn't hungry right now. Well, unless there was more pocket-meat on offer.

When there wasn't, and Ben headed back to the living area, Razor sniffed along the kitchen units since he was there. After that, he moved on to the table, then the sofa and chairs. Slowly, he made his way around the entire lower floor.

Other than Ben's scent, there wasn't a single one of another living soul. How odd. People usually wanted to be around other people, so what was wrong with this guy?

He slunk to the green rug in front of the TV, slumped down, and stared at Ben sitting on the sofa.

"Had a good sniff?" Ben held out a length of rope with knots in it. "Want to play?"

Ben looked relatively normal, but so had Pete. Razor frowned. Had he been stuck with another dud?

"No?" Ben dropped the rope and smiled. "If you want to just lie there and get used to the place, that's fine."

Razor shuffled away. Something was wrong with this place. It was so empty, yet it cried out to be so full of life. What had happened here? What had Ben done to be so alone?

Chapter 27

That night, Ben ambled over to the kitchen from the sofa. "Rio? ... Rio?"

Other than going for another pee and enjoying some kibble on his return, Razor hadn't moved from the rug. He'd struggled to fathom what was going on here, because nothing felt quite right. Ben was the key. But was that in a good way, or...

Ben patted his leg. "Rio?"

Razor watched Ben.

"Rio?" He slapped his thigh again. "Rio?"

Why did he keep making that "Rio" noise? It appeared Ben wanted him to go over there, but if so, why didn't he use his name to make it clear like his man always had?

Razor frowned.

Rio — Razor.

Rio — Razor.

They both started with an R noise, making them quite similar. Ben seemed nice, but was he so slow-witted he thought Razor's name was Rio?

Weirdo had used the "Rio" noise, too, and she'd been a complete loon. Yes, that had to be it. They thought he was called Rio. Why on earth would they think that?

"Rio?"

There was an easy way to find out if he was right.

He dawdled over.

Ben smiled. "Good boy, Rio. Good boy." He fished the bag of pocket-meat out of the high cupboard in which he'd placed it earlier and offered another square.

Okay, so everybody wanted him to be Rio now, did they? That was fine by him if the pocket-meat kept coming.

Rio took it. The smoky aroma mixed with the tangy taste... oh, heaven. But then it was gone.

Ben returned the bag to the cupboard — a place no dog could ever reach.

Rio frowned. *Giving away only one tiny square at a time, zippy? That's verging on animal abuse!*

Ben moved to an area beyond the food bowls.

"Rio, this is for you." He patted a spongy red bed. "Bedtime, Rio. Bedtime."

Ben arched his eyebrows as if he expected something to happen. Nothing did.

He patted the bed again. "Get in, Rio."

Rio didn't move.

Ben pulled Rio by his collar. "Trust me, you'll like it when you try it."

Rio sat on the floor.

Ben winced. "No, don't sit there." He patted the center of the bed. "Here."

Rio stayed put.

"Okay, let's do it the hard way." He picked up Rio and plonked him in the bed. "There you go. Isn't that comfier?"

Staring at Ben, Rio stood in the bed, eyes wide with shock at being manhandled. What the devil was this loon going to do next?

Ben shoved Rio's rump down, making him sit.

"See? Nice, isn't it? Now lie down."

Ben waited.

Rio stared.

"Lie down, Rio. Lie down."

Seriously, zippy? Don't tell me you're expecting me to sleep in this thing. What kind of prissy little princess do you think I am?

Ben shrugged. "Okay, if you want to sit, sit."

In the kitchen, Ben boiled some milk and added it to a mug of brown powder that smelled chocolatey, then whisked it.

"See you in the morning." He ruffled Rio's shoulders, then clomped up the stairs, the mug steaming in his hand. When he reached the top, something clicked, and the room plunged into darkness. He disappeared into one of the rooms off the balcony.

Rio stared into the shadows, bemused. What the devil was going on? Ben looked relatively normal, but he hadn't punched or kicked Rio once yet, hadn't chained him out in the cold, hadn't acted as if he didn't exist. What sick game was he playing?

Other than those hours with Rat, every single day, all Rio had ever known was suffering. That was how it had always been, so that was how it was always meant to be. Even when staying with Weirdo, he'd been caged, had a cone strapped to him, and been intermittently tortured by Vera and her implements. So, this unrelenting pleasantness made no sense. Life was suffering. Period.

And he wanted to suffer. He *needed* to suffer. Suffering was normality. It was belonging. It was comforting. Without it, how was he supposed to cope, to know when he was being good? A world without suffering was a world in chaos — completely alien, totally baffling, utterly terrifying.

And in another few hours, the sky would lighten, then, like all people did, Ben would wake, and this torment would begin all over again.

Rio whimpered. He needed a world he understood. But how could he get that now? If only Rat were there. Or even Weirdo.

Rio's heart screwed up into a ball, crushing itself tinier and tinier, tighter and tighter. The longing for the life he'd lost erupted as he turned his face to the heavens. He howled.

The wail filled the cavernous room, the darkness seeming to amplify it.

He howled again. And again.

The mournful cry echoed his pain, saying more than the noise of people could ever say.

The door opened upstairs, something clicked, and light bathed the room. Ben scurried downstairs.

"Rio, it's okay, buddy. It's okay."

He scooted over and knelt beside Rio. Ben hugged him, cradling his head against his chest, one arm draped over his back, his hand brushing the fur on his stomach.

Glowing pictures of Rat formed in Rio's mind. He clung to them, dreaming of a time they might become real again.

He stopped howling but whimpered. What had he done wrong to deserve being treated like this? Why wouldn't Ben hit him? Cage him? Let him feel normal? It was as if the man didn't want him to be happy.

Ben stroked Rio, his voice as soothing as his hand. "Shhh, Rio, shhh. I know this is a strange place, but I've got you."

Rio whimpered again. He couldn't even stare at his white brick wall. This was a nightmare. A nightmare.

Ben stopped stroking and exhaled loudly.

Rio gazed at him. Was this when the hitting would start? Oh, please, please, please.

"This isn't working, is it?"

Rio whimpered.

Ben stood. Towering over Rio, he sighed again.

Rio pleaded with his eyes. Just one kick. A feeble punch. A girlie slap... Anything. But something. Please, something.

Ben lunged toward him.

Yes! Rio braced for the onslaught.

But Ben scooped him up in his arms. He carried Rio over to the sofa, and like handling a delicate flower, he lowered so Rio was half on the sofa, half in his lap.

Rio gawked. Jeez, what a loser. What the devil did a dog have to do to get beaten around here?

Ben pulled a black throw off the back of the sofa and draped it over them.

"This is only for tonight because everything is so strange, so don't be thinking this is going to happen every night." He clicked on the TV and stroked Rio's head. "I hope you like horror movies."

So this was new. Rio didn't know exactly what *this* was, or if he liked it, but it certainly was different.

With the constant stroking and all the excitement of the day, Rio struggled to stay awake. His eyelids fluttered, drooping lower and lower. He battled to keep them up, needing to monitor what was happening because it was so perplexing, but the world blurred, his eyes closed, and—

Wait...

His eyes popped wide open again. Had he just seen what he thought he'd seen? The greenest green grass beneath the bluest blue sky? Rio glued his gaze to the TV. It couldn't be, could it?

A black-and-white dog leaped across a perfect blue sky. It grabbed a gold disk out of the air and landed in the greenest grass to have ever grown. And a man hugged him. A man with short dark hair and a goatee.

What the...?

Rio sniffed, but the man on the TV had no scent.

With his mouth agape, Rio twisted to Ben. Short dark hair and a goatee.

He flashed his gaze back to the TV, but now a woman was brushing her teeth and smiling like an imbecile about it.

He turned to Ben. It couldn't be, could it? Was Ben the Frisbee heaven man?

Chapter 28

Sunlight flooded the living room, sharp and fresh.

Ben stretched, then looked down at Rio still lying across his lap. Rio didn't move, just peered up from the corner of his eye.

Yawning, Ben rubbed his face, which seemed to have more hair on it than the previous day. Odd.

"I don't know about you, but I'm ready for some breakfast." He nudged Rio. "Up, Rio."

Rio clambered off. He stretched, pushing his butt up in the air and his forelegs out, then lay on the floor.

"Maybe the john first." Ben padded upstairs. A moment later, a toilet flushed, then Ben returned. "Maybe you better pee, too." He opened the cupboard securing the pocket-meat.

Rio sat up. Nose twitching, both ears turned toward Ben, gaze glued to his hands.

Ben retrieved the bag and shook it, heading for the door. "Come, Rio."

Salivating, Rio trotted over.

"Good boy." Ben handed Rio a square. He scarfed it down instantly.

Ben dragged on a black coat and pushed his feet into boots without socks. He attached the leash, and they ambled out.

The early-morning air bit with a savage freshness, making all the scents crisp and raw. Rio savored the cornucopia of smells — trees, bushes, flowers, grass, dew, nighttime critters that had left their mark, daytime critters that were just starting to... so many smells. His library of scents would be positively bursting if he stayed here any length of time.

Ben guided him down the staircase. "Pee, Rio."

And there was his new pee-post. So convenient. He cocked his leg.

"Not there again, Rio. Please." Sighing, Ben folded his arms as Rio peed. "Okay, if you must."

Rio finished.

"Well, you held it in all night, so I guess you deserve a treat for being good." Ben gave him another square. "Ready for breakfast?"

Back in the kitchen, Ben pulled the top off a can and held that up in one hand, a bag of kibble in the other. "Wet or dry?"

Rio sniffed. Last night's kibble had been meaty and crunchy, but the new thing smelled interesting — salty, moist, beefy, sour... he stared at it as he studied its different smells.

Ben raised the can higher. "This one?"

Another scent drew Rio's attention. If he had a choice...

He stared at the cupboard securing the pocket-meat.

"Oh, no." Ben smirked and wagged a finger. "That's not for meals, that's a treat for being good."

Rio stared at Ben, then the cupboard, then Ben again. He studied the man. Though there were two males in the house, only one could be the alpha. It was best they establish who that was early to avoid unnecessary problems later. Strategy: it was what separated winners from losers.

Ben seemed to enjoy giving him pocket-meat for peeing in a good place or for not peeing in a bad place. If the man had mastered that, it suggested he could learn other tricks with the right training. Strategy was a wondrous thing.

Rio wandered to the bottom of the stairs. Yes, this newel post was almost as good as the one outside. He cocked his leg.

"No!" Ben dashed over.

Rio hated that noise. He'd heard it so many times, invariably before being punched or kicked.

He lowered his leg and braced, but punishment never came.

Ben patted him. "Good boy, we don't pee inside."

That was a happy voice. Good. So no punishment. Rio waited for his reward.

His jaw dropped when Ben waltzed back to the kitchen. "So, wet food?"

156

Rio sighed. Poor slow-witted Ben. Rio really had his work cut out if he was going to get this guy to understand even the most basic of commands.

He stared at the cupboard, not Ben and his pathetic little can.

"Rio?"

Ignored.

"Rio?"

Ignored.

"Okay, I guess you're not hungry." He placed the can in the refrigerator.

Rio meandered closer and yipped.

Cracking eggs into a white bowl, Ben raised his eyebrows at him. "What? I thought you weren't hungry."

He yipped again. But still Ben didn't open the cupboard.

Zippy, there's slow and then there's comatose. Do I really have to spell it out?

Rio ambled back toward the staircase post, stopping partway to ensure Ben was watching. Whisking the eggs, Ben peered from under his brow.

Good.

Rio trotted to the post and again cocked his leg. He glanced at Ben.

The man did nothing. Strange. This was supposed to be a no-pee spot.

Ben met Rio's gaze. He snorted, then retrieved the pocket-meat.

Finally, zippy, finally. I knew you had it in you. Rio lowered his leg, his mouth watering. Strategy: there was no beating it.

Ben didn't scoot over like last time but dawdled as if there was no urgency. He folded his arms, gazing at Rio. "You know what? You go ahead and pee."

Rio looked at the pocket-meat, then at Ben. What was happening? Why wasn't he offering a square already?

Ben shook the pocket-meat. "Rio, you've just peed outside. If you can squeeze out, say, five drops, you can have the whole bag."

Rio frowned. That was a lot of noise from the silent man, so it had to mean something, but what? His body language suggested he wasn't conceding to Rio's status as the alpha male but instead was making a direct challenge. Rio couldn't let that pass.

Slowly raising his leg, Rio watched Ben for any hint of concession. Ben nodded. "Go on. Show me what you've got."

Yes, that was definitely a challenge. And that wouldn't do. If they were to be staying here together, Rio had to exert his authority.

Okay, but remember, ace, you've only got yourself to blame for this.

He fully cocked his leg.

And waited and waited.

He glared at Ben. The pee was taking a while, but it was coming. He strained. There had to be something, even just a few drops.

Nothing.

He tensed his muscles and squeezed his entire rear end. He couldn't let the man win. That would set a dangerous precedent.

Straining hard, Rio grunted.

Ben laughed and sauntered away. "Put your leg down, Rio."

Rio dropped his leg. There was no point if there was no pee, and Ben wasn't even watching.

Ben shut the pocket-meat in the cupboard, then dolloped wet food into a bowl and plonked it on the floor.

Rio drooled. There was no denying it smelled good.

Tail drooping, he strolled over and gobbled it down. Ben might have won this round, but that didn't mean he'd won the fight. Strategy — Rio just had to find the man's weakness, then exploit it.

After breakfast, Ben dressed and they went outside again. Rio studied the expanse of grass — it kind of looked like the place where his black-and-white friend leaped across the blue sky, except this sky was a lumpy gray. Maybe this wasn't the place after all. Especially as Ben's stinginess with squares suggested he wasn't the man. The Frisbee heaven man certainly wouldn't deny his friend pocket-meat.

In the wood, Rio discovered more additions for his library of scents, including insects living together underground. Lots of them. More than he could ever count. Fascinating.

Ben answered a phone call. "Hi, Mom."

"Hi, sweetheart. Your dad and I are just heading to that farmer's market I told you about, so I'm calling a little early. Sorry, I know you like to sleep in on a Saturday."

"Actually, I'm out and about already."

"Really?"

"Yeah, I'm walking in the woods."

"Oh, that's so good to hear. It's about time you got out into the world again, Ben. I'm so pleased." Her voice became quieter, as if she'd turned away. "Ben's taking a walk in the woods."

A croaky male voice said, "About time."

Mom said, "Your dad says he's pleased, too. Listen, he can't change his hospital appointment on the twelfth, but I can still fly down to spend the weekend with you."

Ben winced. "Thanks, but I don't want you going to all that trouble, Mom."

"Trouble? Don't be silly. We don't want you spending that Saturday on your own, do we?"

"I won't be on my own."

"What? You mean you've met someone? That's wonderful. You see, I told you seeing that doctor would be worth it."

"I, uh"— Ben rubbed his face —"I'm not seeing Dr. Frazer anymore. I haven't seen him for months."

"What?"

He kicked a pebble lying on the path, and it rocketed away to hide in the shadows under a bush. "I was going around in circles, Mom. It was pointless."

"It's gotten you out walking with someone on a Saturday instead of wasting your day in bed, hasn't it?"

Ben rolled his eyes. "No."

"No? What do you mean no? You're out, aren't you?"

"I'm out because"— he drew a breath —"I got a dog."

"A dog?"

"You know, four legs, a tail, fur. You must have seen one because they're really popular."

"I know what a dog is, Ben, I'm just mystified as to why you've gotten one. Didn't you learn your lesson after the last time?"

"I did. And that's why I got him."

A stronger scent pulled Rio away from his insect find. A scent coming from Ben — his smell of contentment had been replaced by frustration and anxiety. Rio knew the smells well because they were invariably precursors to someone kicking him. He watched Ben for any sudden movements, ready to dodge.

Mom said, "Is it too late to take it back?"

"Why would I want to take him back?"

"Think of the commitment, Ben. How it will tie you to the house. You need something to get you back into the world, not to give you another reason to shut yourself away from it."

Ben looked to the heavens and shook his head. "Rio is a *he*, not an *it*. And as for tying me to the house, who's to say I won't make new friends because of him?"

"How? He's a dog, not a matchmaker."

"Dog owners talk to each other, you know."

"And you'll join in, will you? Because you're so outgoing? You know it was always Evie who was the gregarious one out of the pair of you."

Ben clenched his fist at the Evie noise, his whole body tensing as if preparing to fight.

"That's where Rio comes in." Ben pulled one of Weirdo's leaflets from his pocket and read off the back. "Dog parks, obedience classes, dog hiking clubs... Rio might be the best decision I've made all year."

"I suppose it might. Just make sure you don't start babbling. You know what you're like if you get thrown when you meet someone new."

Ben shook his head. "I meet new people every day, Mom. I do *not* babble."

"That's through work, sweetheart, where you're the expert, so you know exactly what you're talking about. But you get flustered and—"

"Okay, so I won't get flustered. Besides, that's where Rio will help. He'll make a great ice-breaker." He patted Rio. "Won't you, boy, huh?"

"I hope you're right, Ben. I really do."

"I am, Mom. You'll see."

"Okay, sweetheart. Chat soon."

"Bye, Mom."

Ben put the phone in his pocket. He stared at Rio. "Well, that's done it. It's either the dog park or the dog house. Which do you fancy, Rio?"

160

Chapter 29

Back at home, Ben collapsed onto the sofa and pulled the leaflet from his pocket again. He pursed his lips.

Rio sat on the floor. People-stuff. Boy did they have a weird relationship with paper, even though it was inedible. They particularly liked it covered in squiggles. Especially when they folded it and kept it in their wallet. Heaven only knew why because it wasn't like it was valuable. If it was, why did they wipe their butt on it?

Ben wafted the leaflet at him. "You know, maybe we'll leave this till next week. We need to get to know each other before we bring other people into the equation. And of course, I need to know you'll behave in public."

He nodded. More to himself than Rio. "Yeah, we'll give it a week. Maybe two." He opened a drawer in the small table beside the sofa and dropped the leaflet in.

Rio gazed at him. So this was life, was it? Breakfast, a walk through the trees, then lying around the house. He had to admit, it was a cushy number compared to what he'd been used to. Not that it was Frisbee heaven, but neither was it being bitten in a fight or chained up all day every day.

Okay, he didn't have a concrete floor to sleep on, or a white brick wall to stare at, but that was nitpicking. As for suffering? If he was patient, it would come. It always had before.

Ben tapped his phone and studied the screen as if something interesting was happening. A strange male voice talked, then a dog barked, so Rio tilted his head, listening. He sniffed — if it wasn't near enough to smell, it wasn't near enough to attack. Interest lost, he stretched across the floor.

Ben watched his phone for so long the smell of the day changed. The silence was wonderful. Ben really knew how to entertain guests.

Finally, Ben looked up. "It seems we've got some work to do before we venture out in public." He laid his phone down and picked up the knotted rope. "Rio?"

Rio looked from the corner of his eye.

"Come on, boy." He wiggled the rope.

Rio looked away. People-stuff. Nothing to do with him.

"Rio?"

Ignored.

"Rio?" The rope thwacked Rio's side.

Rio jerked around. What the...?

"Interested now?" Ben smirked. He wiggled the rope again, then flashed it out toward Rio.

Rio jumped back.

That thing comes near me again, ace, and you'll get it back in pieces.

Ben wiggled it. "Grab it, Rio. Grab it." He swung it out again.

Rio snatched it and locked his jaws around it. *Don't say I didn't warn you, ace.*

He shook his head from side to side, savaging the thing. Oddly, Ben smiled as if he were happy, which made Rio wrench on the rope even more.

Ben leaned forward, adjusting his grip to pull harder.

Rio thrust his forepaws out in front of him and levered back. He yanked and yanked.

Ben grabbed the rope with both hands and sniggered. "Man, you're strong. I wish I'd started with an easier game now."

Rio heaved harder. He was having this thing.

"Rio, drop it."

He jerked back again and again.

"Drop it."

Rio hauled with all his might, dragging Ben to the edge of the sofa. Just a fraction more and it was his. A tiny fraction, a tiny—

Ben shook the bag of pocket-meat. "Drop it."

Rio dropped the rope and stood, ears pricked.

"Good boy." Ben placed a square on the floor.

Rio gobbled it up. When he turned back, Ben wiggled the rope. "Grab it, Rio."

Rio glared at the rope. *So that's your game, is it, zippy?* He lunged and sank his teeth into it. Ben pulled, but Rio set his powerful muscles and heaved, jerking Ben toward him.

Although he'd let Ben have it once, that wasn't happening again. Twisting his head, he tore at the thing.

"Drop it."

Rio snarled, riving at the rope.

"Drop it."

Rio yanked backward.

Ben shook the pocket-meat. "Drop it."

Rio released the rope, staring at the bag.

"Good boy, Rio." Ben placed another square on the floor, which Rio devoured. Ben grabbed the rope once more and taunted Rio.

This guy just didn't know when he was beaten. Rio snatched it and tugged.

"Drop it."

Rio frowned. That same noise again. Did it mean something? He heaved so hard, Ben lurched forward.

"Drop it." Ben dangled the bag.

Rio released the rope and waited for his prize. It came, but as he munched it, he couldn't help playing back what had just happened.

Every time Rio dropped the rope, Ben gave him a square. A clear pattern. It was as if him dropping the rope commanded Ben to give him pocket-meat. How cool was that? He'd never imagined being able to command a person to do anything. Maybe if he made Ben do the rope trick often enough, the man would learn to give the treat sooner — none of that prolonged "Drop it. Drop it" nonsense.

But what did that "Drop it" noise mean? Did Ben call pocket-meat "Drop it"? Or was this his way of offering Rio a piece?

Did it matter if he was getting free pocket-meat?

Ben sat smiling, holding the rope in his lap.

Jeez, so happy because you've gotten your precious rope back. If only you knew how you'd been played. Sucker.

Rio didn't like taking advantage of someone — especially someone evidently slow — but people had taken advantage of him all his life. This wasn't payback, it was karma.

They played the do-you-want-a-piece-of-Drop-it game a few more times, then Ben set the rope aside. "You're doing well with that, Rio. You're obviously a smart dog."

Rio yawned and lay down. If there was no more game, there was no more pocket-meat, so no more interest.

Ben put on the TV. Rio watched for a while, hoping Sky Dog would appear, but he didn't, so Rio dozed. Later, they enjoyed another walk, then dined.

In the evening, Ben patted the sofa beside him. "Rio?"

Lying on the floor, Rio sniffed. No pocket-meat. He stayed where he was. Not just because there was nothing to be gained by moving, but because a gnawing loss clawed at his stomach. It was that time of day when Rat was supposed to nestle against him. Rio gazed about the room. Maybe he'd find a quiet corner. Bury his head in his paws and—

Ben scooped him up, plonked him on the sofa, and rested a hand on his side.

Rio glared. So now he was property to be shifted around like a sack of old boots? He glanced around for the darkest corner into which to crawl. But...

The warmth from Ben's body, the closeness of his scent, the touch of his hand...

Maybe he'd stay. Ben obviously needed him here, and after the guy had given him so much food, it was a small price to pay. Rio snuggled up against him. And Ben smiled that silent smile.

Lots of loud bangs and bright flashes appeared on the TV. Agog, Ben barely moved for the rest of the night.

Finally, he clicked the TV off. "Bedtime, Rio."

A nudge encouraged Rio to jump down, and Ben guided him to the red bed.

Rio glared at it. This thing again?

Ben patted the bed, his hand sinking into the spongy padding. "In you get, Rio."

Rio sat. No way was he getting into that thing. If anyone saw him, he'd lose all credibility as a fighting dog.

Ben took the pocket-meat bag from the cupboard and patted the bed again.

Rio jumped in and sat, ears pricked, nose sniffing.

"Good boy." Ben gave him a square. "Goodnight, Rio."

Ben strolled upstairs and clomped along the balcony. The room darkened as Ben closed a door behind him.

So only one square, zippy? For sitting in this monstrosity?

Rio jumped out. The floor was good and hard. Not as hard or cold as his beloved concrete, but nothing could ever compare to that. So, where was he going to sleep?

His gaze roamed for the best spot from which to observe the room in case anything happened. But the staircase drew his attention. Why did Ben sleep upstairs? What was so special up there?

Well, there was no better time to find out.

He padded up, his claws *tap-tap-tapping* on the wooden steps. Following Ben's scent, he crept along the balcony, another scent slowly overwhelming Ben's — the perfume of dried flowers.

The door through which Ben's scent disappeared was closed.

Luckily, Rio knew a trick for that. He raised a paw and smacked it down onto the silver handle sticking out. The door opened as if by magic. He ambled in.

"Rio?" Ben leaned up in bed, then slumped back down. "Oh, you've got to be kidding me."

Inside the room, most of the furnishings were white, beige, or chocolate brown, while on the walls hung paintings with thick, sculpted globs of the brightest colored paints — reds, yellows, greens, blues... the pictures kind of looked like the countryside outside, but also kind of didn't, as if the person wasn't seeing it as it was, but how it could be in some wildly exotic dream.

The house had a different vibe up here. Tranquil yet engaging. Yes, he could see why Ben liked it. Now, where would he sleep?

Maybe next to the beige chair, or under the window, or...

He cringed. Not on the far right near the large closet — Rio recognized the smell hiding in there. Dark, dangerous, loud, destructive, terrifying. Why would Ben want such a thing in a room so peaceful?

So, where then?

Ben heaved a breath, then pushed the covers away. "Okay, I suppose you on the floor here is better than me on the couch down there."

He took a blanket from a hamper and laid it on the floor, then tugged Rio onto it by his collar.

"Lie down, Rio." He patted the blanket.

Rio looked at it, then back at him. What was it with this guy and telling him where to sit?

"Lie down."

Rio gazed about the room.

"Rio..." Ben pushed Rio's butt down, making him sit. "That's it."

Ben clicked the light off, then snuggled into bed. "Goodnight, Rio."

Rio stood, staring at Ben.

Ben glared. "Rio..."

Gradually, Rio lifted his right forepaw.

"Stay."

He stepped forward.

"Rio, stay."

He crept forward again.

"Rio, do not come any closer."

Maintaining eye contact, Rio took another step.

Ben held up his palm. "No. Rio, no."

Another step. And another.

"Rio. No."

Rio reached the bed and lifted his right paw. Slowly, so painfully slowly, he moved it toward the bed.

Wagging his finger, Ben said, "Do not put that paw on the bed."

Closer.

"No."

Closer.

"Rio, don't you dare—"

He rested his paw on the edge of the bed.

166

"Rio, you're being very naughty." Ben pointed across the room. "Go back over there."

Rio pushed with his hind legs, raising himself.

"Rio, do as you're told." Ben set his jaw, his brow knitted. "Rio."

Rio rested both forepaws on the bed. He stared at Ben. The man was making more noise then he'd ever heard him make before, but he hadn't yet punched him. That obviously meant this was okay, even though the noises didn't seem particularly happy noises. Talk about mixed messages.

"No, Rio." Ben shook his head.

Rio's eyes now on a level with Ben's, he looked him square in the face.

"Don't you dare get on this bed, Rio. Don't you da—"

Rio jumped onto the bed.

"Rio, get down at once."

Rio slumped, part on Ben, part on the bed.

"Oh, dear Lord. Why did I ever think a dog was a good idea?"

Rio stretched out. Well, that was easy. It looked like it was round two to him. He'd prove himself the alpha yet.

Chapter 30

Sunlight sparkling through a gap in the drapes, Rio lay facing the foot of the bed, his hindquarters on a pillow.

Ben stirred. "What the...?" He shoved Rio's rump. "Get your butt out of my face, Rio."

So, Ben was pushing him away without a single sniff of his butt? And Rio had thought Weirdo was weird!

Ben had seemed to want to be friends, yet any fool knew the best way to become acquainted was through butt-sniffing. It was no wonder people made so much noise. How well someone was, what mood they were in, what kind of day they were having, what they'd eaten recently... all valid questions, and all easily answered with a quick sniff. No noise required. The majority of people-noise would disappear overnight if only they'd sniff butts. What a wonderfully silent world that would be.

But that was people — no logic to them.

After they ate and had a walk, Ben insisted they play the do-you-want-a-piece-of-Drop-it game but with a twist.

Perched on the edge of the sofa, Ben held the bag of pocket-meat and said, "Sit."

For the third time, Rio sat. And for the third time, he received a square.

So, if *Drop it* was Ben's word for a square, what did *Sit* mean? Could it mean *ready*? Obviously, because that explained the logical sequence of events: Ben said he was ready; Rio sat, thereby issuing the command for Ben to give him a square; Ben gave him a square. Marvelous. And so much easier than fighting with that rope. What other educational games could he teach Ben?

They played the Sit game a bunch of times, then Ben picked up his phone. "Okay, Rio, that's it. We don't want you getting fat, do we?"

Rio stood, eager to play. He waited for Ben to say he was ready, but he didn't, so to be safe, Rio sat.

He waited for his square, but Ben didn't look up from his phone.

Rio frowned. Maybe he hadn't signaled clearly enough. Yes, that was it — Ben simply hadn't realized the command had been given. He pushed up, then sat again. And waited.

But no square materialized.

He stood once again, waited a moment, then sat. Yet again, no square was forthcoming.

Hey, I'm sitting here, ace. I'm sitting!

Ben ignored him.

It wasn't fair to change the rules halfway through a game, so Rio barked.

Without looking up, Ben ruffled the fur on Rio's shoulders.

Rio tilted his head to one side. Could it be because the sequence had been broken? The game usually started with that 'Sit' noise, but only Ben could make that sound. That meant Rio could stand and sit and stand and sit all day, yet get nothing.

Not fair.

Rio snorted. If there was one thing he couldn't abide, it was a cheat. Well, two could play that game.

He marched to the bottom of the staircase, looked at Ben, then nonchalantly cocked his leg. It was hours since he'd peed, so this time it was no idle threat — urine jetted onto the post.

Ben scrambled across. "No! Rio, no!"

Rio tensed his muscles to halt the stream.

"Good boy for stopping, Rio. Good boy."

Ben offered him a square on the flat of his hand.

Sucker!

Once Ben spent some time tidying the house, they went for another walk. Then after dinner, they settled on the sofa, and Ben enjoyed more flashing lights and loud bangs.

Later, Ben yawned and nudged Rio onto the floor. "Bedtime, Rio. I trust you're going to try your own bed tonight."

Waltzing to the kitchen, Ben tapped his thigh. "Rio."

Was it pocket-meat time already? Rio trotted over.

Instead of opening the cupboard, Ben crouched to the red bed. He patted the center. "Sit, Rio. Sit."

Standing beside him, Rio stared at the horrible thing. Why was Ben so intent on him sitting in this thing?

Ben patted it again. "Rio, you'll love it if you try it, trust me."

Rio sniffed it. Oh, the stench of comfort was sickening.

He looked at Ben, then back at the bed. The guy seriously expected him to willingly get into this monstrosity. Like any self-respecting fighting dog would want to be seen in that.

He shoved it with his snout. Look at the thing. So fluffy. So spongy. So... cozy.

For crying out loud, as if a fighting dog wanted to be cozy.

He'd bet it wasn't even comfortable, but all show. Like a dog that growled too much — all noise, no bite. In fact, he'd prove it. He sat in it.

Hmmm... it was just as fluffy, spongy, and cozy as it looked. He could see how some dogs would take to a thing like this. The infirm, the soft, the weak-willed. But a hardened fighting dog? A dog's dog? No way!

He stared at Ben.

"See, I told you you'd like it."

Rio snorted.

Okay, zippy, you want me to sit in it, I'll sit in it — for you. I'm getting no pleasure out of this at all.

If the guy had gone to all the trouble of putting it here, it would be rude to throw that kindness in his face.

Rio snuggled into the sumptuous padding. Oh dear Lord, it was beyond doubt the greatest abomination to ever exist in the canine world. He snorted again. However, he'd suffer in silence. For Ben's sake. But he wouldn't enjoy a moment of it. He'd probably be awake all night, uncomfortable, constricted, and self-conscious.

He closed his eyes, though he knew it was pointless trying to sleep.

***

Footsteps clomped along the balcony.

Bleary-eyed, Rio peered from inside the bed. Dust floated on shafts of sunlight beaming across the room. He frowned. It was morning? He glared at the bed. He'd spent all night in this thing?

Rio scrambled out. What kind of a prissy little princess was Ben turning him into? He sat beside the bed — he couldn't risk anyone seeing he'd enjoyed it. Not that he had. The entire night had been a positively awful experience for a hardened fighting dog to have to endure.

"Hey, Rio," said Ben, strolling down the stairs. "Don't like the bed, huh?" He clicked his tongue. "That's unfortunate, seeing as I bought two of the darn things."

Ben grabbed it and strode toward the front door. "Don't worry, we'll figure something else out."

Wide-eyed, Rio watched. Where was Ben taking his bed? Not that it mattered because he hated the thing, but it would be nice if he'd been consulted.

Ben opened the closet near the front door where he kept his jacket and placed the bed inside.

Rio whined. His bed...

"What? You're hungry?" He prepared Rio's breakfast. "Big day today. I hope you're ready."

They ate, had a shorter walk than usual, then Ben went upstairs to his room and clattered about, opening and closing drawers and closet doors. Normally after a walk, Ben would stretch out on the sofa and they'd play one of the pocket-meat games. What was going on?

Rio stared at the balcony. Should he investigate? He moseyed for the stairs but froze, looking toward the front door. Or should he complete another little job first?

Ben wandered into the bathroom. That gave Rio just enough time...

He trotted to the closet near the front door and whacked the handle with his paw. It opened. He snatched his bed in his jaws, scurried back, and dropped it in its spot.

The toilet flushed, so Rio darted to the foot of the stairs and sat upright, ears pricked, tail wagging. It was the perfect crime. Ben wouldn't have a clue it had happened.

Dressed in a matching navy jacket and trousers with shiny shoes, Ben marched down the stairs, straightening his tie.

"Best behavior today, please, Rio. I'm especially counting on you to remember your 'Sit' and 'Drop it' lessons. Okay, buddy?" He tousled the fur on Rio's head.

"Right, let's go." He strode toward the front door but slapped his forehead. "Oops, don't want to forget the magic ingredient in case things go sideways, do we?"

Ben scampered to the kitchen and grabbed the pocket-meat.

Rio's tail wagged harder.

Turning for the door, Ben did a double-take at the red bed.

"Didn't I...?" He waved it away. "Doesn't matter, there's no time for that now. Come, Rio. Come."

Rio scampered after the pocket-meat. Ben attached his leash, and they left, heading for the car.

They were taking a trip? How fun.

Chapter 31

In town, Ben led Rio into the small foyer of a building, a door with squiggles on the glass at one side, a staircase on the other. He unlocked the door.

The room smelled... dead. No plants, no animals, no life at all. The decor was nothing like home either — gone were the ravishing reds, the blazing yellows, the wild greens... here, drab grays and subdued blues dominated.

A pastel blue sofa and armchair sat at one side, and nearby stood shelves with books that smelled dusty, suggesting they weren't opened often. Pride of place went to a large desk with a computer.

Rio sniffed the sofa. Some days ago, a young woman had sat there — flowery perfume, tuna fish salad, cat, sweaty palms on the upholstery, an earthy muskiness on the seat. Before that, a man had sat in the middle. The stench of cigarettes overpowered most other smells, but Rio still detected—

"Rio?" Behind the desk, Ben crouched beside a red bed. "Is there any point in asking you to sit?"

Seriously, zippy? Another one of those dreadful things?

Maybe he'd lie in it later. To please Ben, not because he wanted to.

Rio moved onto the chair. Ben's scent leaped off, suggesting he sat there regularly.

"Okay, important dog stuff. I get it."

Rio's nose clogged with the stench of stale tobacco, he sloped over to lie by the door to reinvigorate his senses with the smells wafting in from the street. He categorized those he knew and stored those he didn't for later investigation when they went outside.

But one smell in particular disturbed him. He sniffed. That wasn't outside.

Turning, he sifted the mixed aromas through each nostril independently to home in on the source. Beefy, salty, juicy... what was that? It was coming from the corner of the room. He moseyed over, the meaty scent getting stronger.

He leaned down to a metal cup with a tennis ball sitting on top and nudged it. They toppled over, the ball rolling away. Beneath lay a meaty treat. Rio gobbled it up, then glanced at Ben. Leaving something precious out in the open for anyone to take? *Sucker.*

What other treasures might be around?

Rio ambled around. Another strange smell lured him to the side of a filing cabinet — another ball and cup reeked of chicken. Ben might be able to drive a car, use a phone, and work the TV, but he knew squat about hiding things.

Although Ben appeared engrossed in people-stuff, an odd smirk played on his lips.

Rio knocked the cup over and devoured another treat. *Sucker.*

For the rest of the morning, Ben played on his computer, chatted on the phone, and had fun with papers. It didn't appear entertaining, but Ben's pheromones suggested otherwise, his mood being content — maybe even with a sense of achievement.

A number of times, Ben guided Rio into a small kitchen at the back while people visited. Once they'd left, he was allowed back to sniff the seats, after which he resumed lying by the door. Except for two occasions when he discovered the cups had magically stood back up, sprouted another treat, and sucked the ball back on their top.

At midday, Ben picked up Rio's leash. Rio wagged his tail — there was another leg to today's adventure?

Side by side, they strolled along the street, Rio sniffing the sidewalk, lampposts, trash cans, passersby... it was wonderful. Until they turned left at a corner.

Rio froze — he knew this place.

Ben gave the leash a gentle tug.

Rio trotted past Ben, dragging him onward.

"Rio." Ben gripped the leash tighter, preventing Rio from racing ahead. "Behave or we're going back."

Rio's tail wagged like crazy, and he didn't care. He was back on his beloved sidewalk. Straining, tongue lolling, he heaved Ben along as quickly as possible. His friend would be waiting. And he'd been waiting for so, so long.

"Rio!" Ben quickened his pace, pulling on the leash.

Big glass windows appeared near a street light.

There! It was there.

Rio raced to cover the last few yards. A glowing picture played in his mind — a black-and-white dog soaring across the sky...

He gasped. What the...?

Mouth agape, he looked around, desperate to find the place he'd loved so much. Had he made a mistake?

But he hadn't — it was the right window. So where were all the TVs?

In the window, cell phones gleamed.

Phones? They'd gotten rid of his friend for phones? Like the world needed more of those contraptions. He barked at the glass.

Ben stroked him. "What's wrong? Did you used to know this place?"

Rio had lost his concrete, lost Rat, lost his wall, and now he'd lost the sky dog. What would he lose next? He whined.

Ben heaved a breath. "I know what'll cheer you up."

Head hanging as low as his tail, Rio tramped after Ben. Everything abandoned him. Everything. Even when he tried to be good.

He glanced at Ben from the corner of his eye. This wouldn't last. Just like everybody else, Ben would find a reason to leave him.

He whimpered, drilling his gaze into the sidewalk.

But his life was suffering, so why was he surprised?

Maybe because he'd dared to dream of something different. If life was supposed to be nothing but suffering, why was he able to dream? It wasn't logical. The simple fact that he could dream and experience nice things suggested that a different life wasn't impossible. There had to be more to life. But what? And if there was, how could he get it?

Dragging his feet, Rio whimpered again, so far behind Ben that the leash pulled taut.

Rio wasn't greedy — he didn't expect unending happiness. But occasionally, very, very occasionally, just a tiny gesture to show that life wasn't only suffering but could shine like the brightest star.

Ben stopped. His voice faltered. "My daughter used to love this place."

Sensing the leash slacken, Rio raised his head. A giant glowing hot dog sign hung over a green food truck. His jaw dropped.

Having been upwind of the place, he hadn't smelled it as they'd neared, but as Ben approached the serving hatch, a haze of succulent sausages, burgers, and hot dogs enveloped Rio. He drooled.

"Two jumbos, please. One plain," said Ben to the mustachioed man inside.

Moments later, they wandered away in a cloud of the most glorious smell Rio had ever savored — barring pocket-meat. They crossed the street on the black-and-white stripes to the bench under which, a lifetime ago, he'd occasionally crawled to shield from the rain or wait for Champ.

What had ever become of Champ? Rio had needed to ensure the dog would never get near Rat, but he hoped it was doing well. Although, that was a thought for another time because, right now, only one thing mattered — what did Ben intend to do with two hot dogs?

Ben laid one in his lap, then tore the plain one in half.

"Here you go, boy." He gave it to Rio.

Fresh hot dog? *For him?*

Okay, so maybe "suffering" occasionally took a day off.

Wanting to savor the experience, Rio took the piece gently. Warm pork juices slipped down his throat. The meat was tantalizingly fresh, not old and cold; the bread soft and moist, not stale and moldy. Heaven.

And he'd believed all people-stuff was nonsense. Occasionally, they got it right — there was no mistaking perfection when it slapped him in the kisser.

Ben tucked into his own hot dog. As he licked ketchup off the side of his mouth, he gave Rio his other half.

Rio devoured it, then sat looking at Ben. It was probably the greatest moment of his life. And it was all thanks to this man. Rio drooled. Thanks to this man still eating a hot dog.

Ben wagged a finger, his noise muffled with his mouth full. "You've had yours. Don't be eyeing mine."

Rio licked his lips.

"Okay." Ben rolled his eyes, bit another chunk out of his, then brushed the topping off the rest into a trash can. "Sorry, but onion is as bad for dogs as chocolate." He offered Rio the last piece. "Don't say I don't treat you well."

Rio chomped into it. The moist, meaty lump disappeared in an instant.

All gone, he stared at Ben.

Ben lifted both hands, showing they were empty. "Don't look at me. You had more than I did."

Rio sighed. *You did good, zippy. You did good.*

Maybe life wasn't only suffering after all. And more importantly, maybe, just maybe, he'd found a new friend.

Chapter 32

The next few days fell into a nice, neat pattern – breakfast, walk, gray room, walk, gray room, home, dinner, walk, TV, bed. Rio enjoyed the pattern, not just because the activities were so fun, but because Ben kept inventing new games. And a good game meant only one thing – pocket-meat.

On the sofa at home, Ben said, "To me."

Rio dutifully trotted over from the kitchen. And dutifully devoured the square Ben presented to him.

"Well done, Rio." Ben cupped Rio's face and ruffled his fur. "What do you say we mix things up a bit?"

Ben put the pocket-meat in the cupboard, then headed to the far side of the room. "Rio, to me."

Rio stared. So the pocket-meat game had ended, had it? He sat down.

"To me."

Rio yawned.

"To me."

Rio didn't even look.

Ben exhaled loudly. He tramped to the kitchen and retrieved the pocket-meat. "So much for mixing things up."

Rio pricked his ears. Was the game back on?

At the far side of the room again, Ben held up the bag and shook it. "To me."

Rio bounded over.

Smiling, Ben placed a square on the floor. It was gone in an instant, then Rio sniffed around the area to ensure he hadn't missed any scraps, while Ben moseyed back to the sofa.

"Rio, to me."

Rio licked the spot where the pocket-meat had been, just to get every last juicy trace.

"To me." Ben shook the bag again.

Rio darted over.

Ben placed another square on the floor.

Rio scarfed it down. Talk about easy money — this was like taking a bone from a puppy. Rio felt almost guilty at taking advantage of Ben like this. Almost...

Sucker!

But what was with all the noise? Ben couldn't seem to decide on which noise to use to start the game — Drop it, To me, Sit, Stay, or Don't pee there... when people-noise was so interchangeable, it was no surprise people made so much of it because it had to be endlessly confusing.

Rio licked his lips, staring at the bag. Thank heaven he could interpret what Ben wanted, despite what the man was actually saying, or he'd never get any squares.

After a few more rounds, Ben put the bag away, then patted the sofa beside him. Rio jumped up, and they snuggled together for the rest of the evening.

Bedtime, Ben again tried to coax Rio into that diabolical, cozy bed. Like that was ever going to happen. Rio sat near the thing, staring into space.

Ben patted the padded interior. "Come on, Rio. You could try it just once."

Rio didn't even look at it.

"Okay, have it your way." Ben tramped upstairs and the room fell into darkness.

Rio jumped into the bed and snuggled down. Oh boy, it was even comfier than he remembered. So soft, so fluffy, so spongy. And Ben slept on that lumpy thing upstairs. People were so crazy.

Come morning, Ben clomped about upstairs. Rio listened, stretched across the comfiest bed ever created. Another minute. Maybe two.

Finally, the toilet flushed.

Rio sprang out of the bed and lay alongside it, his shameful secret safe.

They breakfasted, then went to the gray room.

Rio settled into the comfortable pattern they'd developed, yet no sooner had he done so than it all changed, with the gray room dropping out of the picture.

Ben lounged on the sofa, Rio standing before him. "Sit."

Rio sat.

"Good boy." Ben gave him a square.

Rio stood, it being the signal for Ben to ready himself because the command to give pocket-meat was coming.

Ben confirmed he was ready. "Sit."

Rio gave the command by sitting. And received his square.

He'd loved finding new scents on their trips to the gray room, and the giant hot dogs they'd enjoyed twice now, but playing a squares game couldn't be beaten.

Putting the bag in the drawer in the table beside him, Ben stretched out on the sofa. "I don't suppose there's any chance you can learn to fetch a beer?"

Staring at the man, Rio tilted his head. That was way too much noise to have any real meaning.

"Thought not." Ben sniggered. He flicked through the channels on the TV, but the phone rang.

"Hi, Mom."

"Morning, sweetheart. How's your weekend going?"

"We're doing good, thanks."

"We?"

Ben scratched under Rio's chin. "Me and Rio."

"So you've still got the dog?"

"Of course I have. He's *my* dog."

"Well, if that makes you happy, dear. Does that mean you want me to fly down next week or not?"

Ben sat up. "We'll be fine, Mom. Thanks."

"You say that now, Ben, but what about the anniversary on Saturday? You know how upset you were last year. And that was before... well, you know."

180

Ben rubbed the back of his neck. "I don't want to make a big thing of it this time, Mom. And if you're here, there's no way that won't happen. I think it's best if it's just me and Rio."

"You're sure that's what you want?"

Ben stared at the floor a moment. "I'm sure."

"Then, okay. But I can be on a plane at a second's notice. You know that, don't you?"

Ben's eyes sparkled with moisture. "I do, Mom. Thanks."

"So, how was the dog park?"

"We, uh"— Ben rubbed his chin —"haven't tried it out yet."

"Because you joined the dog hiking club or obedience class?"

"Because I figured Rio and I should get to know each other properly before we bring other people and other dogs into it." He winced at Rio, his fingers crossed.

"That's fair enough."

Ben looked upward, clasping his hands together for a moment, and mouthed, "Thank you."

"How about next Saturday?" said Mom. "Being around other people will help take your mind off things."

"Maybe, yeah."

"Just don't get flustered because of what day it is. You know how you babble when you're uneasy."

Ben blew out his cheeks. "Is that your idea of a pep talk?"

"I'm being serious, Ben. You need to get out. Mix with people. The last thing you want is to be moping about that house all day on your own."

"I won't be on my own. I'll be with Rio."

"You can't talk to a dog."

"You talk to Prune Juice all the time."

"Cats are different. They're old souls."

Ben rolled his eyes. "If you say so."

"Okay, I'll be off, then, sweetheart. Promise you'll call if you change your mind about me visiting."

"I will. Bye, Mom." He hung up.

Ben tickled behind Rio's ear. "We're okay, aren't we, boy?" But he sighed. "Maybe it wouldn't be such a bad idea to try the dog park next weekend."

For the rest of the day and the next, they lounged around or went for walks, but then, the gray room made a return and the old pattern restarted. Ben obviously wasn't happy about it because as the days passed, the silent man became even more silent, their walks became shorter, and the number of games grew fewer and fewer. One evening, Rio pawed the table drawer while Ben slumped on the sofa, staring into space.

Ben had made another fresh batch of squares, and the intoxicating scent taunted Rio. Drool strung from his mouth.

He swatted the handle, but it was different from a door's and refused to open.

Why didn't Ben want to play? They'd played every day, so what had changed?

Maybe if he started the game, it would encourage Ben to join in. Rio stood, then sat, stood, then sat. Ben was oblivious to it.

Rio whined.

Without looking, Ben patted Rio's side, then resumed his slouching.

Rio sniffed. Ben's scent had changed completely. He'd never had a happy scent — more darkly content — but now, it was simply dark. And getting darker.

It was as if...

No, that was too crazy to even consider.

Except, the more Rio studied the man, the more it seemed the only answer to what was happening — Ben was in pain.

But how?

People inflicted pain; they didn't feel it. What was going on here? How was it possible that a person was suffering? Especially when they showed no signs. Ben didn't limp or have scars but looked like any other man.

Maybe Ben's scars were on the inside. Like Rio's for Rat.

Yes, that would explain it. Perhaps that was why Rio had been brought here — it was a pack for those suffering. The problem was that members of a pack were supposed to support each other. What could he possibly do to help Ben?

Chapter 33

The next morning, things seemed normal – they had breakfast, went for a walk, then prepared to leave... presumably for the gray room. But something was wrong. Though Ben was doing all the usual things, Rio had never smelled a scent more forlorn.

He whimpered. Not for himself, but for the pain Ben was obviously feeling.

Ben trudged upstairs like a man three times his age, then, minutes later, trudged back down in his matching jacket and pants. Without a word, he attached Rio's leash and shambled for the front door.

Rio hoped there'd be a hot dog walk later. Nothing cheered him up like a succulent pork lunch, so he was sure it would lift Ben, too. But when Ben turned the door handle, he froze, staring straight ahead as if he'd forgotten what he was doing.

Rio waited. Was Ben sick? If so, how could Rio get him to Vera and Weirdo for them to make him better?

Ben slumped, his forehead banging against the door. He shook his head. Dropping the leash, he heaved himself back to the living room, feet shuffling as if they were chained to rocks.

Ben talked with an apologetic tone to a number of people on his phone, then slung it aside and collapsed onto the sofa. He stared at the wall. Silent.

Rio appreciated the wonders of staring at a wall, and of silence. Normally, he'd have been happy to bask in such togetherness. But with Ben acting the way he was, smelling the way he was...

Rio whined. What could he do?

He looked around for inspiration. The knotted rope lay close by, so he retrieved it and dropped it at Ben's feet. The "Drop it" game would cheer Ben up, which, right then, was even more appealing than any number of squares.

But Ben ignored it.

Rio knew how easy it was to lose oneself in wall-staring, so he picked up the rope and dropped it again.

Nothing.

Rio whined. He nuzzled Ben's hand, not looking to be fussed over but simply for a reaction. Even a kick. Anything. Just something from the man he'd come to like who seemed to be disappearing.

But Ben didn't move.

Rio shoved his snout under the man's hand so the palm lay over the top of his head, but still, it didn't move.

Rio had always known the end would come with Ben and that suffering would return. But now that they were here, he didn't want them. Yet how could he fight them?

The same way he'd won so many fights — strategy.

His plan was risky because it might see him not just kicked but chained outside for heaven only knew how long. But if it meant rescuing Ben...

Rio ambled toward the bottom of the stairs. Halfway, he glanced over to see if Ben was watching. He wasn't.

Rio barked.

Nothing.

Ben was probably calling his bluff. Like he had before. Strategy was a wondrous thing.

Rio cocked his leg against the staircase post. He looked back, praying for Ben to shout "no" and dash over to drag him outside. But the man's gaze remained drilled into the wall.

Rio gulped. It was make or break time.

Closing his eyes, hoping to feel a hand grab him roughly by the collar, he peed. Urine jetted against the post and pooled across the floor.

Ben didn't move. Didn't speak. Didn't even look.

184

Rio whined. This was worse than he'd thought.

Head hanging, he tramped across the room and crawled under the dining table. Peeking out at Ben, he whimpered, chin on his forepaws. Everything was lost. Lost.

The smell of the day changed, going from breakfast time to midday. Ben hadn't moved, so neither had Rio.

Without warning, Ben stood.

Rio lifted his head, ears pricked. Was it over?

But Ben ignored him and strode upstairs, as if on some urgent quest. He came back, and Rio shrank farther under the table. Something was coming with him. Rio's nose was never wrong and it was telling him to be afraid. Very afraid.

He wanted to run, but run to where? And even if he could run, Ben was his pack now. Rio couldn't desert him.

As Ben marched down the stairs, the stench grew stronger and stronger, consuming the whole room with its darkness.

The smell was so loud, dangerous, painful, terrifying... and it oozed from the molded black plastic case in Ben's right hand.

Ben sat in the middle of the sofa and placed the case beside him, then lifted a silver device the size of a small candy bar from his pocket. He clicked a button and held it in front of his mouth.

"Mom, Dad"— he closed his eyes for a moment —"you know I love you, but I can't go on like this. Existing isn't living."

He glanced at Rio.

Rio had prayed for Ben to look at him for hours, but now, there was so much sadness in those eyes, it made Rio's heart ache like he'd lost Rat again. He barked. He had to stop Ben from looking at him like that.

"I haven't updated my will, but when you sell the house, I want twenty thousand dollars donated to Happy Days Animal Shelter. Take Rio there, but please make sure you ask for Hazel."

He stared at the wall.

"I'm sorry."

He put the device on the sofa, then raised his phone. He tapped it with his thumb, the screen lit up, and noise started. And the most wonderful thing happened – Ben smiled.

A woman's voice drifted through the room as if it belonged there — so light, so welcoming, so loving. In reply, a girl giggled, then spoke, her noise young, sparkling, and full of life.

Tears streamed down Ben's cheeks, even though he was smiling. His scent changed, too. The darkness vanished and in its place, a bright tenderness cocooned him.

Rio's tail wagged. And he loved that it did because it said everything he wanted to say to Ben but couldn't.

The woman sang something Rio recognized, "Happy birthday to you..."

Ben's voice joined hers.

The girl giggled again.

"Blow out the candles, sweetheart," said the phone Ben, though the Ben watching mouthed the words, too.

The woman said, "Don't forget to make a wish."

There was a loud exhalation, then both adult voices said, "Yay!"

Someone clapped.

But then the screen darkened and the voices disappeared.

Ben's expression melted, transforming from unbounded joy into the direst despair.

Rio's chest hurt just watching, as if someone was stamping on him to crush, crush, crush the life out of him.

Ben reached for the case.

Rio's jaw dropped. No, please. Not that.

Ben rotated the small dials on the front, each covered in tiny squiggles, then opened the case. Released, a menacing stench consumed the room. Ben removed a black pistol.

Rio barked. He had to stop this, but how? He'd seen a gun only once, but it was something he'd never forget — the noise, the smell, the blood...

That time, a dog had squealed the most agonizing squeal Rio had ever heard, despite all his years of fighting. The poor thing had twitched twice, then never moved again.

How could Rio possibly fight a device capable of doing that?

Ben checked a magazine.

Creeping forward, Rio barked.

186

Ben slapped the magazine into the butt.

Another bark.

Ignored.

What could he do? How could he get that terrifying device back in the closet?

Rio trotted closer. He barked. And barked. And barked.

Ben finally looked at him. And smiled that silent smile of his. "I'm sorry, boy. I'm sure you'll find the life you deserve, but I can't give it to you."

He raised the gun to his head.

Ben's chin trembled and his breath rasped as he stared at the wall. "I'm sorry, Eve. I know I promised I'd build a new life, but there's nothing here for me anymore."

He screwed his eyes shut.

Rio yelped. He had to stop it before it was too late. But he was just a dog. He didn't know people-stuff or how to make people-noise.

What could he do?

What could he do?

Rio did the only thing he could think of — he delicately snagged the sleeve of Ben's jacket in his jaws and eased Ben's gun hand away from his head.

Ben's brow knitted. "You're just a dog." He let his hand fall to the cushion. "How the devil could you do that?"

Rio sniffed. The man's scent was different again, the doom being replaced by genuine warmth. Rio licked Ben's hand.

"If *you* can do something like that, maybe..." Ben rested the gun on the sofa, then wiped his tears away with both hands.

Rio gasped. This was his chance. He grabbed the pistol in his mouth. If he could hide it, it would never thunder to make anything squeal ever again.

Ben gasped, too. "Rio, no!"

He grabbed at the gun but yanked his hand back, then held up his palms. "Easy, Rio. Good boy."

Rio backed away. The doors to the outside were shut, so he couldn't bury it. And this was Ben's house, so where could he hide it that Ben wouldn't find it? How could he make it safe? How?

Ben crouched, locking Rio's gaze. He held out his hand. "Drop it, Rio. Drop it."

Now you want to play, ace? Seriously?

Ben smiled, taking the pocket-meat from the drawer. "Remember the game, Rio? Drop it ... please, Rio, drop it."

Saliva ran over the gun. Oh boy, did he want that pocket-meat. But he had to deal with this thing. It was way too dangerous to be left where someone could get to it.

He glanced to the stairs, but Ben held his arm out in that direction. "Drop it, Rio. Please. You don't know how dangerous that thing is."

Rio glanced about. He had to find a way to make this horrendous device safe, but how?

Maybe...

He backed away, watching Ben for any sign he was about to grab for the pistol.

Grimacing, Ben followed him, stepping as if the floor had suddenly become fragile. "Rio, please."

Rio's butt hit one of the kitchen stools. Finally. He shuffled under the table.

Behind the protective bars of stools and table legs, he lay down, clutching the weapon. He couldn't bury it, couldn't hide it, so he'd do the only thing he could do — guard it. If no one could take it from him, it couldn't hurt anyone.

Ben crouched. "Rio, for God's sake, give me that. Please."

Rio tightened his grip. He had to protect this thing at any cost.

Easing one of the stools aside, Ben leaned into Rio's sanctuary. "Good boy. Stay, Rio. Stay."

He reached.

Rio shuffled back, adjusting his grip. But as he repositioned his jaws to secure the weapon, a small part of it moved between his teeth.

A deafening blast shook the house.

Ben keeled over. Blood pooled across the floor.

Chapter 34

Rio cowered under the table, the coppery stench from the pool of blood clogging his nostrils. It was all he could see, all he could smell.

What had he done? In trying to make the horrible device safe, he'd done the worst thing possible — made it thunder.

He whimpered. If only he could go back and change what had happened. But even if he could, what could he do instead? If he'd done nothing, Ben would've made the thing thunder himself.

Ben?

Rio sniffed. The smell of the day had almost gone full circle — the darkness bleeding in from outside confirmed it. He glanced at the front door. At the trail of bloody footprints Ben had left as he'd lurched out with a towel tied around his leg.

Ben had been gone for hours. After how bad Rio had been, the man would probably never come back. And who could blame him?

Rio whined. He'd tried to be good. Good! How had it gone so wrong?

The night grew colder, but Rio didn't move from under the table. How could he? He was too bad — he'd slipped out of the car when he was supposed to be a fighter for his man, he'd lost Rat when he was supposed to be his protector, and now he'd hurt Ben when he was supposed to be helping him. Bad things happened around him. The best thing was for him never to leave this place so he could never hurt anyone ever again.

Chin on his paws, he closed his eyes. This was his life now. Under the table forever to keep the world a safer place.

A rumble outside made his eyes pop wide open. He angled his ears to track it as it neared.

Light sliced through the front windows, and the rumble of a car engine grew louder. Rio froze, senses straining...

Tires crunched on gravel, then the rumble stopped. A groan came as feet shuffled toward the front door.

Rio held his breath. Heart racing.

It couldn't be, could it...?

Finally, Rio's nose gave him the best news ever — Ben! It was Ben!

Rio longed to rush to the door and lick and lick the man to show how sorry he was, but he shrank even farther back into the shadows. Just because Ben had come home didn't mean he'd come for him.

The door opened and Ben hobbled in using a metal stick for support. He clicked on the lights.

Rio whimpered. Ben's scent was mixed with similar medicine smells to those Rio had experienced in Vera's room. Was that where the man had been? Thank heaven Vera had been able to fix him.

"Rio?" Ben squinted. "Have you been under the table all this time? Awww." He patted his right thigh but screwed up his face and balled his fists as he gasped.

His breath calming, he said, "Not that leg, doofus." He held out his hand, rubbing his thumb and fingers together. "Rio? Don't worry, I'm not mad. Come on, boy."

Rio's insides squeezed together, like everything was curling into a tight, tight ball to hide. He ached to leave the table, but bad things always happened around him, so he couldn't risk it.

Ben draped a towel over the blood. "Come on, Rio. Forget that's there."

Grimacing and sucking through his teeth, Ben lowered himself to sit on the floor.

Rio gulped. Ben couldn't be so close to him. It was too dangerous for anyone to be so close.

"Eve always swore that every life wasn't just precious but special. That there's so much to this world, this universe, that we still don't understand. So much mystery. I loved her passion but never bought into all that woo-woo garbage." He drew a long breath. "But you?"

Ben rubbed his mouth. "I don't know how you did what you did, or why. I mean, dogs don't do that, dogs *can't* do that." He shrugged. "Except, obviously, they can."

He stared into space, as if wanting to make more noise but not knowing how.

He sighed. "I got you because I'd seen the difference a dog can make. How the right one can transform a miserable existence into a life worth living. So, when I saw you, saw you were suffering as much as I was, I figured we might be a good fit." He snickered. "I was even thinking *I* was being a big man for giving *you* a second chance. Can you believe it?" He shook his head.

Rio stared at Ben. For a silent man, he sure was making a heck of a lot of noise, so it had to be important to him. But did it mean anything? Probably not. Anything worth saying never needed so much noise.

But who cared? Ben's scent was no longer mired in gloom — that was all that mattered.

Maybe everything was going to be okay. Maybe it had all been meaningless people-stuff that could be forgotten about so they could get on with the important things in life.

Rio crept a paw out from his sanctuary.

"That's it." Ben smiled and beckoned. "To me, Rio."

Yes, meaningless people-stuff. Rio shuffled below the table's edge.

"To me. To me."

Rio crawled fully out. Ben hugged him.

"Thank God, you weren't hurt." He clung on, fingers digging into Rio's fur, then sniggered. He snagged the pocket-meat bag he'd dropped all those hours ago. "Wow, you were so frightened you didn't even come out for this."

He opened the bag, and the smell burst out.

Holding the table, Ben pulled himself up. He wiggled the bag and hopped for the sofa. "Come on, Rio."

Daring to raise his tail, Rio scampered after him.

Ben put a square on the floor. Rio gobbled it up.

Amazingly, Ben immediately put another one down.

Rio frowned. He hadn't given any sort of command, so what was Ben doing? As if people-stuff wasn't confusing enough, now the guy was going off-book?

Rio looked at the pocket-meat from the corner of his eye, then at Ben. *This isn't a trick, right, zippy?*

Slowly, Rio leaned down and took the square. He cringed, half expecting something bad to happen. But it didn't.

"You get as many as you can eat tonight, boy." Ben put a third one down.

Whoa, what the...? Until now, he'd had to work hard to earn these by training Ben to follow a sequence of actions. Now he was getting squares just handed to him? He was sure the gun had hurt Ben's leg, which explained the limping, but maybe he was wrong. Maybe he'd shot the man in the head. That was the only explanation.

He devoured the square. Again, Ben instantly replaced it.

Yep, the poor guy had lost it. He was little more than a vegetable.

That was tough, but life was brutal. Rio ate the pocket-meat and Ben replaced it.

Rio scarfed down that one too but then gasped. What would happen when the bag was empty? Could vegetable Ben still use a stove?

Chapter 35

Snuggled in his bed, Rio listened to Ben clomping about in his bedroom. Rio closed his eyes again. Another minute. Maybe two. He twisted to see if he could get even comfier. And he did. Wow, this bed was amazing.

He sighed, the comfort overwhelming. So, maybe three minutes. He dozed...

Someone cleared their throat.

Drowsy, Rio opened one eye.

Standing over Rio, Ben smirked, arching an eyebrow.

Both Rio's eyes popped wide open. He was still in bed. In his prissy princess bed!

He scrambled out and sat beside it. How the devil had he fallen so deeply asleep he hadn't heard or smelled Ben approaching? Darn his comfy bed. Still, maybe Ben hadn't twigged, what with his head trauma.

Ben sniggered. "Too late now, dog. Your dirty little secret's out."

Okay, you win this round, zippy. So I like my prissy princess bed — it's a quirk. Part of what makes me so enigmatic. But I'm still a hardened fighting dog who could take your hand off with one bite. You'd do well to remember that.

Ben waltzed away, chuckling.

I said remember that!

Ben started on breakfast.

They completed their usual morning routine, then instead of starting a game, Ben changed into clothes that weren't for the gray room or for lounging around at home. Was something going on?

Ben sauntered to the front door and called, "Rio?"

Rio trotted over.

"Sit."

Rio sat and Ben attached his leash.

"It's time to bite the bullet and keep that promise." Ben snickered. "Talk about an inappropriate pun."

Wait...

Rio frowned. Didn't he used to get a square when he sat? What was going on? Don't say that because he'd enjoyed so many last night, he wasn't getting any today.

No, wait... it was probably Ben's head trauma. Great, that meant going through the whole rigmarole of training the man again. If that was even possible with someone of Ben's diminished mental capacity.

Ben said to himself, "It's not going to be as bad as you think. It's not going to be as bad as you think." He sighed. "Okay, Rio, let's get all the fun over with."

He led Rio to the car.

So, no walk today? Rio had relieved himself earlier but had then been ushered straight back in, only for Ben to spend ages scrubbing the blood off the floor. Why the change in routine?

They drove into town and parked in a lot. Ben remained seated, muttering to himself and staring at the world as if he wasn't seeing any of it.

Rio peered out. What was making Ben so anxious? The scent of other people and other dogs hung on the air, but not to the extent it was anything to worry about.

Ben gripped the steering wheel, knuckles white. "We have to do this. It's the only way." He glanced at Rio. "It's time." He sniggered. "She'd say it was well past time, but..."

He heaved a breath and exited the car.

Ben took Rio out. "It's now or never, Rio. Come on."

Once out, Ben fitted a muzzle to Rio. "Don't worry, this is only a precaution. If you're good, it can come off."

Rio hated muzzles, but if Ben needed him to wear one, fair enough.

Ben guided them toward a path through some trees, the smell of dogs growing stronger and stronger. There could only be one reason for visiting a place with so many dogs.

Rio looked up at Ben. If Ben asked him to fight, he'd fight. Ben had been good to him, so Rio would give him the victory he deserved. That would be odd, though. Ben was a warm, quiet man, not the violent, loud type that frequented dogfights. But why else would they come to a place filled with dogs?

With his heart pounding, Rio straightened up to his full height, puffing out his chest. His opponents needed to see how big and fit he was — a fight started long before the first bite. Strategy.

Through the trees, a grass verge dipped away on the right to where brown rectangles of earth burst with flowers. Rio gave it only a cursory sniff because of what appeared on the left: a wire mesh fence encircled an area covered in wood chips and dotted with trees. Inside were benches, people, and dogs. More dogs than Rio had ever seen at any fight.

Rio stopped, squinting into the area. Everywhere, dogs roamed free, sniffing, playing, investigating, running, lying, rolling...

He frowned.

Where was the fighting? He couldn't smell a single drop of blood, couldn't see a single wound, couldn't hear a single yelp of pain. What the...?

Ben yanked his leash. "Rio, I don't want to be here either, but let's just rip the band-aid off, huh?"

They entered through a gate, Ben breathing quicker than normal and his heart pounding. But not with excitement the way his man's had when they'd attended a fight. Something odd was happening, but what?

Rio strutted along, glaring at anything that looked in his direction. Ben did the opposite, keeping his face downward to avoid eye contact. All around, people talked quietly, sat quietly, played quietly... where was the bravado, the swagger, the aggression? This was the strangest dogfight club ever.

A brown Chihuahua with scratches across its snout shot past him, a huge stick in its mouth. It bolted under a bench, but the branch caught on the metal supports on either side. The dog cartwheeled over the stick and smacked into the muck.

Rio rolled his eyes. *That* was his competition? Some creatures just weren't fit to be called a dog.

Scrambling up, the tiny dog yapped and yapped as if it didn't care, then grabbed its precious stick again and heaved backward, the stick clattering the supports. The dog growled and growled and yanked and yanked, obviously frustrated and unable to fathom why its prize wouldn't fit under the bench.

Way to go, superstar. I've never wanted to be a cat more in my life.

Rio and Ben ambled on. At the far left end of the area, Ben sat on an empty black bench and guided Rio around to sit on the ground at the end of the seat. Ben buried his face in a book while Rio drilled his gaze into dog after dog, looking for weaknesses.

A small black thing had pencil-thin legs — one bite and it would never run again. A white dog had a limp — attack that to put the beast out of action. A brown thing had more rolls of fat than Rio could count — he'd bet that would poop itself if it caught him so much as looking at it.

Cute, infirm, obese... boy, did the organizers have a lot to learn about dogfighting.

A dog with short brown-and-white fur stopped six feet away and sniffed the ground.

Was this the first challenger? Rio's hackles rose. He snarled.

Ben patted him while gripping his leash tighter. "Easy, Rio. We're here to have fun, not to tear something to pieces."

Rio waited for Ben to remove the muzzle. But he didn't. Rio pawed it. How could he fight with this thing restricting his primary weapon?

However, instead of attacking, the dog before him squatted, pooped, then meandered away, wagging its tail. A chubby woman strolled over and collected the poop in a white bag.

Hey, Weirdo wasn't the only one. Maybe there was a club in the area. That would explain why Weirdo had collected every poop he'd ever done. He'd figured she simply couldn't resist collecting the stuff, no matter how many samples she already had, but she was probably swapping it with other members for poop she'd never come across. Smart.

But if Weirdo's friends were here, it probably wasn't a dogfighting place. So, what the devil was it? And if they weren't fighting, why was Ben so anxious?

Rio lay down, chin on his paws. Sniffing, watching, listening. He'd figure out what this place was, even if it took all day.

On the next bench, a gray-haired man laughed with a young brunette and a man with no hair. Two dogs chased around the bench, but without gnashing teeth — just yips of joy.

Farther away, a woman in red threw a yellow ball for a flappy-eared dog. It trundled away and returned, wagging its tail like crazy, as if it had achieved something remarkable.

Near a tree, two brown dogs tussled, no teeth or claws, just pushing and rolling. A black-and-white one joined them, and they fell into a heap.

Everyone seemed so unbelievably happy. How was that possible? So many people — all happy. So many dogs — all happy. Talk about unnatural.

A small black dog with stumpy legs wandered toward them. Tail wagging, it stared at Rio.

Without lifting his head, Rio growled. *Looking for a friend, pumpkin? Look again.*

The dog yelped and scooted away, its stubby legs a blur in its desperation to escape.

You got that right, pumpkin. This here's a fighting dog that could rip you to—

Rio yelped with surprise and jerked his head up as something prodded his butt.

Ben leaned around to look behind them at the same time Rio did. "What the...?" he said.

The brown Chihuahua with scratches across its snout popped its forepaws onto Rio's back and tried to mount him.

A young woman with bright purple hair dashed over. "Woofy, no!"

Rio scooted away, then whipped around and snarled. Mounted? By a freaking Chihuahua! And not just any Chihuahua, but the retarded one with the giant stick. Oh, the indignity!

Glowering, Rio snarled. When he'd finished with it, the thing would be nothing but a smear of blood on the ground. *Say goodbye, superstar.*

Rio lunged, but Ben grabbed his collar.

Ben stroked him. "Easy, Rio. Easy."

Purple Hair shoved a black cane with a silver handle in the shape of a leaping dog under her arm.

"I am *so* sorry." She scooped up the rapist and held the thing before her. "In his head, I'm sure he thinks he's a Rotty or a Great Dane. He'd have a coronary if he looked in a mirror and recognized himself." She stared the dog in the face. "Lord Wooffles Mountbatten III, that was so naughty! What have we said about not humping things?"

"Lord Wooffles Mountbatten?"

She shrugged. "Blame my grandma. The problem is that once he gets overexcited, if you don't use his full name, he won't listen."

The thing whimpered, its huge bulging brown eyes seeming to bulge even more.

"Awww, how can I stay mad at you?" She kissed him on the head, then looked at Ben. "Again, I am *so* sorry."

"Don't worry, no harm done. Though, Rio will be upset he can't wear white to his wedding now."

"I wish I could say it's the first time something like this has happened, but I'm afraid Woofy is very 'affectionate,' not to mention very gender-inclusive. Even species-inclusive. We visited my grandma yesterday, and he tried to mount the cat — hence the scratches on his nose."

"I'll have to remember not to bend over to tie my shoelaces when he's around."

Purple Hair laughed. "Thank you for being so understanding." She looked into Woofy's face again. "Are you going to behave if I put you down?"

The thing licked her. She laughed and released him.

Woofy looked at Rio.

Ben holding him at bay, and still muzzled, Rio glared.

Woofy barked the yappiest, most pathetic bark Rio had ever heard. Rio narrowed his gaze at it.

Instead of running, it doddered closer, sniffing at him.

"Awww, he wants to be friends." Purple Hair leaned down and stroked Woofy. Her floppy bangs parted to reveal a long scar across her forehead.

198

"I don't think we do friends," Ben said.

"'We'?"

"Rio, my dog." Ben patted him. "Sorry, I don't know why I said 'we.' I'm Ben, a man, not a dog, so of course, I do friends." He rubbed his mouth, his face reddening.

She grinned. "Well, thank you for the clarification, Ben, a man, not a dog."

Ben's face grew redder. "Yeah, I, uh... sorry, I can usually, uh, talk and, uh, use words. And sentences. Good ones. Big ones. Not like these. You heard I could before, today."

And even redder.

"That is, you heard it previously. I don't mean 'before today' in a historical sense — I put a comma between 'before' and 'today,' which obviously I didn't mention because I was speaking. Unless you think I should mention it, which would make speaking quite a lot harder. Period. That was punctuation, not another reference to a span of time. I don't think I'll include punctuation."

Sweat beaded on his brow. He wiped it on the back of his forearm.

"But you heard me talk properly earlier — that's the word I wanted, 'earlier', forget that comma thing — so, you heard me talk earlier when I was..." He gulped. "Talking..."

Purple Hair said, "And do you want to stop talking now?"

"Yes, please."

"Okay, you can stop."

"Oh, thank God." Ben slumped, gasping as if he'd been running.

Rio stared at Ben. What was the man doing? He'd never made so much noise. And why was he stinking of dread and dripping with sweat?

Purple Hair said, "So, as you're such a linguist, let me pose a question."

"Do you have to?"

She sat on the bench, a quizzical look knitting her brow.

"Obviously you do. Okay." Ben squirmed, gazing at the exit.

Rio glared. What was this woman playing at? If she didn't leave, this tiny monster wouldn't either.

She said, "Do you ever wonder what the word 'dog' is in dog?"

"Excuse me?"

"The dog word for dog."

Ben squinted. "The dog word for dog? You've lost me."

"Dog language."

Ben arched his eyebrows. "Sorry, my high school didn't offer that class."

She snickered. "But don't you ever wonder?"

"Not really. Rio doesn't say much."

"No, I mean in their heads. Every dog recognizes another dog, so when"— she pointed at a random dog —"that guy walks down the street and sees another dog, in his mind he must think, 'Hey, there's a dog.' Except, obviously, he'll use his own word for *dog*."

"Obviously." Ben gazed around, as if hoping a tree might fall on him.

"Hey, I'm serious."

Ben scratched his head. "I, uh, I hadn't thought about it, but yeah, I suppose when one dog sees another dog, then in dog language, it must think the word *dog*."

"It's a game changer, ain't it?"

"Is it?"

"Don't you see what it means?"

He shook his head.

She said, "If you extrapolate that basic idea, what you get is staggering."

"Uh-huh?"

She smirked. "You're yanking my chain, aren't you?"

Ben twitched a smile but then shook his head. "If only I was."

"Well, if they have a word for dog, then they must have a word for other things too — food, water, walk, leash, toy... before you know it, the only conclusion is that they have an entire language. We're just too dumb to speak it."

"Hmmm..." Ben's expression brightened. "I'd never thought about it, but yeah, I suppose they must have a language. How else could they think?"

"I sometimes wonder what Woofy calls me."

"I know what Rio calls me — the-guy-who-screams-'don't-pee-there'."

Purple Hair laughed. "He's not housebroken?"

"He is, but he's smart and likes to see how far he can push me."

"Ah. Two alphas battling it out for superiority."

"Maybe. But I can't blame him. He's a rescue, so he hasn't had the best of lives."

"So far."

"Excuse me?"

"The best of lives *so far*. I get the idea that things have turned around for him recently." She smiled.

"I hope so."

"Anyway, we'll leave you two boys — sorry — dog and man-not-a-dog to get back to your fun." She stood. "Woofy, come."

She waved at Ben, then wandered away, resting on her cane. Woofy scurried at her heels.

Still red-faced, Ben leaned down and petted Rio. Under his breath, he said, "Touch and go for a moment there, Rio. But luckily, she's a bit of a kook, so I think we got away with it."

From twenty feet away, Purple Hair called out, "By the way, I'm Izzy, a woman, not a dog. And I do friends, too." She laughed. "Scratch that — I *make* friends, not *do* friends. That makes me sound as bad as Woofy!"

"So, it's safe to bend over in front of you."

She sucked through her teeth. "Ohhh, I don't know. A butt like that, I can't promise I won't spank it."

Ben's face glowed again, and he glanced about anxiously. People on a nearby bench stared, smirking.

He gulped. "You haven't seen my"— he lowered his voice —"butt."

Izzy laughed. "Sorry, I couldn't resist seeing how red a person's face could get." She winked and sauntered away.

Rio lay down, watching Izzy and Woofy leave. What a pair! Thank heaven it was the last he'd ever see of them.

Chapter 36

Face still red, Ben ruffled Rio's fur. "Shall we beat it before someone else collars us?" He sighed. "Though mixing with people was the whole point of coming. For both of us." He picked up his cane. "Who'd have thought it could be such a train wreck?"

Rio leaped up. They were leaving? Thank heaven!

But Ben leaned back on the bench again. "She was kind of fun, though, don't you think? The type who makes life interesting."

Rio whimpered. Were they going or not?

Ben toyed with the gold band on the third finger of his right hand. "But what's so special about fun and interesting? Now, snuggling up on a sofa, just the two of us, that's special." He stood. "Home?"

Rio yipped. Were they going this time?

Ben led them back to the car. Once underway and scents they'd passed earlier suggesting they were heading home, Razor melted on the rear seat, the stress of the trip draining from him. Thank heaven he'd never have to suffer that ordeal again.

Apart from a "To me" game, the evening was wonderfully silent. They snuggled on the sofa together, everything finally just as it should be.

But the next day, Ben led him to the car again. He wasn't wearing his matching jacket and trousers, so they weren't going to the gray room.

Rio cringed. Surely they weren't going to that awful place with those awful characters.

As the car entered the parking lot, Rio whined. It was *that* place.

Ben stroked his head. "Relax, Rio. It'll be better today. I mean, it couldn't be any worse, could it — you sexually assaulted and me socially embarrassed? So, yeah, today will be fun, you'll see."

This time, Ben chose a bench at the opposite end of the enclosed area. Rio constantly checked behind him, while Ben buried his face in a book again. Dogs played, people chatted, members of Weirdo's fraternity collected poop...

Rio let his chin sink to his paws. He still sniffed and rotated his ears for signs of trouble, but it was strangely soothing being around his own kind, especially when they were having fun instead of tearing each other to pieces. Even the muzzle didn't bother him. There was something to be said for a boring life.

A high-pitched *yap-yap-yap* disrupted the solitude, and a small brown shape on spindly legs tore toward him.

Rio cringed. Oh, please, no!

Woofy skidded to stop before he slammed into Rio but tripped in the wood chips and tumbled over and over. He leaped up and ran in a circle, yapping and yapping.

Izzy ambled over, leaning on her cane.

Ben said, "Hello, again."

She smiled. "It looks like your dog's got a new friend."

"I'm not sure Woofy has. Sorry."

She stroked Woofy. "He's like a bad haircut — accept him for what he is, and before you know it, he's grown on you so much that you can't help but love him."

"A sound philosophy in general."

She nodded. And sat on their bench.

Rio glared at her. *So we're doing that now, are we, duchess? Just thank your stars I'm muzzled.*

He growled. He couldn't bite her, but he could sure put the fear of—

She tickled him under the chin. "A rescue, you say?"

Oh, yeah. Right there. That's it.

Ben said, "Some monster had used him as a fighting dog."

Her jaw dropped. She reached down and tickled with both hands. "Oh, you poor angel. Thank heaven you've found a nice man like Ben."

Double the tickling? Okay, so maybe the day wouldn't be a total bust if she stuck around.

She lifted her cane. "I see you're a fellow enthusiast."

Ben rolled his eyes. "Fortunately, it's only temporary."

"I guessed from the standard hospital issue. Did you have an accident?"

Ben drew a slow breath. "My dog shot me. You?"

"Zombie apocalypse. I was bitten and they had to amputate."

"No, seriously?"

Izzy frowned. "What? I thought we were making stuff up."

"No, straight up — Rio shot me. I put my gun on the table to clean, but Rio snatched it, and it went off."

"You're sure it was an accident? Maybe you're buying the wrong kibble."

Ben laughed. "Maybe." But his joy faded, consumed by an inner darkness. He sat twisting his wedding band around and around.

Rio nuzzled him.

"Hey, boy." Ben stroked him.

Izzy said, "Has it been long?"

"Hmmm?"

"Your ring. It's on your right hand, not your left."

Ben shifted on the bench and gulped. "I... uh..."

His fingers dug into Rio's fur as if he were in pain, yet nothing had happened. Rio glanced around for anything he should bite. There was nothing. So what was wrong?

Izzy said, "Sorry, I didn't mean to pry. So, how about you don't ask about these"— she lifted her cane with one hand and her bangs with the other to reveal her scar —"and I won't ask about that." She nodded to the ring. "Deal?"

Ben almost smiled. "Deal."

"So how long have you had Rio?"

"Just a couple of weeks. You and Woofy?"

"My grandma moved into a retirement home six months ago and was horrified at what would become of him, so I took him. We visit once a week." She beamed. "I tell you, the look on her face when Woofy trots in. She's like a kid at Christmas."

"And she's the one who named him?"

Izzy nodded, then rolled her eyes. "Lord Wooffles Mountbatten III."

"Wait. The third? There have been three dogs all called Lord Wooffles Mountbatten? Isn't that animal abuse?"

Izzy giggled. "Okay, you've uncovered my family's deep dark secret — my meemaw is in the state pen on three counts of inhumanely naming a dog."

As Ben and Izzy continued chatting, Ben managing not to turn bright red today, Woofy stared at Rio from a couple of feet away.

Appearing to feel braver, Woofy trotted closer.

Rio cringed. He didn't want to have to kill this thing, but he was in no mood to be friends with his attacker.

Woofy came to within a few inches and yapped. Rio glowered, willing him to leave.

But Woofy play bowed, sticking his forelegs out in front of him and butt up in the air.

Rio prodded him with his snout, and Woofy fell over. He leaped up and yapped as if it were play.

Was this the stupidest dog ever?

Rio growled.

Ben shook the leash. "Rio, play nice."

After glaring at the interloper, Rio rolled onto his side so he didn't have to look at the thing.

Instead of getting the message, Woofy jumped onto Rio and stood over him, yapping.

Rio twisted, throwing Woofy off balance. The little dog tumbled into the muck but again bounced back up and yapped for more. He sprang back onto Rio, as if they'd invented a fun game.

Writhing, Rio sent Woofy cartwheeling into the dirt again. And up the little thing jumped. Yapping and yapping with glee. He ran and launched himself onto Rio's side, where he triumphantly yapped louder, as if he'd conquered a mountain.

Instead of frustration and anger, a warmth welled up in Rio as glowing pictures formed of Rat and their over-the-mountain game.

This time, Rio didn't jerk violently but wriggled just enough for Woofy to lose his footing and slide to the ground.

Woofy immediately clambered onto Rio again, and the over-the-mountain game continued.

Izzy said, "It looks like Woofy does have a new friend after all."

"I think so." Ben sniggered, then scanned the perimeter. "I wish I could let Rio off leash to play properly, but he could easily jump that fence."

"Do you think he would when he's got it so good with you compared to the life he had before?"

Ben rubbed his chin. He looked at Rio, then around the enclosure. "You know what, I'm going to risk it."

He leaned down and cupped Rio's head. "Don't make a fool of me, please, Rio. I can't chase you after *someone* shot me."

He unclipped the leash.

Rio stood. Woofy play bowed again, then ran under Rio's stomach, out the other side, and away. Rio tore after him.

When he caught him, Rio slowed to give the tiny dog a chance to keep up. Again, Woofy shot under Rio, then he circled in front of him. They raced around the enclosure, Woofy yapping.

As they rounded a bench, Woofy lost his footing and tumbled across the ground, wood chips flying everywhere. The moment he was steady, up he leaped and away they shot again.

Rio had to hand it to Woofy, he sure had heart. Nothing fazed the little fella — no obstacle or accident, of which there were many. They played until Woofy stopped dead and pricked his ears.

"Woofy, come!" shouted Izzy.

Woofy bolted toward the bench. Rio followed.

"To me, Rio. To me."

Rio ran over to Ben, who stroked and stroked him. "Good boy for coming back, Rio. Excellent job."

Wait... didn't I used to get a square for this, too? What's your game, zippy?

What was happening to all the squares he was earning? He hoped Ben was putting them aside for a pocket-meat blowout later.

Ben attached his leash, and Izzy did likewise to Woofy. Together, they ambled through the gate, chatting.

"I'm this way." Izzy pointed left.

Ben gestured right. "You'll get me that number?"

She waggled her phone. "I've set myself a reminder. See you, Ben. Bye, Rio."

"So long, Izzy."

They separated. Ben marched along the path, his stride long and steps solid, not short and shuffled like when they'd arrived.

"Looks like you have a new friend, Rio." He pursed his lips and rubbed his face. "And it looks like I have, too." He sighed. "If only I was sure I really wanted one."

Chapter 37

At home, Ben paced from the sofa to the kitchen and back. He shook his head. "I can't do this. I know you told me I had to, but I can't. I just can't."

Back and forth, back and forth.

"And if that means breaking my promise, then..." He covered his face with his hands and snorted a deep breath. "But I didn't promise only you, Eve, did I? I promised both of you." He dragged his hands down his face. "Oh, God, what am I supposed to do?"

Lying on the green rug, Rio watched. Why was Ben walking and walking? And why was he talking to himself? He'd seemed to have recovered much of his mental capacity, but perhaps the trauma went too deep.

"Get a grip. She's just a friend. A *friend.* It's not like we're dating. Jeez, we've only met twice." Ben clasped either side of his head. He grimaced and clawed his fingers into his hair. "Dating? Oh, freaking..." He exhaled loudly. "What if she already thinks this is a *thing?*"

He marched across the floor again.

"I have to say something. I can't do this, so I have to say something."

Collapsing over the dining table, he slumped onto his elbows.

"Look what you've done, Eve. I know that promise was only because you wanted the best for me, but look at the mess it's made."

Rio wanted to help, but what could he do? He scampered to the knotted rope. The "Drop it" game usually cheered up Ben, so he nudged Ben's leg.

No response.

Rio yipped.

"I can't win. I just can't win. I don't want to meet someone else. But do I want to be alone forever?" He cupped his hands in front of his face.

Rio yipped again.

"Any ideas, Rio? Because I'm all out." He gripped the rope and Rio yanked.

They played for some time, but then Ben's phone rang.

He tramped over to it on the sofa, but as he reached for it, he slapped his forehead.

"Oh, darn it, I forgot to call." He answered the phone. "Hi, Mom. Sorry, the day kind of got away from me."

"Thank goodness. I was getting worried."

"No, everything's cool, Mom. We were out a little longer than I figured we would be, is all."

"Anywhere fun?"

"Uh..." Ben covered his eyes. "Oh, boy." He bit his lip. "Mom, I want to tell you something, but I don't want you making more of it than there is. Can you do that for me, please?"

"Why? Is everything alright?"

"Fine, Mom. Everything's just fine."

"You're sure?" Her voice faltered. "Because it doesn't sound it, and I couldn't bear it if anything happened to you as well, Ben."

"Seriously, Mom, everything's good. I just need some advice, but it's a tricky subject, so I need you to be as impartial as possible. Okay?"

"I can try."

"Okay." Ben covered his mouth with his hand for a moment, as if he didn't want to say more. He heaved a breath. "I've made a new friend."

"We're not talking about the dog again, are we?"

He rolled his eyes. "No, Mom. We're talking about a person."

"But that's wonderful. Why is it a problem?"

"Because"— he flopped onto the sofa —"it's a woman."

Mom gasped. She whispered as if talking to someone else. "Ben says he's met a woman."

Ben rubbed his brow. "I can hear you, Mom."

A gravelly man's voice in the background said, "Fantastic. How long has he been keeping that a secret?"

Ben said louder, "No secret, Dad. She's just a friend. *A friend*. I can't stress that enough." He grimaced. "See, this is exactly why I didn't want to say anything."

"I'm sorry, but it's just such good news," Mom said.

Ben heaved off the sofa and paced. "It's not news, Mom. That's why they don't have stories like this on the TV — breaking news: man meets woman for platonic relationship. It's the opposite of news."

"If it's so unimportant, why are you making such a big deal of it, sweetheart?"

"I..." Ben stopped and leaned his head against the wall. "That's the problem — I don't know."

"Could it be you like her and want it to be news?"

"Mom, whether I like her or not isn't the point."

"So what is?"

"I..." Ben shook his head. "It's..." He groaned. "That's the problem — what *is* the point?"

"Evie wanted you to be happy."

"I know."

"She'd be upset you haven't moved on."

Ben pushed off the wall and wiped his eyes. "I know."

"So you know what you have to do."

"But how? Eve was..." His face twisted into unimaginable pain. "She was everything."

"It's been years, Ben, years. It's time. And I think you finally know it is, or we wouldn't be having this conversation. Don't you think?"

"No... maybe... I don't know." Ben slumped onto the sofa.

"Why don't you talk to Evie about it? Getting it all out might help you see things more clearly."

"Maybe."

"Do you want me to fly down? I can be there tonight."

"No. Thanks, Mom. Bye."

"Call if you need anything, sweetheart. Anything. Take care."

He slung his phone aside and stared into space.

Rio whimpered. He'd known suffering, but he'd rarely known this kind — the kind that only hurt inside. What had happened in Ben's life that the wounds tormented him so? Had Ben lost someone in the way Rio had lost Rat?

Rio rested his chin on Ben's knee, his eyes filled with such concern. How could he help his friend? Rio could fight any dog any size and win, but he couldn't beat an opponent he couldn't see.

Ben wiped his eyes again, then his hand fell to Rio. "Hey, boy. I think it's time for another trip."

Chapter 38

Whining, Rio pawed at the inch-wide gap at the top of the car window. That scent. He knew that scent!

Ahead, a black metal fence in front of tall bushes came into view. Trees, hedges, dirt, birds, flowers, people, gravel, insects... all blended into a uniquely identifiable smell: the park filled with tiny walls. And that meant only one thing — Rat!

The car stopped. The moment Ben opened the door, Rio lunged to run to Rat.

Ben hauled him back. "Rio, please. Not now."

Gripping the leash tight in one hand, Ben opened the trunk with the other and removed the single red rose and bouquet of pink flowers he'd bought en route. He turned for a gated entrance.

Rio drove forward, pulling on the leash so much he choked.

"Rio!" Ben heaved him back. "Behave or you'll wait in the car."

Okay, Ben wouldn't let him run. Rio had waited this long, so a few more minutes wouldn't hurt. He slowed to Ben's pace, glowing pictures forming in his mind: Rat playing hide-and-squeak, Rat chomping kibble, Rat snuggling into Rio's fur...

Rio sped up. When Ben matched him, Rio quickened his pace again, his collar digging into his throat.

"Rio." Ben stopped dead, leash taut. "Last chance."

Again, Rio calmed. It was only weeks since he'd seen Rat, but it felt like a lifetime. Oh, Rat was going to love living at Ben's. He'd love Ben's games, too. This was wonderful. Wonderful!

They walked along a tree-lined avenue, row after row of tiny walls covered in squiggles stretching away on either side. Approaching a big tree, Rio cringed and sniffed, remembering his last encounter here. With no sign of the Gray Man, he relaxed.

The tiny building with the hedge around it was away to the right, but Ben turned onto the small gravel path on the left.

Rio pulled to go right, but Ben pulled harder.

This made no sense. Why bring him to Rat but not let him go to him?

Ben trudged to two small black walls, each containing squiggles in gold. He placed the pink flowers before the first one and picked a couple of dead leaves off the ground. "Hey, sweetheart."

Rio stopped pulling. Ben's scent and the way he dragged himself about suggested that he was hurting inside again. Allowing Ben a moment to compose himself was the least Rio could do after the man had brought him here for Rat.

"I miss you so much." Ben wiped his eyes, then patted Rio. "This is Rio. Talk about a handful. He's a very different character from you-know-who, but no less special. You'd absolutely adore him. I do already."

Ben kissed his fingertips, touched the wall, then turned to the neighboring tiny wall and laid the single red rose on it. Bowing his head, he clasped his hands in front of him and stood silently.

Finally, he said, "Eve, I've tried to do what you asked but"— he gazed into the distance, then returned to the wall —"it just feels so wrong. And I-I don't know how it can ever be any different."

He wiped his eyes.

"I know I promised you"— he glanced at the other tiny wall —"promised both of you, but I never dreamed it would be so difficult. It feels like..." He gazed into the sky, tears rolling down his cheeks. "It feels like cheating."

Ben hung his head and swallowed. "I've met a woman. She's only a casual acquaintance, but the thought she could become anything more horrifies me. Mom thinks it's time, Dad, too. And on some level, I suppose I do. But I just can't." He shook his head. "I can't. I'm sorry."

He walked away. Rio scurried alongside. The man seemed utterly broken. Why had he come here if it hurt so much? People-stuff — there was no understanding it.

On the main avenue, Ben turned toward the car, but Rio lunged for the next big right-hand path.

His voice wearier than Rio could recall hearing before, Ben said, "Okay, you've been good, so we can walk a while."

Rio struggled, gasping with the effort of hauling Ben along. The excitement of his and Rat's reunion boosting his energy, he heaved Ben closer and closer, down one path, cutting to another, making turns...

"You're not just walking, are you? You're going somewhere specific." Ben quickened his pace, so Rio drove on harder.

Finally, a tiny building surrounded by a hedge appeared. They were there. Rio yipped.

Ben frowned. "Do you know someone buried here? Has someone brought you here before?"

Rio pulled toward the building, the chipped blue paint of its door bright in the sunlight. He nuzzled between the right-hand wall and hedge.

"Here? What is this place to you, Rio?" Ben squeezed in, twigs jabbing into him.

Pulling around to the rear, Rio sniffed. Rat was still there!

He frowned, but something was very wrong. He lunged, pulling Ben.

"Easy, boy. I'm bigger than you, so it's not that easy to squeeze through."

Rio rounded the rear corner and froze.

Rat lay on the ground. Or part of Rat. Holes dotted his body, the flesh sunken and taut, while his scent was tainted like meat left in the sun. The sight made Rio's heart feel like someone was standing on his chest and stamping, stamping, stamping. The pain crushed everything he knew, everything he loved.

Rio whimpered. He nudged Rat with his nose, but Rat didn't move.

He yipped. The same yip that had always brought Rat scuttling through the rusty pile to him. But still Rat didn't move.

Ben peered over. "A rat? This is what you've come to see?"

214

Rio stared down. It was Rat, but it also wasn't. As if the best part of him — the part that made him Rat, the part that differentiated him from Ben, or a tree, or pocket-meat — had disappeared.

How? How could Rat be both there and not there? And if he wasn't there, where was he?

Rio whined. He'd imagined Rat creating a cozy secret lair and cramming it with food. Rio whined again. This was his fault. If he hadn't let the Gray Man take him, he'd have been here for Rat.

Ben scraped against the wall as he crouched and hugged him. "It's okay, Rio. It's okay. I don't know what this is, but I'm here. And I promise, all that foolishness from before is done — I'm not going anywhere."

Ben took a Swiss Army knife from his pocket and dug a small hole. Gently, he laid Rat in it, then covered him and patted the dirt flat.

Rio didn't know why, but the process made him feel a little better. As if Rat had disappeared into one of his shadowy holes to sleep for the day and would return once darkness fell.

Ben hugged Rio again. "Come on, boy, let's go home."

Rio trudged around the tiny building. He'd never again play hide-and-squeak, never curl around someone to sleep, never yip and have someone run to him full of love. Oh, for just one more day...

Chapter 39

On the sofa, Ben shook the pocket-meat bag again. "To me. ... To me. ... Rio, to me."

Rio lay under the table, gaze welded to one of the table legs. It wasn't as good to lose himself in as his white brick wall because, it being so slim, too many distractions surrounded it, but it was better than nothing.

He'd known bad things happened when he was out in the world, which was why, after Ben's accident, he'd determined never to leave this place. But then he'd changed his mind and left. And what had happened? He'd lost Rat forever.

Bad things happened when he went out. Bad, bad things.

However, if he stayed here and never left, bad things could never happen. It was the only way. Strategy: it was a harsh mistress, but its logic was undeniable.

He huddled in his sanctuary. Huddled as small as he could make himself. He was never going out again. Never.

Ben limped over. Resting a hand on the table, he peered under. "Come on out, Rio. Please. This isn't healthy — and I should know."

Rio stared at the table leg.

Wincing, Ben lowered to the floor and scratched Rio under the chin.

Rio hardly felt it, as if someone had removed the part of him that felt nice things. Feeling nice things was too risky. They could tempt him to do things he shouldn't, and he couldn't allow that.

Ben offered a square. Normally, Rio would be drooling with the pocket-meat so close, yet he ignored it, the smell barely registering.

Ben stroked him and talked soothingly. For hours. Rio dozed on and off, and every time he woke, there was Ben, stroking.

The house in darkness, Ben said, "I'm sorry, Rio, but I'm going to have to lie down." He caressed his injured leg. "This leg is seizing up with sitting on the floor for so long."

Ben groaned as he stood. "Dear Lord, I feel like an eighty-year-old."

He staggered upstairs.

The next morning, Ben again tried to coax Rio out with pocket-meat and then for a pee. Rio wasn't hungry, and because he hadn't eaten or drunk anything, he didn't need to relieve himself.

Later, Ben peered under the table dressed in his jacket and trousers — gray room time.

"Rio, I have to go into the office, but I don't want to drag you out by your collar and upset you even more, so I'm leaving you here." He ruffled Rio's neck fur. "But I'll pop back at lunchtime to check on you, okay?"

Ben left.

Hours later, he came back. He stroked Rio, offered food, spoke gently... all the usual stuff.

Rio didn't budge.

He didn't later either when Ben came home in the evening.

The next day was the same. Except at one point, Ben tried to force water into Rio's mouth. Rio clamped his mouth shut and turned away.

"You've got to drink, Rio. You're going to make yourself ill." Ben blew out his cheeks. "Oh boy, look who's talking."

Rio stared at the table leg. Suffering was his life. Always had been; always would be. How stupid he'd been to imagine it could be any different. Why wouldn't Ben leave him alone to it? Didn't the man realize Rio was doing this to keep everyone safe, not just himself?

His hands on his hips, Ben stared down at Rio and shook his head. Finally, he said, "Just remember, you made me do this. If it all goes sideway, it's your fault."

He took his phone from the table and tapped the screen. A woman answered.

"Hi, Izzy, it's Ben."

"Oh, hi, Ben. This is a nice surprise."

"Sorry to call so early, but I have a problem with Rio. Are you going to the dog run today?"

"No, I'm working, then I've got plans. Why? What's happened?"

Ben rubbed his brow. "It's kind of weird, but we went to the cemetery to leave flowers, then after, he took me off to a tool shed at the far side as if he knew the place, and behind it, we found a dead rat."

"Sorry, did you say a dead rat?"

Ben paced to the sofa. "Yeah, and his reaction... well, it was like he'd lost his best friend. And now, he won't come out from under the dining table. This is the third day."

"Didn't you say he'd been a fighting dog?"

"Yeah. He lived on the street for a while, too."

"Could he have lived in the cemetery? Behind that shed?"

"I guess so. But how does that explain the rat?"

"Animals make friends, just like we do."

Ben frowned. "But a dog and a rat?"

"Google, I don't know, 'Owen and Mzee.'"

"Owen and what?"

"Mzee – M-Z-E-E. It's an amazing story about hippo and a tortoise who became best friends. Or there's a goat called Jack who helped Charlie, a blind horse, get around. Or Kamunyak, a lion who adopted antelopes. The point is, they're all incredible stories about animal friendships, so maybe Rio *has* lost his best friend and is grieving just like we would."

Ben plonked down on the sofa. He gazed at Rio. "So what do I do?"

"What are your plans for tonight?"

"Sofa, TV, bed. It's a packed schedule in our house."

"It is now — dog hiking with my group. I'll text you the details."

"But he won't budge from under the table."

"Just get him there. Carry him to the car, if you have to. Once he starts interacting with other people and dogs, there's a good chance he'll start feeling better, just like you or I would."

"Thanks, Izzy."

"Hey, what are friends for?"

Ben ended the call, limped over to Rio, and held a stool to lower himself. He stroked Rio. "I have to go, Rio, but I'll be back in a few hours, and later, we're going to see Izzy and Woofy. I don't know what happened, Rio, but we'll make it better, again. Promise."

He left.

***

That evening, Ben crouched to Rio under the table. "Believe me, this is going to hurt me a darn sight more than it's going to hurt you."

He grabbed Rio's collar and hauled him forward.

Rio thrust his claws against the floor, but on the polished wood, there was little traction, so he slid farther and farther out.

He twisted to break away, but Ben had him tight.

Rio writhed and bucked. He couldn't bite Ben, but he had to get away. The man had no idea what he was doing — the bad things he'd unleash if Rio was back out in the world.

Ben's face twisted in pain. He groaned and cursed, but he dragged Rio out and scooped him up in his arms. Sweat beading on his face, Ben carried Rio outside, dumped him on the car's back seat, and fastened him into his harness.

They drove farther into the countryside, where trees crawled over hillsides and the sky grew bigger and bigger until it caressed distant mountains.

Rio whimpered. Bad things would happen. Bad, bad things.

At a trailhead, Ben eased to a stop. A number of cars were already parked there, people and dogs milling about. Ben got out.

Izzy scooted over, Woofy yapping and yapping alongside. "How is he?"

Ben shook his head.

She peered in through the window. "Awww, the poor thing. Is he secure?"

"Yes."

She opened the door and stroked his shoulders. "I'm sorry you're suffering, Rio, but bad things can happen to those we love — real bad sometimes. But we're here for you."

Rio didn't move. He ached to run back to his table and be left alone.

She held his harness and looked at Ben. "May I?"

He nodded. "Please, anything you think will help."

She unclipped his harness. "Come on, baby, let's get you out."

Holding his leash, she pulled on his butt, dragging him toward the open door.

He didn't struggle because there was no point — Ben would just manhandle him.

Dropping out, Rio sat on the asphalt, head down.

Woofy yapped and play bowed. Then yapped again, as if believing Rio couldn't have heard him. When Rio didn't react, Woofy sat and tilted his head at him, as if wondering what was going on. It was the quietest he'd ever seen Woofy.

A chubby man with a graying beard wandered over and held out his right hand. Ben shook it.

"Tom Jenkins, hike leader." The man gestured to a black-and-white mutt at his side. "Bully, second-in-command."

"Ben. This is Rio."

"If he's nervous around other dogs, maybe hold back and bring up the rear, so he doesn't feel so overwhelmed. Does he need a muzzle? I've got a spare."

Ben patted his pocket. "I've got one, thanks. But it's not nerves that's the problem. We think he's depressed because he lost a friend. Sounds silly, but..." Ben shrugged.

"Nothing silly about animal emotions, Ben. They feel them just like we do." He glanced at his watch. "Look, time's getting on, so if you want to give him a few minutes to get a feel for the place, then catch us up, that's fine, but we have to set off to make the circuit before nightfall. That work for you?"

"Fine, thanks, Tom."

"You're welcome. Good to have you both with us." He strode away, pointing to the path. "Okay, guys."

The group of dog hikers moved out.

"You get off with them, Izzy. I don't want to spoil your night."

"Yeah, right. Like I'm going to abandon an animal in distress." She sat cross-legged on the ground, caressing Rio. "I know you're hurting, Rio, and I know you understand squat of what I'm saying, but trust your instincts. Feel how much we want to help you."

Rio needed to leave. He couldn't guarantee anyone's safety unless he was under his table. He whimpered.

Ben said, "I don't think he's going anywhere anytime soon."

Nodding, Izzy winced. "It would be cruel to literally drag him through the countryside."

Ben pointed down the road. "My place is only a few miles away. You're welcome to a coffee. Or a beer. Especially since I've ruined your plans."

She leaned down to whisper into Rio's ear. "Has he trained you to do this, Rio? Is this how he lures vulnerable young women back to his lair?"

Ben held up his hands. "I'm sorry, I didn't mean to be forward. It's just, Rio enjoyed playing with Woofy the other day, so I hoped getting them together might spark something."

She laughed. "Any wine?"

Chapter 40

Under his table, Rio peered at Ben, Izzy, and Woofy, all sitting on the floor, staring at him. Why couldn't they leave him alone? Couldn't they see he didn't deserve friends because he only hurt them? He'd hurt Rat, hurt Ben — who would be next?

"Let me try." Izzy plucked a square from Ben's hand. "Bacon, Rio. Lovely bacon." She sniffed it. "Mmmm... meaty, smoky..." She offered it.

Rio didn't budge.

She said, "Maybe if he sees us enjoying ourselves, he'll come out to join in."

"Okay."

Izzy stood, but when Ben tried, he grimaced and clutched his leg. Izzy grabbed his arm to support him.

"Thanks." He straightened, then limped to the kitchen.

"So, this is the scene of the crime, huh?" Izzy smirked. "The dog in the kitchen with the revolver." She laughed. "Makes a change from Miss Scarlet in the library with the candlestick. Maybe you should pitch Hasbro an update."

Ben arched an eyebrow. "You realize I could've died. And not only would Rio have shot me, but he'd have then had to eat me to survive."

"Ah, the perfect crime — eating the evidence."

He laughed, holding up two bottles. "Red or white?"

"Red?"

Ben opened the red, then took two glasses from a cupboard and gestured to the sofa. They moseyed over.

"How are you liking the dog run?" Izzy kicked off her shoes to sit cross-legged and turned toward Ben.

He shrugged. "It has dogs. And they run."

"What were you expecting?"

"To be honest, I figured it might be a decent place to meet new people without any pressure, you know? Not like at a bar or something."

"Yeah, I figured that from how you always choose an out-of-the-way bench and stick your head in a book. It just screams warm and approachable."

He nodded. "Chapter three of *How to Win Friends and Influence People*."

She smiled, sipping her wine.

He cleared his throat. "But seriously, it's tough meeting new people."

"You're telling me."

"You? It must be a breeze for you."

She frowned. "Why?"

"You're so happy and outgoing."

"You forgot charming and beautiful."

"Sorry. You're so happy and outgoing, not to mention charming and beautiful."

She playfully slapped his arm. "Stop, you'll make me blush." She squinted at him. "But I notice you didn't say 'smart.' Are you trying to tell me something?"

"Actually"— Ben exhaled loudly —"there is something I need to tell you, yes."

"This sounds serious."

He grimaced. "It kind of is."

"Just a second." She shook herself to loosen up. "Okay, this amount of serious?" She sat upright with a neutral expression. "Or this amount?" She folded her arms, knitting her brow.

Ben rolled his eyes. "You're not making this easy."

"Am I supposed to?" She smirked.

"Look, all I want is to be up-front from the get-go." Ben rubbed his brow. "I'm not looking for a romantic relationship, so if that means we can't hang out..."

"Why? Because a man and a woman can't be friends? I bet you know every single line from *When Harry Met Sally*, don't you?"

"What? No, I..." Ben frowned. "What?"

"Look, I didn't want to say this but"— she drew a breath, then gestured to Rio and Woofy —"I'm only here for the sake of the kids. Once they go away to college, I'm out of here."

"Do you ever take anything seriously?"

"Fenugreek."

"Fenugreek? The herb? You mean you're allergic?"

"No, I just think it's a stupid word."

"Stupid?"

"Can you think of a word that sounds more made up? Fen-u-greek. I mean, come on, put in a little effort for crying out loud." She counted on her fingers. "And don't even get me started on *piffle, bupkis, diphthong...* what were they thinking?"

Ben studied her, silent.

"So, every month, I choose a word and email a different member of Congress using details that make me look like a constituent. Although all my alternatives have been rejected, it's fun to waste their time, because they have to reply or risk losing my vote."

Smirking, Ben nodded. "I can believe you do that."

"You bet I do. Politicians?" She blew out her cheeks. "Scheming, self-serving, money-worshipping parasites."

Ben sniggered. "Don't hold back on my account. Feel free to say what you really think."

She wagged a finger. "Trust me, I could rail all night about the injustices that could be fixed like that"— she snapped her fingers —"if only those in power would get off their butts, so we better change the subject." She sipped her drink.

"Okay, what's your favorite color?"

Laughing, she spluttered wine.

Ben handed her a white tissue from his pocket.

Izzy wiped her chin. "Oh, I know, apart from the attempted murder in the kitchen, what's the craziest thing that's ever happened to you?"

Ben arched his eyebrows. "Wow, uh... I don't know. I mean, what could possibly come close to being shot by your own dog?"

She wrinkled her nose. "Mmm, I suppose so."

"How about you?"

She snorted into her glass, shooting him a sideways glance. "I was expecting you to come up with something that wouldn't make me look so awful."

"It's that bad?"

"If you look at it in a certain light."

Ben twisted toward her. "Oh, I'd never do that."

She exhaled sharply. "Okay, I French-kissed a pug."

Izzy stuck her face in her glass, peeking at him over the rim.

"French-kissed a pug? You know, I'm struggling to see what kind of light might make that look bad."

She snorted again. "It's really bad, isn't it?"

"Why on earth would you French-kiss a pug?"

"In my defense, I did save its life."

"And then molested it? I think they cancel each other out." Ben took a drink.

She held her arms wide. "It was an accident."

"Don't tell me, you tripped with a pug standing in front of you and stuck your tongue out to break your fall."

She giggled. "Something like that."

"Come on, spill."

"The dog fell in that pond in the park near the mall and drowned. I gave it the kiss of life."

"That's not exactly French-kissing. I want my money back."

"That's not the end of the story." She held her hand up and sipped her wine. "See, to give a dog mouth-to-mouth, you massage its chest, then hold its snout shut to breathe into its nose. Easy, right? Except a pug has a squashed-up face, making it fiddlier. Anyway, after I'd massaged its chest, I leaned down to blow into its nose and gulped a breath. But I'd forgotten I was chewing gum, and it dropped into the dog's mouth. Instinctively, I flicked my tongue out to catch it."

"Ewww." Ben's face twisted as if he'd tasted something horrible.

"Unfortunately, the owner figured I wasn't saving his beloved pooch but Frenching it, so he went ape. Luckily, the dog started breathing, so all was forgiven." She shrugged. "I should qualify this by saying I took

225

a class on advanced first aid for animals. I wasn't prowling the local waterways, waiting for a victim to fulfill some weird fetish."

"So, you can really give a dog mouth-to-mouth?"

"Oh, yeah. You can resuscitate most animals. But when they come around and find you fondling them, you have to remember no means no." She winked.

He laughed.

At the sounds of people enjoying themselves, Rio peered out from where he lay under the table. The world appeared so warm and inviting. Who'd ever have guessed at the turmoil lying just below the surface, waiting to suck the unwary into its tendrils?

It had been a close call tonight. He'd thought Ben was going to drag him away with those other people and dogs. Away into more chaos, more suffering. Thank heaven Ben had made the sane choice and brought him back to his sanctuary.

Woofy stared at Rio, head tilted to one side. He hadn't yapped once, hadn't tried to clamber onto Rio, hadn't tried to play. He'd just stared. Rio appreciated the little thing leaving him in peace. In different circumstances, maybe they could be friends.

But that wasn't what life was about. At least, not his life.

For Rio, life was suffering. It always had been, so he'd been stupid to fight it.

The world was what the world was. Simple.

Woofy tilted his head the other way, drawing Rio's attention. When their gazes met, Woofy wagged his tail.

Rio closed his eyes. He couldn't be a part of Woofy's world.

Quiet tapping on the wooden floor lured Rio into peeking. Everything seemed exactly the same — Ben and Izzy chatting on the sofa, Woofy sitting nearby with his head tilted. Rio snuggled down again but then frowned. He squinted at Woofy. Was Rio imagining it, or was Woofy closer?

Woofy didn't move, just stared with those big, bulging brown eyes.

Rio nestled behind his tail again.

Tap-tap-tap.

Seriously? Rio peered out again. His brow furrowed. Woofy was sitting with his head tilted, just as before, but something didn't feel right. Rio scanned the floorboards. Hadn't Woofy been sitting behind that joint a moment ago, not across it? Who cared? Maybe the dog had shifted to scratch an itch.

Rio settled back down, shutting his eyes.

Tap-tap—

Rio jerked his head above his tail, eyes popping open.

Woofy instantly dropped his butt to the floor so he was sitting. Sitting closer. His bulging eyes seemed even wider, as if he was fearful of being punished for being bad.

The little dog slowly lifted his right forepaw and crept it forward. He hovered it above the floor, studying Rio. When Rio did nothing, he lightly rested his paw on the floor and moved his left to join it. He froze for a moment, as if trying to judge whether he was getting away with his subterfuge, then shuffled forward and sat again.

Woofy waited.

Maybe Rio wasn't the only one to appreciate the brutality of the world and that hiding away was the only safeguard against the endless suffering. If Woofy was smart enough to figure that out, Rio could share his sanctuary.

Woofy slowly reached forward again, while watching for a reaction from Rio. When none came, he moved another step closer. Then another. And another.

There was room for two under the table, so Rio closed his eyes and snuggled down.

Tap-tap-tap.

Rio ignored it, but then something prodded his tail. He jerked up, eyes wide.

Woofy nuzzled under Rio's tail, wiggled between his legs, and nestled against his belly. His big bulging eyes stared, and when Rio did nothing, Woofy closed them.

Glowing pictures materialized in Rio's mind of his cozy nights with Rat. For the first time in days, the darkness that had consumed his thoughts lifted. Warmth flooded his body, joy caressed his thoughts, and togetherness cocooned his spirit.

Rio had believed he couldn't be a part of Woofy's world, but it appeared no one had informed Woofy. Thank heaven!

A new glowing picture formed for Rio to treasure. He'd lost Rat, and there was nothing he could do about it, but he was going to make darn sure he lost no one else. No matter what he had to do to protect them.

Izzy looked at the time on her phone. "We better be making tracks. Thanks for a nice evening."

"You're welcome."

She turned to the kitchen. "Woof—" She clutched her chest. "Awww, that's so beautiful."

Ben craned to look. "Oh, wow. That must be the happiest Rio's been for days. It's going to be awful having to disturb them."

"Maybe we don't have to."

"How do you mean?"

"Do you have a guest room?"

"Yes."

"Then Woofy can stay where he is, and if I'm not driving, I can have a refill." She handed Ben her empty glass.

Taking it, Ben stood. "It's getting a little chilly, so I'll turn up the heat, since you're staying."

"Don't waste the energy." She pulled the throw off the back of the sofa. "We can share, can't we?"

Chapter 41

As motes of dust danced in the sun shafting through the windows, Rio licked Woofy, who still lay curled up with him. He dragged his tongue over the tiny dog's torso the way he had with Rat. Awake, but with his eyes closed, Woofy basked in the attention.

Ben stirred on the sofa. His eyes flickered open, then popped wide as he saw he was nestled against Izzy's chest, both of them sharing the throw.

"Sorry." He jerked his head up.

"Shhh." She pointed at Rio and whispered, "Look."

Ben's jaw dropped and he froze, still leaning on her. Together, eyes filled with wonder, they stared as Rio washed Woofy.

Woofy rolled onto his back and stretched, so Rio dragged his tongue over the little dog's belly. Woofy moaned with delight.

Izzy grinned. "I think it's safe to say Rio does do friends."

"Yeah." Ben eased off her. "Sorry, about... you know."

"It's okay. I don't want to soil my angelic image, but it's not the first time a man has touched my boobs." Straightening her blouse, she did a double-take at a wet patch. "Though, it is the first time one's fallen asleep on them and drooled."

Ben winced. "Sorry."

She laughed. "No worries. What time is it?"

Ben checked his watch. "Nearly seven. I have to start moving if I'm going to make it into work on time."

"Your boss isn't a dog lover to understand the situation?"

"He is — it's me — but I've a meeting I can't postpone again."

Wagging his tail, Woofy wandered from under the table. *Yap, yap, yap.*

Izzy said, "Someone's up and ready for breakfast."

"If it will make things easier, you can shower and have breakfast here."

"And have to do the walk of shame without anything to be shameful about?"

Ben floundered. "I, uh..."

She winked. "Get the coffee on while I use the bathroom. Woofy will have whatever Rio's having." She stroked Woofy. "Have you made a new special friend, Woofy? Aren't you lucky?"

Ben ambled to the kitchen. "Cereal, muffins, eggs and bacon...?"

"Any pancakes?"

Ben opened a cupboard. "Pancakes it is."

Izzy sauntered upstairs while Ben busied himself. He gave Woofy a bowl of kibble and some water, and the dog gobbled away.

Ben crouched and stroked Rio under the table. "Your friend's eating. Any chance you'll join him?"

Rio looked at Ben, at the concern oozing from his eyes, then at Woofy as crunching noises came from the bowl. Maybe he was looking at this all wrong. The previous night, everyone had been happy and snuggling — like a proper pack should — and nothing bad had happened. Maybe the sanctuary wasn't the table but the whole house.

Rio eased up.

Ben beamed and patted his thigh. "That's it. Come on, Rio. Come on out."

Rio tottered forward, his legs stiff.

Ben sat on the floor and hugged Rio. "I was so worried about you, buddy. You gave me such a fright." He scratched Rio's head. "Now, do you need a pee first, or are you going to eat? Oh, I know." He held up a finger, pushed up, and opened the refrigerator. "A special occasion calls for a special meal." He showed Rio a pack of pinky-red meat. "Bacon."

Rio licked his lips. Woofy forsook his kibble and stood beside Rio, gazing up at the meat.

Ben laughed. "A table for two, is it?"

He cooked while Rio and Woofy sat side by side, glued to the proceedings. Rio drooled, the meaty smell intoxicating after not eating for days. Ben put the fried strips on a plate and left them while he set the table and prepared other food.

Izzy strolled down the stairs, smelling of coconut, her hair wet.

Ben pulled out a stool with a green cushion. "Please."

Izzy sat.

Ben pointed to different items on the table. "Bagels with cream cheese, blueberry muffins, and"— he set down another plate —"pancakes." He gestured to various containers. "Maple syrup, chocolate, peanut butter, caramel sauce, strawberry jam. Need anything else?"

"After all this, liposuction might be a good idea."

Ben smiled. "I can do coffee."

"White, two sugars, thanks."

Ben nodded and turned back to the kitchen.

Lifting pancakes onto her plate, Izzy nodded to the dogs sitting so patiently. "Is this *Invasion of the Body Snatchers* or something?"

"Huh?"

"What's happened to the real Rio and Woofy?"

He held up a plate. "Bacon."

As Ben swept the plate in various directions, Rio turned his head to track it, with Woofy mirroring his every move.

Izzy snickered, pointing her phone at them. "Cool trick."

"Yeah, we open in the Ambassador Lounge, Caesars Palace, on Thursday."

Ben touched one of the rashers. "It was too hot earlier but should be okay now." He cut the pieces up, divided them between two plates, and placed those on the floor.

Rio dove in, as did Woofy, and slobbering noises filled the air.

Izzy poured maple syrup on her pancakes. "It's great to see Rio lively again."

"In no small part thanks to you and Woofy." Ben placed two cups on the table, one for her, then helped himself to pancakes, smothering some in strawberry jam, others in chocolate. "Dig in."

They ate.

Cutting into a pancake, Izzy said, "If you don't mind me asking, why the dog run?"

"Because I've got a dog." Ben pointed at Rio. "You must have seen him — a big furry thing with a tail."

Izzy raised an eyebrow. "I mean, why the need to meet people? You're a nice guy, with a great house, so obviously, a good job. You must have friends. What went wrong?"

Ben sighed. "My wife and I had friends, yeah. And after I lost her, I kept in touch with many of them, but then..." He heaved a breath. "After everything that happened with my daughter, many folks didn't know what to say, and I didn't know what to say to them. It was just easier to shut myself away."

She clutched her mouth. "So, you didn't just lose your family, you lost everything."

"Some friends made an effort, for a while, but there are only so many times you can bear to see an eye roll because you're talking about some game or movie you streamed — again — because you can't bear to talk about their family vacation, or their family celebration, or their family's report card successes."

Ben looked away, biting his lip.

Tears in her eyes, Izzy touched Ben's arm.

He shrugged. "Life happens."

"So, you got Rio for companionship?"

"He needed someone as much as I did..."

"And you fixed each other. That's beautiful."

"Fixed?" Ben snickered. "As recent events have proven, I think we'll both be works in progress for some time yet."

"Any way I can help, just ask. Okay?"

He patted her hand on his arm. "Thanks, Izzy. That means a lot."

They resumed eating.

Rio lay on the floor, near his table but not under it, and Woofy nestled alongside him.

It was good they were all living here now — there was strength in numbers — but he knew Ben and Izzy would be wanting to go out to do people-stuff. That presented a problem because they were too innocent to understand what a truly brutal world it was. They'd be waltzing into the worst dangers imaginable, totally oblivious to them, so how could bad things not happen?

Strategy. They didn't have one because they didn't know they needed one. Luckily for them, strategy was his superpower.

His table was his sanctuary and the house appeared safe too, but he couldn't stay here. He couldn't be safe and warm, knowing that those he cared for were facing untold nightmares. His earlier strategy was wrong – he couldn't hide away from the world. On the contrary, he had to be out in it to fight for those he loved.

Everything he'd suffered, everything he'd discovered, everything he'd mastered had all been preparing him for this moment. He'd believed the world spun in perpetual chaos, but it didn't. He just hadn't understood his place in it. Now he did – he was to bring order to that chaos, using all the skills at his disposal. He was a hardened fighting dog, so bad things were *not* going to happen. Not on his watch.

After breakfast, Ben put on his jacket and trousers.

They were going to the gray room? Rio bolted to the front door. Woofy yapped and trotted over, too.

Izzy said, "Someone's definitely feeling better."

"Thank heaven for that."

Izzy crouched and petted Woofy. "Ben says thank you, heaven."

He smiled and petted the little dog, too. "Yes, I don't know what you did, Woofy, but thank you."

Yap-yap-yap. Woofy licked Ben's hand.

They left the house. Ben opened the car and Rio leaped in, but as Ben secured his harness, Izzy and Woofy didn't get in with him. Instead, they entered the two-door red car they'd arrived in.

Rio barked.

Ben patted him. "Easy, Rio. You'll see them again soon."

Rio lunged to jump out and stop Izzy and Woofy leaving alone, but his harness held him fast.

He barked again. They couldn't go alone. Who'd protect them?

Ben rolled his eyes at Izzy. "He doesn't want you to leave."

"Sorry, Rio." She blew him a kiss. "We'll see you soon." She strapped Woofy in and opened the driver's door. "Let me know how things go."

"Will do. So long, Izzy. Thanks for everything." Ben got into the car and fired up the engine.

Rio twisted around, barking, barking, barking. Izzy and Woofy — they were defenseless.

Izzy's red car pulled away.

Izzy...

Woofy...

He'd had one job to do — one — to protect the pack. And he'd already failed. Rio whined. Bad things were coming. Bad, bad things.

Chapter 42

As soon as they arrived at the gray room, Rio patrolled it, ignoring the usual treats strewn about in cups. He had a job to do, so he couldn't afford distractions.

Sniffing the sofa informed him that a number of people had been since his last visit — an elderly couple, a young woman with a boy who'd wiped chocolate on the arm, a man who smelled of fish... none of them appeared to be a threat.

Ben went into the kitchen. Rio followed and searched the area, then inspected the little bathroom. Satisfied the location was safe, he took up a guard position, lying at the side of the desk nearest the foyer. Anyone trying to reach Ben would have to get through him — as if that was ever going to happen.

Ben returned from the kitchen with a steaming mug of coffee. Hand on his hip, he stared at Rio glowering at the entrance. "Real welcoming, Rio. Are you trying to scare my clients away?"

Everything was fine, for a while — Ben enjoyed his usual games of shuffling papers, chatting on the phone, and playing on his computer. However, midmorning, Ben opened the door to the small rooms at the back.

"To me, Rio. To me."

Rio didn't take his gaze off the foyer door.

"Please, Rio. I have an appointment in a few minutes."

Rio remained on guard.

"God, give me strength..."

Ben traipsed back, grabbed Rio's collar, and hauled him toward the kitchen.

Rio pushed his forelegs out and dug his claws into the gray carpet. He had a job to do; he was going nowhere.

"Rio, if you're not going to behave, you can't come here." Ben heaved.

Rio's grip wavered and he jerked forward. He thrust his claws into the floor afresh, making Ben stumble.

"You're going in the kitchen, dog." Ben dragged Rio closer and closer.

Rio could have broken free by brute force, but he couldn't risk hurting Ben. Thankfully, his superpower was strategy.

Rio collapsed and lay on the floor, a floppy mass. He shot Ben a sideways look. *Let's see you move me now, ace.*

Ben glanced at his watch. "Rio, I don't have time for silly games." He slung his jacket on his chair and scooped Rio up. "You're going in there, whether you like it or not."

He dumped Rio in the kitchen.

Rio jumped up and fought to nuzzle out, but Ben held him at bay while blocking the doorway, then pulled the door shut, imprisoning Rio.

Rio yelped. He was Ben's only line of defense. Had the man had gone crazy?

He raked the door and barked. He had to get out. Had to.

But Ben didn't free him.

Rio glared. As if a closed door was going to stop him. He swatted the silver handle with his paw, but instead of it being a lever, it was a knob — the door didn't open.

What devilry was this?

He tried again, but his paw slid off without doing anything. He'd seen Ben open the door, but how, when the thing employed such trickery?

Rio clamped his jaws around it and rived, but his teeth couldn't grip the slippery metal either.

He howled. He hadn't been able to save Izzy and Woofy, and now, Ben had a death wish. Rio's pack was disintegrating, and he couldn't do a thing about it.

He howled and howled.

Ben muttered, stomping toward the door. He opened it a crack. Finally, sanity prevailed.

Rio stuck his nose into the gap and wiggled to get through.

Ben threw a handful of squares behind Rio. "For Pete's sake, Rio. Give me a break."

Squares? He was a hardened fighting dog, and his next fight could come at any second — he had no time for squares.

Grabbing Rio's snout, Ben shoved him back and closed the door.

What was Ben playing at? Did he want bad things to happen? Rio whined and clawed the door. There had to be a way out. Had to be.

The gray room foyer door clicked open and Ben spoke. A high-pitched voice Rio didn't know replied.

Rio's jaw dropped. It was too late — someone was here.

He howled. Ben had to run. Run for his life.

The voices neared, as if from the desk area. Rio sniffed. Female, not young, but not old either, recently eaten the kind of spicy food his man had enjoyed. He focused harder, dissecting the scent for those telltale elements that revealed more than any amount of people-noise ever could. She was healthy, menstruating, and a little anxious.

Anxious? That was better than angry, fearful, or frustrated, but not as good as sad, happy, or excited. Such an emotion suggested there was a fair chance she wasn't a threat, but Rio couldn't risk it. He howled again.

Ben opened the door a crack. "You're sure it's okay?"

"Of course. I have a rescue myself, so I know they can have issues."

Blocking the doorway, Ben squeezed in. He wagged his finger. "Continue acting up and you'll be spending the day at home, alone. Understand?"

Rio nuzzled him. Thank heaven the man had come to his senses. However, before Rio knew it, Ben slipped the muzzle on him. Rio twisted away, but it was too late.

He glowered at Ben. Come to his senses? Yeah, right. The guy had completely lost it.

"Be good and you can stay with us. Okay?" Taking Rio's collar, Ben led him into the room.

A blonde woman smiled, sitting in front of the desk. "Awww, he looks so sweet, bless him."

Rio glared at her, testing how well the muzzle constrained him — it had him good. He lurched to take up his guard position beside the desk, but Ben yanked him behind it and pushed his butt down, making him sit.

Ben said, "Again, my apologies for the interruption. Now, where were we?"

The two people made lots of noise, but none of it changed in volume or tone. Their scents confirmed neither of them was feeling aggressive. Nevertheless, Rio continued monitoring the situation. He'd let his guard down when Bushy Beard and Pete had found Rat, so no way was he making that mistake again.

The woman left, and shortly after, a young couple arrived.

Finally, Ben took the correct precautions — he kept Rio at his side.

This new people-stuff sounded and smelled similar to the earlier stuff. As did the stuff with an elderly man later.

Midday, Rio and Ben enjoyed a walk and something to eat. They took a route they'd walked before, but instead of reveling in any new scents and adding them to his library, Rio was on high alert for danger. Ears pricked, nose sniffing, eyes flashing, he prowled past the store where the sky dog used to appear.

A young dark-skinned couple approached, laughing loudly — Rio studied them for any hint of a sudden movement. Two teenage girls by the wall chattered so quickly their noise was just a blur — Rio sniffed, checking for alcohol or other substances that had often been a precursor to violence when he'd lived with his man. A woman in a motorized chair scooted along — Rio listened for any suspicious sounds that suggested concealed weaponry.

Nothing passed him without at least one of his senses scrutinizing it for a threat.

Back in the gray room, people-stuff resumed. After a young man with an earring left, Rio squinted at the room. Fun and life happened at home, so it was filled with dazzling colors, but this place? This place was for people-stuff, so it was gray because everything that happened here was gray.

Rio winced. Ben spent the majority of his life doing gray people-stuff and only a small proportion of it actually living. Why? What made people-stuff so fascinating that people put their real lives on hold to do it? Why did they choose to stagnate in a sea of gray instead of choosing to flourish in a world of dazzling color? Were they too stupid to realize what they were missing? Or was something preventing them from truly living?

He'd always figured people were in control of their lives, not least because they'd always been in control of his, but maybe they weren't. Poor people.

Maybe he'd been too hard on them in the past. All those people who'd ignored him when he'd needed help on the street — they were probably struggling with the grayness of their own lives, so they'd needed help just as much as he did. Unfortunately for them, it appeared they didn't realize that, which explained much of the chaos and misery drenching the world.

The afternoon was as action-packed as the morning, then in the evening, they returned home. Rio strode in and slumped on the rug, the stress of being on constant alert draining from him. He stretched and looked at Ben.

Okay, zippy, about those squares...

Ben busied himself in the kitchen. His phone rang and Izzy's voice appeared. "How's the patient?"

"The patient is doing just fine, but I can't say the same of his nursing staff."

"More problems?"

Ben stirred a saucepan. "He's constantly on alert, like he sees everyone and everything as a threat. I don't know what he thinks might happen."

"I suppose if he's lost one friend, he'll be wary of losing another."

"Yeah, I get that, but it doesn't help when I'm dealing with a client and he's glaring at them as if he wants to rip out their throat."

She laughed. "Don't you have anywhere you can put him during meetings?"

"Oh yeah, then he serenades us by howling."

"What's he sing? Bach?"

Ben rolled his eyes, adjusting the heat under the pan. "Very funny."

She giggled. "I thought so."

"You know, it says a lot about someone when they laugh at their own jokes."

"What? That they're super intelligent with an incredible sense of humor?"

"And... what was it?" Ben scratched his head. "Happy and outgoing, and charming and beautiful."

She clapped. "Yay, you got it. Tell me again, why are you single?" She gasped. "Oh, Ben, I'm sorry. It just slipped out. Me and my big mouth."

"Izzy, forget it. But do you want me to add that to the list?"

"Add what?"

"Happy and outgoing, and charming and beautiful. Big mouth."

She laughed again. "Listen, do you want us to come over tonight, or is everything cool?"

"I think we'll manage, thanks."

"Okay, call if you need us."

They ended the call. Ben finished cooking and ate while Rio had kibble, then they went for a walk.

Rio couldn't smell people in the wood, but that didn't mean he could let his guard down – people were the greatest threat, but they weren't the only one. Striding along their usual path, he glared at a branch that hung out too far. As Ben approached, he barked.

"I see it, Rio, thank you." Ben snickered and ducked under it.

Rio led Ben by a rock, giving it a wide berth, then the long way around a tree because its exposed roots could trip a person.

People were so fragile, it was a wonder they survived more than a few years. Those pink bundles of bawling stress they called babies were the worst. What the devil was the point of those? They couldn't do anything. Except poop and vomit and poop and cry and poop.

Children weren't much better. Okay, they could at least walk around by themselves, but all that meant was they could cause more trouble in more places. It was only once people got bigger that they seemed to ever achieve anything, though most of it was pointless people-stuff. If only they could run and jump and fight like dogs... the wonders they could accomplish then.

After only a few minutes, Rio pulled to go home. The longer they were out, the longer bad things had to happen.

Back in the living room, Ben pointed upstairs. "Are you going to let me go to the bathroom alone, or do you need to make sure it's secure first?"

Rio yawned on the rug. The house was safe, so his job was done for the day.

Ben chuckled and wandered away.

The next day in the gray room, Rio's duties began anew. He sniffed all around the sofa area for anyone who might have crept in while he'd been away.

"Rio, no one's here. No one's been here since we left. Relax."

Ben ambled into the kitchen and reached for the coffeemaker, but he stopped as Rio squeezed past him to patrol the area first.

Ben glanced upwards. "Give me strength."

He grabbed Rio's collar, hauled him into the main room, and plonked him in his bed at the back. "This ends now, Rio." Ben stabbed at the bed. "Stay... stay."

Ben was using his unhappy voice. But Rio couldn't let that stop him from doing his duty. He put a paw out of the bed.

"No."

He pulled it back in.

"Good boy."

That voice was softer, so... Rio put his paw out again.

Ben shook his fists at the heavens and grunted.

Rio looked up, too. He was trying his best, but had he missed something? He must have because something was upsetting Ben.

"Come on." Ben marched for the door. "We can't go on like this."

Chapter 43

Trapped inside the car, Rio whined, staring across the parking lot. Where was Ben? He'd been gone for hours. Or it felt like hours.

Rio clawed the gap at the top of the window, but couldn't make it any bigger to escape, so he sniffed at it. He didn't know which way the wind was blowing, but there was no trace of Ben. Bad things could be happening right now, and he couldn't do a darn thing to stop them.

Whimpering, he stared out. On two sides, cars blocked his view; the front and back were a little clearer, but there was still nothing to see but cars.

Rio froze, mouth agape. What if Ben never came back? Rio had been so worried about a bad thing happening to Ben, he hadn't stopped to think that maybe *he* was the bad thing.

Rio curled into a ball and mewled. That explained why his life had always been suffering — he reaped what he'd sown. He'd created problems for his man, so his man had abandoned him; he'd created problems for Rat, so he'd lost him; he'd created problems for Ben, so...

Life was suffering. Why did he keep forgetting that and imagining it could be anything other?

If only he could—

Air gusted through the window. Rio gasped. He leaped up and pressed his face to the glass. Ben!

The man strode over, holding a brown paper bag with squiggles on it.

Rio yipped. It was Ben. Ben coming for him!

Ben opened the car door to unfasten Rio's harness, but Rio lunged and licked and licked him.

"Okay, okay, I've only been ten minutes." Ben laughed. He took Rio out on his leash.

Jumping up, Rio licked anything he could reach, tail wagging. Ben hadn't abandoned him. He was here. *Here.*

"Yeah, I missed you, too." Ben grinned, shielding himself from the tongue-lashing. "Now, we've only got forty-five minutes before my first appointment, but you're smart, so that should be enough. Come on."

Ben led him through the cars toward trees and bushes at the edge of the lot. Rio scanned the gloom beneath the leafy canopy. A new place. That meant the potential for new threats. He pricked his ears, sniffed the breeze, and peered into the shadows. Whatever bad thing lurked here, he'd rip it to shreds.

But when they emerged at the other side of the trees, Rio stopped dead and gawked.

Lush greenery sprouted everywhere, punctuated by splashes of color where flowers exploded from the ground with such stunning coordination, it was as if they'd been put there.

In three directions, paths led through the vegetation like secrets begging to be told.

They ambled down a path that curved to a lake shimmering in the glorious sunshine.

But the most amazing sight was the people. People who weren't "people." They weren't grumpy or bustling or loud, but quiet and laid-back and happy.

Rio squinted at them. A place with no people-stuff and no people-noise? It was a miracle. Gone was the aggression he'd known on the streets — here, people meandered, their voices light, their scents sparkling like the sunlight on the rippling waters. How was that possible?

Bombarded by more scents than he'd ever encountered, Rio dawdled down to the lake alongside Ben and around to a huge expanse of grass. Rio frowned at it. Even though he'd never been here, it felt as if he knew this place. But how?

243

Putting the bag down, Ben crouched to him. "I've held off doing this in the open, but I think I can trust you. Please, don't make a fool of me."

He unclipped Rio's leash.

"Now, you're going to discover we don't have to be joined at the hip. I hope." He took a tennis ball from the bag and held it under Rio's nose. "Have a good smell, okay?"

Standing, he pulled back his arm and hurled the ball. "Fetch, Rio. Fetch."

Rio watched the ball soar through the air, then hit the ground and bounce away. He looked at Ben. Now what? Weirdo used to do that, then go and pick it up. Was Ben here to exercise?

Hands on his hips, Ben stared at Rio. "No worries. Maybe balls don't float your boat."

He pulled an orange rubber rod from the bag. "How about a stick?" He let Rio sniff it, then prepared to throw. "This time, Rio."

He flung the stick.

"Fetch, boy. Fetch."

Rio watched the rod cartwheel through the air. Yeah, that was more interesting than the ball because it moved more, but... he looked at Ben. And?

Under his breath, Ben said, "You're really making me work for this, aren't you?"

He pulled out a curved, bright yellow blob and held it for Rio to smell.

Rio leaned forward to oblige, but Ben squeezed it. The blob squeaked, and Rio jerked his head back.

"Ah, interesting, huh? Is this the one? A squeaky banana?" Ben tossed it far, far into the air.

Rio watched, but the thing didn't squeak again, so he looked back at Ben before it had even landed.

Sighing, Ben crouched and ruffled Rio's fur. "Rio, this is for your benefit. You can't spend every second at my side. It's not healthy. Especially because, sometimes, it's just not possible. If you'll fetch just one of these, you'll see you can leave me and I'll be here when you come back."

He picked the bag up. "This is the last one, Rio. Please, try for me."

Ben took out a piece of gold plastic. A disc-shaped piece of gold plastic.

Rio's jaw dropped. It couldn't be...

Instead of Ben pulling his arm back past his shoulder, he swung it sideways in front of his waist.

Rio gazed on. No, this wasn't possible. His life was suffering, it wasn't—

"Fetch, Rio. Fetch." Ben launched the disc. Like magic, it seemed to hover, skimming through the air in a kind of slow motion.

Rio shot after it. This was it. This was the moment he'd dreamed of but never imagined could ever happen.

Floating in a gentle arc, the disc spun on. Rio tore after it. He gazed up, up into a perfect blue sky. He could almost see the black-and-white sky dog leaping to catch the disc. And now, he was going to do it, too.

He pounded his paws into the ground and soared into the air. The world stopped as the disc all but hung, waiting for him. Rio glided behind it, plucked it out of the sky, and dropped to the greenest green grass to ever grow.

Clutching the disc, he shot back to Ben. The man's silent smile had vanished, replaced by a smile that showed more teeth than Rio had ever seen.

Ben crouched and flung his arms wide. Rio raced into them.

"You did it, Rio. You did it." Ben hugged him. "I knew you could."

Rio yipped. He'd done it. *He was a sky dog.*

Chapter 44

Ben held up the disc to Rio. "I know I said this five minutes ago, but this really is the last time. Okay?"

Dancing with excitement, Rio yipped. *Throw it, zippy. Please, please, please, throw it. Throw it!*

Ben skimmed the disc and Rio tore after it.

Floating and yet not floating, flying and yet not flying, the disc did its magic thing. Rio closed in on it, the wind rushing through his fur. He jumped, and feeling like he was floating with the disk, he closed his jaws about it.

He landed and bolted back to Ben.

Frisbee heaven was real. *And he lived there.* Who'd have thought it possible?

"Sorry, Rio, time's up." Ben took the disc. "But don't worry, now we've discovered what you like, we'll have plenty of fun with this."

They ambled back around the sparkling lake and up the incline toward the parking lot. All the way, Rio couldn't stop gazing at Ben. This was possibly the greatest day of his life. Possibly the greatest day of anyone's life.

Leaving the tree line, they strode between parked cars.

"Excuse me?"

Ben turned.

A man in a black jacket approached. "What's the best route to the church on Bleaker from here, buddy?"

Ben pointed away behind them. "If you hang a—"

The man scooted closer and held a knife toward Ben. "Wallet and phone."

Ben froze, mouth agape, eyes wide.

"Wallet and phone. Now!" The thug jabbed the knife, its blade glinting in the sun. He stank of fear mixed with fury.

Open-mouthed, Rio stared. He might be wrong but... with the thug's stench and the fright-filled reek now coming from Ben.

Bad things...

Rio leaped. He slammed into the thug's chest, knocking him over. The thug crunched into the asphalt, Rio falling on top of him.

Rio clamped his jaws around the thug's arm. The thug wailed as Rio gnashed his teeth.

The thug hammered at Rio.

Seriously? That's all you've got, peaches?

Rio had been battered by the best and come back stronger, so some loser who'd dared to bring bad things into Ben's world was going to be taken apart. Literally. Rio ground his jaws together, shaking his head. A coppery taste oozed into his mouth.

The thug shrieked and struggled to push Rio off.

Rio headbutted through the thug's arms and chomped at his throat, but the thug ducked, twisting away. Rio's teeth sank into the thug's cheek.

The thug wailed.

"Stop, Rio! You'll kill him." Ben yanked his leash. "Stop!"

Between the thug pushing and Ben pulling, Rio lost his balance. Ben wrenched him away, but he lost his footing and crashed against a car, jerking Rio with him. They fell in a heap.

Rio scrambled up and lunged to attack.

Ben grabbed him around the body. "Rio, no, you'll kill him."

The thug clambered up. Clutching his face, blood oozing between his fingers, he staggered away.

Rio barked and barked, lunging to get at the monster, but Ben held him back.

Finally, the thug disappeared between two cars.

Ben stared at his hands, his face ashen. "Oh God, Rio. Why's there so much blood?"

Released, Rio leaped to chase the thug, but wooziness made the parking lot spin. He tottered a few steps, then slumped sideways.

Ben caught him. He scrambled up with Rio in his arms. "Oh God, no, no, no."

He raced for the car and laid Rio on the passenger seat. The engine roared, and the car sped away. Tires squealed as it took a bend, then the vehicle hurtled down the road.

Ben pressed his hand on Rio's side. "Hold on, boy."

The car swerved. A horn blared. Ben shouted, "And you, buddy."

Tires squealed around another corner, and the car shot along again.

Rio's side felt warm and wet. Odd. He didn't remember swimming, but maybe he had. Maybe in that sparkling lake. He closed his eyes. The best day ever...

Despite him and Ben sitting side by side, Ben's voice came from far, far away. "Rio, hold on. Please, hold on."

Ben held him in the seat as the car skidded to a dead stop. He darted around and scooped Rio up, then raced toward a one-story stone building with big square windows.

Ben battered the door with his shoulder and barged in. "Help. Please. My dog's been stabbed!"

Chapter 45

Light flooded through Rio's eyelids and scents cocooned him. Pure and fresh. The sweetest birdsong drifted on air caressed by perfumed blossoms. Enveloped in a wonderful peace, he lay, floating through the world like the golden disc in Frisbee heaven.

Rio's eyes flickered open. A blur of brightly colored shapes greeted him. He lifted his head, but it was so heavy, it dropped back down.

A soothing voice he didn't recognize said, "Hey, Rio, how are you feeling?"

Again, he lifted his head. It wobbled as if it didn't really belong to him, but this time, it stayed up. The world slowly came into focus — a cage with white plastic walls in a room similar to the one Weirdo lived in. But the soothing voice wasn't Weirdo's. He frowned. Where was he? And more importantly, where was Ben?

He sniffed. No trace of the man's scent.

Ben! Rio lunged to run and find him, but his body didn't seem to belong to him either — it jerked but didn't lift a fraction of an inch off the floor.

A dark-skinned woman smiled. "Nice to have you back with us."

Behind her, air gusted through an open window looking onto a cherry tree swathed in pink-and-white flowers. Somewhere within the foliage, a bird tweeted.

Rio barked. He had to protect Ben.

Soothing Voice reached into his cage and caressed his neck. "Easy, boy. Easy. You'll be home soon."

He barked and jerked to get up, managing to raise a few inches before crumpling to the cage floor once more.

"Easy. You'll hurt yourself if you struggle."

He needed to find Ben. Now. He barked and barked, fighting to scramble up. He had to stand. He couldn't run to Ben if he couldn't stand. He kicked and lurched, twisted and writhed.

Soothing Voice stopped smiling. "Oh my, you're determined to do yourself some mischief, aren't you?"

She left the room.

Ben. Where was Ben? He barked and barked.

The door opened again and a man entered. Ben! Rio yipped.

"Hey, Rio. How's my little hero?" Ben wiped his eyes. He turned to Soothing Voice. "Is it okay to stroke him?"

"Please. We don't usually let owners back here, but Rio's so distressed, if he doesn't settle down, he'll either open up his wound again or pull out his IV."

Ben rested his hand on Rio's side. "Lie down, Rio, good boy. You're going to be fine, but you need to rest."

Rio lay down. Ben was safe, so his job was done. For today at least.

Now do you see, ace? Now do you see? It's chaos out there. From now on, no one does anything without my say-so. Got it?

Soothing Voice said, "So, I understand my colleague briefed you on the extent of the injury?"

"Yes."

"Good. Rio will be in here for another thirty minutes for us to monitor him, then we'll move him to a recovery room. He can even have a little walk, if he's up to it."

The people-noise continued for a while, but Rio ignored it, closing his eyes and basking in Ben's closeness.

***

Ben's car stopped outside the house. Rio sniffed. Someone was making fresh squares! He frowned. But who? Ben was here, so who was inside? He strained to identify the intruder, hoping he wouldn't have to fight again so soon, but the intoxicating smell of cooking squares overpowered everything else.

Ben unclipped his harness. "There's a surprise for you inside. Though, with your nose, I figure you've already guessed that."

On the path to the house, two scents lingered, drawing his attention — Izzy and Woofy.

As they reached the door... *yap-yap-yap* came from the other side.

Ben opened it. Woofy yapped and jumped and yapped and spun and yapped. He nuzzled Rio.

Izzy dropped a spatula in the kitchen, dashed over, and crouched next to Rio.

"How's my little crime fighter?" She ruffled the fur on his neck, then kissed his forehead. "You did good, Rio. Real good." She stood and glanced at Ben. "And he'll make a full recovery?"

"Yes, the knife missed anything vital, but he lost a lot of blood, so he was darn lucky."

"Thank God. And no cone. That's good."

"They said he shouldn't be able to twist enough to reach the wound."

"What did the police say?"

They ambled into the kitchen. "They're not hopeful, but they're going to ask the local hospitals and surgeries to report any dog bite injuries."

"Let's hope they catch him."

"I'm just thankful we both walked away from it."

Izzy adjusted the heat under a saucepan. "It's a pity Rio didn't have your gun. Though, on second thought, with his marksmanship, he'd probably have shot you again." She grinned. "Imagine trying to explain your dog shooting you a second time to an ER doctor."

Ben stared into space. Silent.

"You okay?" Izzy touched his arm.

"He was willing to die to protect me, Izzy. He's only known me a few weeks, but he was prepared to die for me."

"That's the power of a dog's love. There's nothing like it." She snickered and pointed to Woofy and Rio sitting side by side and staring at the stove. "Who knows, one day, they may even love us as much as they love bacon." She handed Ben a plate. "This is cool, but you should be the one to reward Rio. I'm doing another batch for later."

Ben sat at the table and offered pieces to both dogs.

Rio wolfed square after square. Frisbee heaven, a good fight against a bad thing, and squares… life didn't get any better than this.

Izzy said, "I know I said I'd cook, but I picked up a couple of pizzas. Okay?"

"Fine."

She wrinkled her nose. "My cooking is what you might call an acquired taste — no pun intended — and I didn't want to spoil the big homecoming."

"Really, it's fine. I'm only pleased you could make it."

"Are you kidding? Woofy would never let me hear the end of it if he missed Rio's first party."

"He could've had a doggy bag."

Izzy arched an eyebrow.

"Sorry," said Ben, "that was bad, wasn't it?"

"So bad I'm surprised they didn't bite you." She nodded to Rio and Woofy, then patted a pizza box with each hand. "Ham and mushroom or pepperoni?"

"We could share?"

"Sure." She nodded to the sofa. "You go relax while I warm them up. Stress can really take it out of you."

"You're telling me." Ben trudged to the sofa and collapsed while Izzy filled Rio's water and food bowls, then placed two more beside them for Woofy.

After eating, Rio ambled over to Ben. His right shoulder and side felt stiff, as if someone was pulling his hind leg back while someone else pulled his foreleg forward to stretch him taut. Odd.

Woofy scampered over, ran underneath Rio, and play bowed, emitting the kind of growl that would make a dogfight aficionado laugh.

"Is Rio okay to play?" asked Izzy. "I can keep Woofy out of the way, if you like."

"The vet said light exercise is fine, so it should be okay."

Ben offered the knotted rope to Rio. "Fancy playing tug with Woofy?"

The instant Rio took the rope in his mouth, Woofy grabbed the other end and wrenched, growling. Rio didn't budge, but Woofy's paws skidded on the floor and he repeatedly fell on his butt with the effort.

Woofy heaved, obviously believing he could win. He shuffled right and jerked but got nowhere, so shuffled left and tugged and tugged.

The angle at which Woofy pulled strained Rio's side, so he yanked his head right. Woofy lifted clean off the ground, swinging around. Rio was so stunned, he opened his mouth, only for Woofy to hurtle through the air and crash to the floor.

Far from disheartened, Woofy scrambled up and scampered back with the rope, as if wanting another airborne adventure.

Ben grabbed Rio's collar and guided him onto the sofa. "Maybe we'll have you up here with me. We don't need another trip to the vet today."

Woofy dropped the rope and yapped at Rio.

"Can you fetch, Woofy?" Ben dangled the rope in front of him.

Izzy said, "Of course he can fetch. He's a dog. It's built in."

"Not into Rio. You won't believe the trouble I had getting him to do it." He shook the rope. "Ready, Woofy?" He tossed it across the room.

Yapping, Woofy bolted after it. When he tried to stop, he skidded on the polished wood and tumbled across the floor. Leaping up, he grabbed the rope and raced back. But Woofy was so small, the dangling rope trailed on the floor. Woofy tripped over it, somersaulted, and splattered in a heap.

Yapping with glee, he jumped up, snatched the rope again, and scurried back.

Rio watched Woofy play. When the little dog fell, he sprang back up; when he missed a catch, he wanted another chance; when he tugged and lost, he came back for more. Woofy was awkward, careless, and inept... and utterly endearing. His never-say-die spirit could teach many a fighting dog a lesson. Strategy it wasn't, but there was something to be said for a bullheaded refusal to accept failure. Or maybe it was strategy: Woofy strategy.

Izzy carried pizza over on two plates and handed one to Ben. She kicked off her shoes and sat cross-legged on the sofa.

"Thanks for doing this, Izzy."

"Don't get too excited. It's only reheated pizza." She munched a slice of the pepperoni.

"No, I mean for being here for Rio."

Rio lay on the sofa, watching the people-stuff, listening to the people-noise. When he'd first come here, he'd figured Ben might one day become as special as Rat. And he had. But the two couldn't be more different characters.

Rat was independent, streetwise, and adventurous. Ben? He was great at people-stuff, but out in the real world? A total catastrophe. Rio had to constantly watch out for the guy — the parking lot incident being a prime example. So while Rat was a friend, an equal, Ben was more... a pet.

And now Izzy and Woofy had joined them. Rio sighed. Training Ben had been fun, but hard work because the man struggled so. He hoped training Izzy and Woofy would be easier. He hadn't realized pet ownership came with such huge responsibilities and commitments.

Still, he had more than he'd ever imagined he would — three pet friends. There couldn't be many dogs — or people — who could make such a bold claim.

Izzy said, "Listen, after such a stressful week, why don't we have a day out on Saturday?"

Ben picked up a hunk of pizza, cheese stringing from it. "What do you have in mind?"

Izzy shrugged. "I was thinking maybe a picnic at the lake. We could hike along the river, see the waterfall, let the dogs have a swim..."

"We'll have to skip the swimming part — Rio shouldn't get his wound wet — but, yeah, sounds good."

"Great. It's a date."

Ben arched an eyebrow.

"A platonic date," said Izzy, "which is the best kind of date because I don't have to make any sort of effort, yet you still have to treat me like a princess." She smirked.

Rio eyed them warily. Yes, he could imagine having problems with such a big group to control, each unruly in their own way. Thank heaven they rarely left the safety of the house.

Chapter 46

In the valley's wide bottom, Rio cringed at the biggest expanse of water he'd ever seen. Probably the biggest anyone had ever seen. Not that it was the water that was the problem. People. So many people. They swarmed over the area like flies over poop. How the devil was he supposed to protect the pack with potential dangers everywhere?

Sounding like animals, children yipped and yowled on a wooden jetty as they leaped and splashed into the water. Farther out, canoes glided over the depths, people in orange life vests paddling through sun-kissed ripples. And around the shore – people. Laughing, talking, playing, feasting, lounging...

On a leash beside Ben, Rio stood next to Woofy and Izzy on a tree-lined path that curled around the water. Vegetation crawled over the hillsides surrounding the lake but for one spot where a cliff rose out of the watery depths, defiant and unforgiving. From the top, water crashed into the lake like never-ending thunder.

Ben gestured left or right. "Any preference for where to set up camp?"

She nodded to the cliff, a backpack slung over her shoulder. "It's always quieter up there, so the dogs will be able to roam free. Can you make it with your leg?"

Ben arched an eyebrow and hoisted a cooler under his free arm. "Shall we?"

Izzy pointed to the left of the waterfall. "The steps are ten times quicker than the ziggy-zaggy path, but they get slick from the spray, so it might be a struggle with the dogs."

"The path it is." Ben limping, they strolled along a dirt path.

Rio glared at everybody they passed. Obviously, his pack was never going to learn from its mistakes — thank heaven he was there to save the day if need be. Again.

Smoke billowed across the path and the smell of cooking sausages filled the air. Ignoring the delicious scent, Rio clung to Ben's side. He couldn't risk any distractions. Not with threats all around.

Ben patted Rio. "You're behaving very well. Good boy, Rio."

He took a bag of pocket-meat from his pocket. Rio had smelled it in the car but was too perplexed at being dragged away from their nice and safe house to bother with it.

Ben offered a square.

Rio wolfed it down. Not because he wanted to, but purely to keep his strength up for the task at hand. Ben threw a square for Woofy, too.

They drew closer to where the crashing water shattered the stillness of lake, a rainbow dancing in its spray.

A steep stone staircase climbed up the side of the waterfall, cutting back on itself a number of times, its steps gleaming wet. Izzy guided them to a path alongside, the moist ground smelling earthy fresh.

They tramped up the switchback path, zigzagging higher and higher, the rocks along the way heavy with moss, as if the place was rarely dry. At the top, they emerged into a forested area beside the river feeding the waterfall, its waters rushing from away in the distance.

Rio panted, his shoulder throbbing from the climb. But there was good news — scents revealed only a scant few people up there and none close by. That was more like it.

Ben wiped sweat from his brow, breathing hard.

"Is it your leg?" asked Izzy.

He nodded. "I don't know how Rio's coping, but it might be wise not to push him too much."

Woofy lay down, his tongue lolling.

Izzy said, "Woofy, too. It's a long way when your legs are so short." She gestured ahead. "There's a clearing not too far."

They strolled along a path that hugged the sloping riverbank and reached a grassy clearing dotted with rocks.

Izzy said, "What do you think?"

"Looks good."

Izzy laid a blue blanket from her backpack on the grass, then unpacked various items while Ben took stuff from the cooler, including dog bowls.

He filled the bowls. "Rio? Woofy?"

They guzzled water and kibble.

"Do you think it's safe to let them off their leashes?" asked Ben.

"I haven't seen anyone else, so..." She shrugged.

Ben released them.

Rio wandered away to sniff the perimeter. It appeared safe, but he couldn't be too careful.

Woofy ambled after him. He play bowed. *Yap-yap-yap.*

Rio ignored him — he had a job to do.

Woofy headbutted Rio's leg, as if Rio might not have heard. Again, Rio didn't react.

Yap-yap-yap.

Woofy ran between Rio's legs, but instead of shooting out the other side, he stayed underneath and peered between Rio's forelegs to sniff what Rio was.

Rio stepped over the little dog to continue his patrol.

Woofy spotted something under a bush, so scampered over to investigate. He snatched one end of a large stick and heaved, but it was caught by the tangled undergrowth. Never one to refuse a challenge, Woofy tugged and tugged, growling louder and louder the more the bush denied him.

He dug his claws into the ground and jerked backward. Finally, the stick came loose and Woofy fell over.

Leaping up, Woofy yipped, his eyes bulging even bigger at his prize — a branch around five times the length he was.

He grabbed it in the middle and ran around, proudly displaying it. Unfortunately, its size and weight made it seesaw, so as Woofy tore around the clearing, one end hit the ground. The jolt flipped Woofy, and he tumbled over and over to sprawl in the dirt.

Sitting on the blanket, Ben moved to go to him, but Izzy grabbed his arm. "He'll be okay. Trust me, he has more lives than a cat."

Woofy barked at the stick, then picked it up and trotted away, only to clonk it against a tree trunk and fall over again.

Izzy snickered. "It's a good thing because, as you can see, he's not the most athletic of dogs."

Ben snickered. "More chess club than Little League."

"Chess?" Izzy winced. "Now, a coloring book club? Maybe. I love the little guy, but he's about as smart as a puddle."

Ben offered her one of the containers, pointing at various parts. "Tuna, ham and cheese, egg salad."

"Thanks." She took a sandwich and chomped into it.

Ben took one, too, gazing at the trees and mountains. "It's nice here."

"You've never been before?"

"To the lake, yeah, but not up here. It's nice to be somewhere new. I enjoy my work, but I get so sick of staring at those same walls."

Izzy finished chewing and said, "I don't want to do the whole boring twenty questions thing, but what is it you do while staring at those walls?"

"I'm a notary public."

She clutched her mouth. "Get out of here!"

He smiled. "What?"

"Wow, that's like one of my top five dream jobs."

Ben frowned. "Really?"

"Yeah, it goes"— she counted on her fingers —"data entry clerk, accountant, notary public, insurance claims adjuster…" Her eyes closed, her head dropped, and she snored.

She giggled. "Sorry, I couldn't resist."

"So, don't tell me, you're an astronaut who volunteers part-time for Doctors Without Borders?"

"Let's see, I've taught meditation at a retreat in California, toured with a rock band as a backing singer, worked in a New Age store, was an extra in an *Avengers* movie, trod grapes at an organic winery, wrote a book about angel dogs, trained to teach doga… oh, and I fought with Godzilla against Mothra — we won. In black and white, of course — the classic Godzilla, not that Hollywoodized version." She took another sandwich.

Ben squinted as if not sure what to believe. "That's some list."

"You should see my full résumé."

Ben offered her a beer from the cooler. "Godzilla against Doga, huh?"

Izzy accepted a can. "Godzilla against Mothra. Doga is a form of exercise you do with your dog. Dog yoga — doga. Get it?"

"Dogs can do yoga?"

"Well, duh. Don't tell me you've never seen Rio standing in Dancing Shiva?" She sniggered. "Actually, it's more about strengthening the bond between a person and their dog than about flexibility, but it's fun."

They continued chatting and eating, then tidied everything away into the backpack and cooler before lounging on the blanket and chatting further.

After a while, Ben called Rio and Woofy over and showed them the knotted roped. He hurled it. Woofy raced after it, but Rio stared at him.

This again, zippy? I'll let Woofy handle this one.

Ben shook the bag of squares. "Fetch, Rio. Fetch."

Well, if you put it that way. Rio darted after Woofy.

The little dog sniffed at something in the long grass, ignoring the rope. Until Rio snatched it up. Woofy scampered in front of Rio, leaping and leaping to grab it, but missing each time and stumbling twice by not looking where he was going.

Rio dropped the rope for Ben and received his reward.

So easy to please. Sucker!

But when Woofy also got a square, Rio frowned. Woofy hadn't fetched it, he had. Did that mean squares were given simply for participating?

Ben threw the toy again. Woofy shot after it, but Rio lay down to watch. Spectating was a form of participation, wasn't it?

Ben wagged his finger. "Nah-huh. No play, no treat." He pointed toward the toy. "Fetch, Rio."

Rio bounded after Woofy and retrieved the rope. They each got a square, even though it was Rio who, again, had done all the work.

They continued playing, Woofy chasing Rio more than the rope. One time, Rio retrieved the rope and was returning when Woofy finally got his aim right and clamped his jaws around one end. Too light to pull it from Rio's grasp, Woofy dangled, swinging like a pendulum as Rio trotted back.

Izzy laughed, pointing her phone at them.

Rio released the rope for Ben, dropping Woofy to the grass. As Woofy was still holding the rope, he claimed credit for having recovered it by yipping and yipping.

They each got another square.

Woofy ate his, then wandered away and savaged the big stick he'd found earlier.

"Okay, that's enough bacon for now." Ben put the bag away.

Rio sniffed. There were plenty of squares left. Woofy might be finished, but he wasn't. He nuzzled Ben.

"Okay, one more. Then that's it." Ben gave him another.

Sucker!

Growling, Woofy gnawed his stick, then lugged it around the clearing again. While Woofy played, they all lay on the blanket, but clouds cast a shadow over the area.

Izzy shivered. "It's a little cool when the sun goes in."

Ben peered upward. The odd patch of blue dotted a lumpy gray sky. "I think that's it for the day. Do you want to make tracks?"

Chapter 47

They all meandered along the riverbank path, Woofy bringing up the rear, scampering back and forth with his huge stick. Rio hung back, too. His shoulder throbbed, so Woofy's pace couldn't be more welcome.

Woofy scooted up carrying his stick and growled playfully. Rio grabbed one end and tugged, yanking Woofy around with it.

The little dog tensed, thrust his forelegs out so his claws scraped through dirt, and jerked backward, growling. Rio teased him by letting him gain ground, only to yank him all the way back. Woofy retaliated, straining to retain his beloved prize.

Up ahead, Ben beckoned, shouting, "To me, Rio. Woofy, come."

Rio released the stick and ambled on, now limping from the pain in his shoulder.

Having triumphed, Woofy taught the stick a lesson by giving it a good savaging. He then dropped it and growled at it, as if daring it to challenge him again.

Izzy shouted, her voice now competing with the crashing waterfall. "Woofy! ... Woofy!"

Woofy snatched his stick and bolted to catch up. He hurtled along the path, but the stick seesawed and one end jammed into the ground. Woofy fell and reeled across the path. Too close to the bank, he pitched over the edge. The little dog tumbled down the muddy slope and splattered into the water, the current instantly swirling him around a mossy rock and away.

Rio gawked. He barked as Woofy's tiny legs paddled like crazy, but they were no match for the river that carried him farther and farther out.

Woofy yapped, but not his usual gleeful yap — now it was filled with fear.

Rio barked and barked. He had to save Woofy, but how?

Ben looked back and beckoned. "Rio. To me, boy." But he frowned, scanning the area.

Izzy stopped, then screamed and stabbed a trembling hand at the river.

Ben ran back toward Rio.

Rio looked at him, then Woofy. Ben wasn't a hardened fighting dog; he was just a man. He wasn't equipped for a life-and-death situation. That left only one option.

Rio tore over the ground. Not toward Ben, but at an angle toward Woofy.

"No, Rio. No!" Ben waved his arms.

Reaching the bank nearer Woofy, Rio shot down the muddy slope and leaped out over the gushing water. He soared through the air like the sky dog he was, then splashed into the river. Sinking into the dark depths surrounded by bubbles, he fought to claw his way back up to the light.

Rio broke the surface and gasped for air. A few feet away, Woofy yapped, the sound drenched in desperation.

Far more powerful than Woofy, Rio struck out for him, closing the distance as the current dragged them both downriver. Rio pushed harder. He had to reach his friend. Had to. Not just for Woofy's sake but his own — he hadn't been able to save Rat, so he'd never forgive himself if he lost another friend.

The water swept Woofy past a boulder. Struggling to keep his head above the surface, he yapped and yapped, but the yaps were getting weaker as the vicious current drained his strength.

Rio fought on. If Woofy could just hold on another few seconds...

Woofy sank, the darkness swallowing every trace of him.

No!

Rio powered on to where he'd lost sight of Woofy, then dove.

Swirling murkiness enveloped him. He kicked on through underwater plants and passed submerged rocks and branches. Woofy? Where was Woofy?

Gasping, Rio broke the surface. He was too late. Woofy was gone.

From somewhere nearby, a spluttered yap...

Rio glanced over the tumbling water. There!

Ahead, Woofy struggled beside a boulder. He clawed at it, fighting to get a grip. But the river was too strong for someone so tiny. It dragged him, his nails raking through the moss and scraping over stone beneath.

Woofy lost his hold with all but one paw.

Rio drove on as the little dog's claws slid farther and farther along the boulder. In a second, he'd be gone.

And ahead, the sound of the crashing water consumed everything.

Woofy was only inches away. Rio almost had him. Almost...

But Woofy cried as his claws skidded on the stone, and the current took him.

Rio lunged. He clamped his jaws to the back of his little friend's neck.

Yes!

He flung his paws toward the boulder. If he could get a hold, maybe he could save them.

His claws slid over the wet stone. He scrambled for a grip as the current fought to sweep him on. Pawing and pawing, his nails scraped the surface. Finally, one claw lodged in a crack. Safe. For now. But how could they escape the punishing waters?

Maybe they could climb onto the rock and wait for rescue.

Rio pawed at the boulder with his other foreleg, but again and again, his claws slipped off it.

The water buffeted them, draining Rio's strength. What could he do? How could he save them?

"Rio!"

Ben! That was Ben! But where was he?

Straining to keep Woofy's head above the water, Rio desperately glanced around.

"Rio!"

Rio heaved with his one secure hold on the rock, hauling himself high enough to see over it. Ben!

Ben hung out over the water diagonally ahead, clinging one-handed to the branch of a tree at the bottom of the muddy riverbank.

"Rio!" He beckoned.

The water swirled around another rock close to Ben. If Rio could make it to that, Ben might be able to reach them to pull them out.

Rio gulped. To get to that rock meant letting go of this one. And swimming across the current.

His legs already trembling with the effort of his rescue attempt, he stared at the far rock. Did he have the strength to make it and then to fight for another hold?

He stared ahead.

The river disappeared in a haze of spray as the crashing water plummeted into the lake. If he missed that rock...

But did he have any choice?

Strategy. He was a master. He couldn't stay here – the longer he did, the weaker he'd become. The answer was obvious.

Kicking off the stone, he pumped his legs, aiming at the rock near the tree.

Ben shouted, "That's it, Rio. You can do it."

Izzy stood at the top of the bank, clutching her mouth.

Paddling with the last of his strength, Rio broke for the rock. The current battered them, desperate to drag them into the crashing water and oblivion.

Rio looked to where the water plummeted over the edge, then at Ben. The river was dragging them too fast. They were going to miss him.

His lungs burning, muscles aching, Rio battled to swim toward the shore. He had to reach that rock. If he didn't, he and Woofy were lost.

Ahead, Ben shuffled to hang farther out over the water. He obviously feared they were going to miss, too.

Rio kicked and kicked. Fighting harder than in any fight he'd ever had.

Struggling for breath because he was holding Woofy, Rio spluttered when his nose momentarily submerged. Woofy coughed on what he'd swallowed, so Rio battled to crane his neck higher above the surface.

The rock was so close. So close.

Rio pounded his legs through the water with the last of his strength and stretched to reach it.

But the rushing current swirled around the rock, spinning Rio — he bounced off the stone. The water grabbed them, aching to carry them away to their end.

But Woofy thrust out a tiny paw, and a tiny claw wedged in a tiny crack. Woofy strategy! Thank heaven for the little dog's bullheaded refusal to accept failure.

Rio pawed with his forelegs and pumped his hind legs, scrabbling at the rock. Raking and raking, his nails skidded over the wet stone, unable to find anything to latch on to.

From above, Ben's hand clawed at them, but he was too far away.

Woofy yelped, the current desperate to rip his little leg from his body so it could whisk them away.

They weren't going to make it. The water was too strong. There was nothing to hold.

As Rio's claws scraped the boulder for the umpteenth time, they raked down and below the surface. And lodged in a hole.

"Hold on, Rio. I'm coming."

Ben shuffled his feet in the mud, slithering this way and that, while jerking his hand farther and farther along the branch. Leaning out almost horizontally, he clawed at Rio, fingers raking the air barely an inch from them.

Rio pushed against the rock to lift his head as high as possible, and Ben's fingertips brushed his ear. But it wasn't close enough.

Groaning as he strained, Ben stretched and stretched. Fingers splayed. Trembling. Reaching. Closer and closer. Almost...

Ben snagged Woofy's collar. He lifted the little dog out of the water and swung him toward the bank.

"I'm coming," said Izzy, stepping onto the muddy slope.

"No! It's too slippery. If you fall in, I won't reach you before you hit the falls."

Shuffling back along the branch, he twisted around. "Can you catch Woofy, if I throw him?"

"I think so."

"On three."

Ben swung Woofy back and forth. "One ... two ... three." He flung Woofy up the bank. But too short.

Izzy lunged, sliding partway down the slope, and caught the little dog. While she crawled back to the path cradling Woofy, Ben eased along the branch again.

"I'm coming, Rio. I'm coming."

Straining, Ben's hand reached nearer and nearer. Rio kicked to lift higher, but his legs hurt so much he wasn't even sure they were moving.

"I'm coming."

Ben's feet skidded in the mud. He grabbed the branch with both hands to save from falling in.

Repositioning his feet, his shoes caked in mud, he once more stretched a hand toward Rio and jerked farther and farther along the branch with the other.

His face twisted with the effort, Ben leaned down, hand trembling. But it wasn't far enough. His feet slid in the mud again, one splashing into the water.

Strategy.

Rio had lived his life by it. Fought by it. Survived by it. And now, it was telling him he had to let go of the rock.

He didn't want to. But if he didn't, Ben would lean too far to save him. And bad things would happen. Rio couldn't let bad things happen. Not to Ben. Not when it was his job to be the protector of the pack. He'd saved Woofy, and now, he was going to save Ben.

Rio whimpered, his plan making him tremble as if the water were ice. He didn't want to let go, but he had no choice.

He gazed up one last time at Ben straining toward him. *Thank you, Ben.*

Rio kicked off the rock.

The current clutched him. But as it feverishly dragged him away to his doom, it also dragged him closer to Ben.

Ben's hand grasped his collar. He hauled Rio up, out of the water.

Ben smiled. "I've got you, buddy."

They'd done it!

An almighty creak came from the tree, and the branch snapped.

266

Rio and Ben crashed down.

"Ben!" shouted Izzy.

Rio plunged underwater and slammed into a submerged rock. His ribs crunched against the stone, forcing a yelp. The hungry water rushed into his mouth and down his throat, eager to consume him, so when he broke the surface, he coughed and coughed, struggling to breathe.

That was when he saw Ben floating facedown, at the river's mercy. A coppery trail of blood snaked through the water from the man.

Ben!

Finally, Rio heaved a sputtered breath.

Rio struck out after Ben, deafened by the crashing water now so close. Ahead, the spray haze hung in the air with nothing beyond but gray sky.

Rio battled to reach the man. A fight harder than any he'd ever fought.

Kicking, kicking, kicking, Rio closed in inch by inch. At last within reach, he lunged. He clawed Ben's arm and managed to roll him over. Blood flowed from a gash on Ben's forehead.

Rio bit the man's jacket and kicked for the shore. But Ben was so heavy, the river so strong, and Rio so, so tired...

Spluttering and kicking vainly against the current, he watched helplessly as the edge where the foaming water finished and the gray sky began loomed closer and closer, like they were being sucked into the mouth of some ravenous monster.

He had to save Ben. Had to. But how?

Dragged closer to the monster, Rio's gaze whirled desperately for an answer.

There!

Right on the lip where the river disappeared, a scraggly bush clung to life on a boulder. They were heading for that. If he could claw something, he could save them. But this wouldn't be like last time when he had umpteen chances – this would be one shot. One. If he missed, they'd be lost over the edge.

Unless...

If he bit the bush, he could hold on until help arrived. That couldn't fail because his bite strength was phenomenal. This current didn't stand a chance against his bite.

But to bite, he'd have to let go of Ben. Ben would fall over the edge.

What should he do? Risk saving both of them, knowing the chances were almost zero? Or save himself, knowing he'd be to blame for losing Ben to the monster? What should he do?

The thundering of the water deafening, Rio stared at the tiny boulder. So close now. Time was almost up. He had to decide. Had to. What should he do? He stared.

He'd be within reach any second.

Save himself or save Ben?

Closer...

Any second.

Save himself or save Ben?

Almost...

Save himself or—

Now.

Rio gripped Ben tighter and lashed out with his paws. He'd found holds on other rocks, so he could do it again.

He scraped the boulder, frantically digging with his claws, desperate for the tiniest of holes...

And one nail found one tiny cranny.

They were saved!

He gasped for air, bracing against the slamming water that ached to drag him and Ben over the edge.

But his claw slipped a fraction. Then a fraction more.

Mauled by the rushing water, he fought to thrust another claw into another hole, scraping and scraping at the stone. He would not lose this fight. Never!

But every attempt only skidded off heartless rock.

And his one tiny claw with its one tiny hold faltered...

Then failed.

The water took them.

And over the edge they plummeted.

Falling, falling, falling...

And just when he thought it was never going to end, it ended.

Rio smashed into the lake. The crashing water pounded him, as if furious at him for having dared to challenge it. It pummeled him, thumping and kicking and punching and stomping more than all the times his man had combined.

Down, down, down he sank, the water battering him farther and farther into the murky depths.

Crushing, crushing, crushing...

His life sliding away from him, the cold darkness of the watery abyss suddenly felt so inviting. He ached to rest, to dream, to quit fighting a world that didn't want him in it. Strategy — a dog had to know which battles it could win. And which it couldn't.

Except...

The river didn't know one thing: he was a hardened fighting dog. *A hardened fighting dog!*

Rio snarled. The river would not win. It *could* not win. He fought it with every strategy in his arsenal. He kicked and clawed, gnashed and twisted...

And when he thought he had nothing more to give, glowing images of Ben revitalized him. He savaged and raked, bucked and ripped...

But it wasn't enough.

The brightness of the sky drifted farther and farther away as he sank lower and lower, away from the light, away from the world, away from his life. Until...

There was only blackness.

Chapter 48

Birds sang.

Rio had never truly listened to birdsong before. How beautiful it was — the melody, the intricacy, but above all, the joy.

And those scents.

Flowers. Lots of them. Nearby.

He'd stored so many scents in his library, he could picture an endless array of plants without needing to see them just from one quick whiff. But though he'd catalogued each scent in such meticulous detail, he'd never stopped to simply smell it — to lose himself in its fragrance.

He sniffed. Intoxicating. Perfumed wonders that stroked the inside of his muzzle the way Ben stroked the underside of his chin.

Ben...

Rio's eyelids fluttered up.

He was lying in a grove of trees swaying in a breeze, their ancient timbers creaking as if they were snoring. Rio stretched, then stood, energy coursing through him as if he'd woken from the most satisfying sleep.

Now to find Ben.

He turned to look across the lake, hoping to see Ben wading out.

The lake was gone.

What the devil was going on?

He sniffed. There was no big expanse of water anywhere nearby. But that was impossible. It had to be somewhere.

He ambled through the mighty trees. Pools of golden light dotted the ground from shafts filtering through the canopy, and the white parachute seeds of dandelions drifted on the air.

Leaving the trees, Rio strolled into a meadow. Flowers of red and yellow and blue waved in a sea of green. Where was he?

He sniffed. He'd never been here, yet he felt perfectly at home. Why? He scoured his library, searching for something resembling the combination of scents surrounding him. Nothing. How odd. Maybe he'd missed something.

Sniffing again, he frowned. The tiniest hint of a scent wove its way through those of the flowers, the trees, the grass... It was so faint. Like a thought he half-remembered that just wouldn't form. What was that?

Rustling.

Through the grass.

He angled his ears as the sound neared. And the scent grew stronger and stronger.

His jaw dropped. And the grass parted.

Eeep.

Rio leaped in an explosion of joy. Rat. It was Rat!

He lay down to be more on Rat's level and licked his oldest friend. Wherever this incredible place was, he'd have to remember so he could find it again with Ben. Ben would love it. Izzy and Woofy, too.

Rat nuzzled him, then ran around to his side, scrambled over his ribs onto his back, and down the other side. It was as if they'd never been parted.

Rat scampered back and squeezed in between Rio's front paws to nestle under his chin. They lazed together in the sun as a blue butterfly flitted by and the gentle chirrup of a cricket caressed the air.

Rio sighed. Days didn't get much better than this — fun with his new pack, a reunion with his old one, and a stunning victory in the fight of his life. Magnificent.

Weaving through the blades of grass, cascading over petals as bumble bees collected nectar, a scent wiggled its way to Rio. He gasped. Ben!

Sniffing to confirm the direction, Rio sprang up, his heart pounding and a glow in his chest warmer than any sun could ever be.

Yes, over the slight brow of the meadow. Ben. It was Ben.

Rat peered up questioningly. Rio licked him and yipped for Rat to follow, then trotted farther into the meadow as birds swooped overhead.

Oh boy, they were going to have such fun, the three of them. Such adventures.

Rio quickened his pace, tail high. The sooner he found Ben, the sooner the adventures could begin. He ran. Faster and faster. Shooting through the grass faster than he'd ever run before.

As Rio crested the brow, Ben's scent became overpowering. And then...

There!

But Rio skidded to a stop. Ben wasn't alone. He hugged a slim woman with short hair and a girl with flowing black hair and a pale complexion. A brown dog yipped beside them.

Ben was part of Rio's pack. Who were these interlopers?

Rio tensed his muscles to bolt over and drag Ben away to be with those he was supposed to be with, but...

Love oozed from the small group. *Oozed.* It was the most beautiful thing Rio had ever witnessed. He ached to join them, to feel that love, to have it envelope him, warm him.

Except, he knew he couldn't because they weren't the interlopers — he was.

He whimpered, the joy draining from him as quickly as the water crashing over that cliff.

And that was when Ben turned. And smiled. Smiled just for him.

Rio's tail wagged like crazy and he didn't care. In fact, he was glad — Ben needed to know how thrilled he was to see him. Maybe that's what his tail had always been for.

Ben wandered over. He crouched and hugged Rio.

Rio whined. Everything was going to be okay. Ben had come for him. *For him.*

But Ben pulled away, a sadness in his eyes. "I'm sorry, Rio, but you don't belong here with us."

Why was Ben sad? They were together. And Ben hadn't even met Rat yet, which was sure to be the highlight of his day.

Ben grasped Rio's collar and led him to the edge of the meadow where shadows lurked in the wood and the birds didn't sing. Rio didn't want to go in there, but Ben pulled him on.

The trees closed in, tighter and tighter, gloom devouring the place. Rio's heart raced, his breath coming in pants. He trembled as the darkness crept ever closer.

He looked up for reassurance from Ben, but...

Rio spun. Where was Ben?

Around and around.

Where was Ben? And Rat? Hadn't Rat followed him?

He peered into the dense army of trunks, searching for blue sky, praying for the green of the meadow. But darkness engulfed him.

His heart hammering, he couldn't breathe.

He fought. Fought for himself, for Ben, for Rat. But it was as if someone were squeezing his mouth shut and blocking his nose.

Rio fell. Tumbling, tumbling, tumbling into the deepest, darkest blackness.

He couldn't breathe.

Couldn't breathe.

Couldn't...

Chapter 49

Rio's eyes flickered open. Izzy's hand was clamping his muzzle, squeezing his mouth shut, as she leaned down to blow into his nose.

He rived his head back.

"Oh, thank God." She hugged him. "I thought we'd lost you."

Groggy, he glanced about. Hey, the lake was back. And Ben. But what were those men doing to him?

He scrambled up. He needed to help Ben.

Izzy clutched him, tears in her eyes. "No, Rio. They're trying to save him."

Woofy yapped, his leash around her ankle.

Ben lay on his back beside a canoe pulled ashore. A mustachioed man in an orange life vest knelt, pumping Ben's chest with his hands. He stopped and a bald man, also in orange, pinched Ben's nose and blew into his mouth.

What the devil was happening?

He barked. They had to stop or they'd hurt Ben.

Mustache Man pumped Ben's chest again.

Ben jerked and water spluttered from his mouth.

Izzy whimpered, smiling, yet tears streaking her cheeks.

The two men in orange high-fived, then, taking an arm each, eased Ben over to sit against a tree.

Izzy led Rio over by his collar.

"Hey." She smiled. "Some picnic, huh?"

Ben nodded.

Rio whined and nuzzled Ben. Ben stroked him.

Mustache Man said, "The paramedics are on their way. Rest up until they get here."

"Thank you," said Izzy.

The man waved, then wandered away.

Izzy patted Rio. "He tried to rescue you, you know."

"Yeah?"

"He could probably have gotten out, but he went over the falls trying to save you."

Ben gazed at Rio. "They said he was a fighting dog, but I never dreamed he'd be fighting for his life — and mine — so often."

Izzy squeezed Ben's arm. "He's very special. I hope you appreciate that."

Ben cupped her hand. "It's time I appreciated many things."

She squinted, as if asking a question, even though she said nothing.

He said, "I think it's time to move on. If that's okay with you."

"You're sure?"

"You only live twice." He snickered.

She smiled and held his hand. "So there are no secrets, I should tell you that I Frenched your dog."

Ben shrugged. "With your track record, it was only a matter of time."

She laughed.

Rio snuggled against Ben. They were all going to be fine. Just fine.

But what a day. Maybe he was wrong about life. He'd figured life was suffering because that was all he'd ever known, but it wasn't. It was a fight.

Before meeting Ben, his life had been one endless fight. Against other dogs, against his man, against unrelenting hardship and punishment... and it was a good thing. If it hadn't hardened him, hadn't trained him to become the master strategist he was, he wouldn't have been prepared for his most important fight of all — the fight for those he loved.

Suffering? Suffering could bring it on. He was a hardened fighting dog; there wasn't a fight against anyone or anything he couldn't win.

A scent drew his attention. There was still pocket-meat in Ben's jacket. After the battle he'd just waged, it was selfish of Ben to keep that to himself.

Rio tried to wiggle his snout into the pocket, but it was zipped.

"What? The bacon?" Ben chuckled. "I guess I can't refuse now, can I?"

"You can say that again," said Izzy.

Ben offered Rio a handful of pocket-meat all at once.

Rio's eyes widened. So many squares? For one little fight? *Talk about easy money. Sucker!*

The End
If you haven't already, discover the dog who started it all.
Read As the Stars Fall to explore how compassion can
make us whole again and friendship can heal
even the most broken of hearts.

Use this link:
www.stevenleebooks.com/stars

Interview with Steve N. Lee

In the back of your last dog story, you said the next one would have a guest appearance by someone from As the Stars Fall *or* When the Skies Cry, *but that was underplaying things a little, wasn't it?*

I didn't want to let the cat out of the bag and spoil the surprise, but yeah, most of the old characters get at least a walk-on part, with some getting leading roles. It made this book an absolute joy to write because I could spend time with "old friends."

Did you always intend to bring back all these characters?

No. For example, originally, Izzy was supposed to be little more than a bit player who was only there to add color, so in early drafts of Harley's book, *When the Skies Cry*, she didn't make it to the end. However, I loved her so much, I changed the story so if I wanted her to, she could make a reappearance.

Rio, on the other hand, was always going to be the hero.

Which is a huge departure from his introduction.

Massive, yeah. You see, a villain is never a villain in their own eyes — in their story, they're the hero. I figured it would be fascinating to turn things around and show what had made Rio into the dog he was and to reveal the world from his point of view. To show that far from being a villain, he was a misunderstood victim. And a hero in his own right.

Rat was such a great character. And such an unusual choice. How did you come up with him?

The section where Rio is stuck as a guard dog would have dragged like crazy without something to spice it up, so I knew I needed something, I just didn't know what.

More events wouldn't cut it without having someone for him to share them with, and a person was out of the question, so it simply came down to finding a suitable friend that would fit in such a place. A rat was obvious, so I brainstormed possible interactions and I loved them.

Those chapters are one of my favorite parts of the book. And it's such a moving friendship. It's strange that there are no people involved and yet it's as loving a relationship as anything between two humans.

Will there be another dog story?

I have some ideas, yes, but at the risk of upsetting readers, I'll be taking a break from dog stories for a while.

I found truly unique dogs with unique stories in Kai, Harley, and Rio, but the other ideas I have don't add anything new. I don't want to give readers new books that are essentially the same old story dressed up with different characters, so until I can come up with a storyline that's equally unique, it's time to hang up the leash, so to speak.

So what's next if it isn't another dog story?

Something incredible that I'm really, really excited about. And something that could never have come about if it wasn't for the dog stories. Readers love these emotional roller coaster the stories taken them on. That was something new for me. Until *As the Stars Fall*, I'd only written thrillers, so I was used to taking readers on a very different kind of roller coaster — one of pulse-pounding action — but the dog stories opened up a whole new way of connecting with readers.

So, next I'll be combining the heartbreaking emotional impact of the dog stories with the edge-of-your-seat suspense of the thrillers to write novels about the Holocaust. Two books are already drafted, inspired by true stories I came upon while on my travels in Eastern Europe, the first titled *To Dream of Shadows*.

I never imagined I'd ever write something like historical fiction. And never ever dreamed I'd write a love story, but that's what I've done — one of the true tales I uncovered features the kind of love that "stories are written about," so how could I not write it? To give you an idea of what it's like, think *Schindler's List* meets *The Tattooist of Auschwitz*.

So, it's a historical romance?

Well... "love story" is a more appropriate term than "romance". It's like the difference between a holiday romance and a love that lasts a lifetime. It's the kind of emotional connection that means you'll sacrifice anything for the other person, that life without them isn't life.

And that's what this love story is about?

Yes. That even in the nightmarish hell of a concentration camp, two people can find that spark that makes life worth living, worth fighting for. I found the true story both incredibly moving and extremely surprising, so couldn't resist telling it.

This true story has never been told in a book before, so it's guaranteed to be something completely new for readers to enjoy. *To Dream of Shadows* is a kind of *Schindler's List* meets *The Tattooist of Auschwitz*.

I did months of research — reading books, watching documentaries, scouring the web — and took a research trip to Poland to visit locations and study material in various museums.

It was hard work, and grueling at times with the things I had to read about, but I wanted to make the books as authentic as possible. Not just to do the individual stories themselves justice, but to be respectful to all those who suffered through that hellish period.

It sounds fascinating. But the dog stories will return at some point, won't they?

The first one took me by complete surprise because I had no intention of ever writing anything like that. Then, two more turned up out of the blue. So, a fourth? Let's just say I wouldn't bet against it.

***

To learn more about *To Dream of Shadows*, please use this link:
www.stevenleebooks.com/Shadows

To enjoy an extended interview with Steve, please use this link:
www.stevenleebooks.com/called

Will You Help?

This book has over 82,000 words in it, yet if you write as few as ten or twelve words in a review, it will make a huge difference to how many people read Rio's story.

If you enjoyed *Where the Echo Calls*, please help me spread the word by posting a short review now (no spoilers, please).

Thank you!

Either search for the title or type this link to go straight to it:
www.stevenleebooks.com/ReviewRio

FREE Book

If you enjoyed *Where the Echo Calls*, you need this exclusive ebook written by Steve especially for you. In it, you will:

> discover who was originally going to be the story's human hero
> read Steve's startling confession about the first draft
> unravel how the characters were created
> enjoy a revealing extended interview with Steve
> choose from a selection of Book Club Questions
> and uncover much, much more.

To get *Where the Echo Called*, please use this link:
www.stevenleebooks.com/called

As The Stars Fall

Discover the dog who started it all! Meet Kai.

A Desperate Dog. A Scarred Girl. A Bond Nothing Can Break.

An injured, young dog trudges the city streets, trembling from cold, from fear, from lack of food. Battered by the howling wind, he searches desperately for his lost family, yet day after day, week after week, all he ever finds is heartbreaking loneliness. But then, one magical spring morning...

Across town, a little girl sobs into her pillow in the dead of night. Her life devastated by a family tragedy, she can't understand how the world can just carry on. Her days once overflowed with childhood joys, yet now, despair, darkness, and emptiness smother her like a shroud. But then, one magical spring morning...

... the dog and the girl meet.

Read *As The Stars Fall*. Use this link:
www.stevenleebooks.com/stars

When The Skies Cry

Meet Harley!

Sometimes, the one you're saving is really saving you.

Harley loses everything when his master dies - his home, his best friend, his reason for living. Day after day, he trudges the streets, trembling from the biting cold, whimpering from the gnawing hunger.

Across town, Rachel has an alimony hearing looming and a make-or-break deadline hurtling toward her, yet they aren't her biggest worries - her autistic son has withdrawn so far into his own private world, he barely acknowledges she even exists.

Luckily, the magic of life is in the surprises no one ever sees coming...

Read *When The Skies Cry*. Use this link:
www.stevenleebooks.com/when

Crime Thrillers

⭐⭐⭐⭐⭐ Karen Bryan
"Absolutely loved it!"

⭐⭐⭐⭐⭐ J. Alexander
"Fast-paced and action-packed"

⭐⭐⭐⭐⭐ Stephen Crowe
"Bloody fantastic"

As *The Stars Fall* is a clean, relatively gentle story. If you also enjoy dark, fast-paced thrillers laced with gritty realism, you'll love my action-packed *Angel of Darkness Series* (book #1, *Kill Switch*, has over 1,000 5-star ratings).

★★★★★ *"Fast-paced and action-packed, it takes you on a ride you don't want to stop!"* J. Alexander

★★★★★ *"Reacher fans should enjoy this … a thrill-packed adrenaline rush."* AJ Norton

★★★★★ *"A good fast-paced read with a fabulous female lead."* Julie Elizabeth Powell

★★★★★ *"Fast paced thriller with suspense packed onto every page. Loved it."* Michael Miller

★★★★★ *"Gripping stuff — I couldn't put this one down, read it in one go."* Jan Simmons

Dive into this pulse-pounding action series today with this link:
www.stevenleebooks.com/angel

Printed in Great Britain
by Amazon

16835352R00162